WILDERNESS GIANT SPECIAL EDITION

Twice The Action And Adventure On America's Untamed Frontier—In One Big Volume!

ATTACK!

All hell broke loose. Loud splashing was punctuated by shrieks and undulating yells. A gun cracked, then another. Bow strings twanged. There was the thunk of arrows hitting home, the sickening squish of clubs rending flesh, the heavy thud of bodies striking the ground.

All of which registered in the back of Nate King's mind as he struggled for his life against the Pawnee who was slowly but surely choking off his windpipe. The pain was excruciating. Nate tried to take a breath, but couldn't.

The Pawnee's features were aglow with brutal glee. Grunting, he shifted to throw more of his weight against the long club.

Unless Nate did something, and did it quickly, he was going to die....

The *Wilderness* Series published by *Leisure Books:*

 # 1: KING OF THE MOUNTAIN
 # 2: LURE OF THE WILD
 # 3: SAVAGE RENDEZVOUS
 # 4: BLOOD FURY
 # 5: TOMAHAWK REVENGE
 # 6: BLACK POWDER JUSTICE
 # 7: VENGEANCE TRAIL
 # 8: DEATH HUNT
 # 9: MOUNTAIN DEVIL
#10: BLACKFOOT MASSACRE
#11: NORTHWEST PASSAGE
#12: APACHE BLOOD
#13: MOUNTAIN MANHUNT
#14: TENDERFOOT
#15: WINTERKILL
#16: BLOOD TRUCE
#17: TRAPPER'S BLOOD
#18: MOUNTAIN CAT
#19: IRON WARRIOR
#20: WOLF PACK
#21: BLACK POWDER
#22: TRAIL'S END

GIANT SPECIAL EDITIONS:

ORDEAL
PRAIRIE BLOOD
HAWKEN FURY
SEASON OF THE WARRIOR

WILDERNESS

THE TRAIL WEST

David Thompson

LEISURE BOOKS NEW YORK CITY

Dedicated to Judy, Joshua, and Shane.

A LEISURE BOOK®

March 1996

Published by

Dorchester Publishing Co., Inc.
276 Fifth Avenue
New York, NY 10001

Printed in the United States of America.

WILDERNESS

THE TRAIL WEST

Prologue

When Richard Ashworth felt a hard object pressed against the base of his spine, he froze. Moments before, the handsome New Yorker had stepped out of the bright midday sun into a dimly lit restaurant. His eyes had not yet adjusted to the gloom. He had no idea who was behind him or what was gouging his back.

A voice as rough as sandstone and with an accent as thick as pea soup snarled in his ear, "Didn't you see the sign on the door, mister? This place is closed until six. Come back in a couple of hours."

Most anyone else would have done as the speaker demanded. But Richard Ashworth had too much to lose to let himself be scared off by an underling. Squaring his shoulders, he gave his name and said, "I believe I'm expected. I was told to meet the Brothers here."

The Brothers. From the docks to the heights of Harlem, from Governor's Island to the rustic cabins that fringed the city inland—that was how the notorious pair were known. Everyone Ashworth knew had advised him to stay away from them, but he was desperate.

The pressure on Ashworth's spine went away. Hulking shapes loomed out of the shadows. A man the size of a small carriage lumbered around in front of Ashworth and raked him from head to toe with a look of ill-concealed contempt. "No one said anything about a meeting to me. Lou, go check while we keep our friend company."

Ashworth put on an air of casual calm. Inwardly, though, his stomach churned. He suspected that, if the Brothers failed to remember his appointment, the monster who served as their watchdog would haul him back into the alley and break half the bones in his body.

The man's thick lips split in a cruel smirk. "We don't often see your type around here, friend."

Ashworth knew to keep his mouth shut, but he couldn't resist asking, "My type? What exactly do you mean by that?"

The man's smirk widened. Fingers as thick as walking canes jabbed at Ashworth's attire. "Fancy beaver hat. Fancy cloak. Fancy clothes and shoes. You look like one of those newspaper advertisements for a store on Fifth Avenue."

Gruff laughter issued from several throats. Ashworth held his temper and said, "I should think, my good fellow, that it would be in your best interest to keep a civil tongue. I doubt that your employers like to have their business acquaintances treated in so cavalier a fashion."

More laughter greeted the remark. The huge man said, "A lot of fancy words, too. I bet you were born with a silver spoon in your mouth, weren't you?"

Before Ashworth could show his resentment, the one named Lou returned and whispered in the huge man's ear.

"You're in luck, Silver Spoon. Follow me."

The Brothers sat at a corner table, stuffing food into their mouths. Both were big, corpulent men. Their balding pates glistened as if slick with grease. Their suits were finely made, but seemed ready to burst at the seams. Napkins dotted with sauce and bits of pasta had been tucked into their collars.

Neither glanced up when Ashworth halted. Clearing his throat, he introduced himself. "First off, I want to thank you for agreeing to hear me out," he said, beginning the speech he had carefully prepared. "You have no idea how much this means to me—"

One of the Brothers—Ashworth did not know if it was Salvatore or Antonio—held up a hand that resembled a ham. "We are busy men, Mr. Ashworth. Get to the point. Tell us why you have come."

The man's brusque manner annoyed Ashworth. Rudeness was a trait he rarely tolerated, but in this instance he made an exception. "I have a certain business venture in mind. To put it into effect, I need capital, and the word on the street is that you have money to loan. So I thought—"

Once more Ashworth was interrupted. The other Brother—and again, Ashworth had no idea whether it was Antonio or Salvatore—fixed flat brown eyes on him.

"So you thought that you'd waltz on in here and talk us out of the money with no problem? You think you can pull the wool over the eyes over a couple of old-country bumpkins just off the boat?"

"I never thought any such thing," Ashworth said.

"That's good to hear," the Brother said. "Because we're not a charity. And we're not a bank either. If you borrow from us, you pay thirty-percent interest on your gross profit. Plus you'll sign over your house on Long Island and the estate on the Hudson as collateral. Fail to make good and they become ours."

Ashworth was startled, both by the amount they demanded and their intimate knowledge of his personal resources. "How do you know so much about me?"

The Brothers exchanged glances. "Honestly, Mr. Ashworth," the same one said, "didn't it occur to you that we would take the precaution of having you checked out? We know that your family was once one of the wealthiest in New York. We also know most of the money is now gone and you want to rebuild the family fortune."

Ashworth could not help but be impressed. His financial state was a closely guarded secret to keep creditors from baying at his door.

The other Brother wagged a fork at him. "Now do as I told you and get to the point. The guy who set up this meeting for you told us a little about what you have in mind. We want to hear it all."

In complete detail, Ashworth revealed his grand scheme. He was scrupulously honest, and to his immense relief, they listened without batting an eye. When he was done, he waited expectantly for their decision.

"I don't know," one said. "The risk factor is terribly high. We stand to lose our fifteen-thousand investment if you don't make it back."

"On the other hand," the other argued, turning to his sibling, "we stand to make twice that or more if he does half as well as he thinks he might."

The Brothers huddled. Ashworth strained to hear what they were whispering, but he could not make out a single word. At length they straightened up. Without being aware that he was doing so, he held his breath.

"You've got yourself a deal," the Brother who had liked the proposition said. "On one condition."

"What might that be?" Ashworth asked, so overjoyed that he was ready to grant any request they might make.

A thumb as squat as a sausage was jabbed at the huge watchdog who had escorted Ashworth in. "You have to take Emilio along."

Ashworth and the giant said in unison, "What?"

The Brother smiled. "That's the deal. Take it or leave it."

Ashworth hesitated. The last thing he needed was someone looking over his shoulder every step of the way. But it made sense for the Brothers to want to keep track of how their money was being spent. "Fair enough. I agree."

"Good. Meet us here tomorrow at the same time and we'll finalize the arrangement."

That was it. The meeting was ended. Emilio led Ashworth to the entrance and opened the door for him. Sullenly watching the happy man walk off, Emilio mentally cursed the fool for ever crossing the restaurant's doorstep. In his anger he slammed the door and did something he had never done before: He marched back into the dining room and over to his employers.

"Forgive me," he said in the language all three of them had spoken for decades before they ever came to America, "but I must know. Why me? What did I ever do to make you so mad?"

"You make it sound as if you are being punished," Salvatore said.

"Nothing could be further from the truth," Antonio declared. "We need someone to watch over our investment and you are the only one we can trust to get the job done. It is as simple as that."

Emilio fidgeted. "Again, forgive me. But do you know what you ask? Have you not heard the stories? There are wild beasts out there that can tear a man to pieces. And there are savages everywhere."

Salvatore leaned forward. "Don't tell me that you are afraid, Emilio?"

The suggestion brought scarlet to Emilio's cheeks. "I have never known fear. You know that."

"Then quit complaining," Antonio said. "You will be well paid. In fact, you will get your heart's desire when you return. All we ask is that you make sure Ashworth does not run off to the Oregon Country with our money."

"And if he succeeds in his venture," Salvatore said, "you are to wait until he has sold the furs. Then kill him and bring the entire proceeds to us."

Emilio's pulse had quickened at the mention of his fondest wish. "I understand," he said, bowing his chin. "As always, I am yours to command."

The Brothers smiled.

Chapter One

The brute caught Nate King unawares. One moment the mountain man was riding westward across the prairie without a care in the world, his powerful buckskin-clad frame perched astride his superb black stallion. The next, there came a violent snort from out of the high grass and a riled bull buffalo reared up in a wallow off to the right.

Nate instantly drew rein. He wanted to kick himself for not having noticed the wallow sooner, even though he could hardly be blamed. It was well hidden, for one thing. For another, the rank scent of urine and sweat was being wafted to the southeast by the stiff breeze.

A heavy Hawken rifle rested across Nate's thighs, but he made no attempt to use it. He hoped that the bull would amble off and leave him be. Having three pack animals in tow, he wasn't hankering for a clash.

Besides, Nate already had enough buffalo meat to last his family a long spell. He had spent the past two days butchering a cow almost as large as the shaggy specimen balefully eyeing him, and the packhorses were burdened with the results of his handiwork.

Nate saw the bull toss its horns, then snort again. Still, Nate made no sudden moves. No one knew better than he did how unpredictable buffalo could be. The simple act of lifting a hand might cause the creature to charge.

The bull cocked its massive head. It couldn't seem to make up its mind whether Nate was a threat or not. Uttering a third snort, it began to turn and leave.

"Good riddance, you mangy critter," Nate said under his breath, pleased the encounter had turned out so well. More often than not, random incidents like that one resulted in life or death situations. And he could do without that.

Just then one of the packhorses let out with a strident nicker. In a flash, the bull whirled. For an animal that weighed close to half a ton, it could move incredibly fast when it wanted to. In a flurry of pounding hooves and bobbing tail, the behemoth swept up out of the wallow and plowed through the grass toward the interlopers who had presumed to disturb its rest.

Nate King let the lead rope to the pack animals drop, reined his stallion to the right, and applied his heels. His intention was to lure the bull off, to have it chase him instead of the packhorses. In that, he succeeded all too well.

The bull angled to intercept the stallion, its broad brow and curved horns parting the stems in front of it like the prow of a great ship would ply the sea. Able to cover ground as swiftly as any horse, it narrowed the gap rapidly.

Nate goaded his steed into a gallop. Holding the Hawken in his left hand, he fairly flew northward. Between the drum of his mount's hooves and those of the onrushing bull, the plain around him rumbled as if to the boom of thunder. He cast repeated glances over a broad shoulder to ascertain exactly how close the bull was.

The brute proved amazingly quick. In a span of heartbeats, its flared nostrils were nearly brushing the black stallion's tail. For a few harrowing seconds it appeared that the bull would bowl the horse over.

Nate bent forward, lashing the reins for all he was worth while praying to his Maker that he wouldn't end his days stomped to a pulp by a cantankerous four-legged cuss that had fewer brains than an adobe brick.

The mountaineer thought of twisting and firing, but discarded the notion. Hitting a vital organ at that angle would be next to impossible. The only plain target was the bull's brain, which happened to be housed in solid bone so dense that a lead ball could never penetrate.

Nate contented himself with fleeing. He knew that buffalo were swift over short distances, just as he knew they lacked stamina. Within a few hundred yards the one behind him should play itself out, he reasoned, and he could escape.

The afternoon sun bathed the gently waving grass in a shimmering golden glow. Any other time, and Nate would have been entranced by the natural beauty the pristine landscape offered. Even after more than a decade of living in the wilderness, he never tired of nature's scenic wonders. It was one of the reasons he had enjoyed living in the majestic Rocky Mountains for so long.

As Nate had learned the hard way, everything worthwhile in life had its price. Life in the mountains might be paradise on earth, but it was a paradise rife with hostile Indians and bestial wildlife. A free trapper had to stay alert every minute of the day and night or he'd pay for his folly with his life.

An irate bellow reminded Nate to concentrate on the matter at hand. The bull was so close that it forked a horn at the stallion's rear legs and nearly hooked one. Nate flailed his limbs to inspire the horse to even greater speed.

Over a minute went by. Then two. Nothing else moved on the vast ocean of grass. It was as if Nate and the bull were the only living things in all existence.

The fact that one was by itself indicated to Nate it was an old bull that had been left behind. Such rogues were extremely belligerent, always ready to fight at the drop of a feather. They had to be, in order to stave off roving wolf packs and prowling panthers.

It compounded Nate's dilemma. The bull just

might chase him until it or Nate's horse dropped from sheer exhaustion. Nate had managed to gain a few yards, but the buffalo showed no sign of giving up any time soon.

Bending low and shifting his torso backward, Nate tucked the Hawken's smooth stock to his shoulder. It was difficult to fix a steady bead. The barrel kept bouncing up and down. He did the best he could, sighting on a spot just above the bull's right eye. Holding his breath, he thumbed back the hammer, pressed his forefinger to the trigger, and started to squeeze.

Suddenly, inexplicably, the bull veered off. It bore to the east at a steady trot, bobbing its head and rumbling irately deep in its chest.

Nate uncoiled his finger and eased the hammer down. Straightening, he looped around to the west to return to his packhorses before they strayed too far. Hardly had he gone 50 yards when the harrowing ordeal was all but forgotten. It had, after all, been nothing exceptional a typical occurrence in a typical day, one of countless near-fatal episodes he'd lived through since taking up residence on the frontier.

A brisk canter brought Nate to the vicinity of the wallow. Two of the packhorses were there, grazing peacefully. But the third, the one that had nickered and caused the bull to attack, the one that had given him no end of trouble during the whole trek, had somehow slipped the lead rope and wandered off.

"Damned nuisance," Nate grumbled. Gathering up the other two, he rode in a small circle until he found where the third had headed to the southwest.

"If I were an Apache, I'd eat it," Nate complained as he followed the trail of bent grass. Talking to himself had become a habit he no longer shunned. It relieved the monotonous quiet that sometimes bore down on a man's soul like a heavy weight. And it fostered the illusion of companionship when there was none, a needed antidote to the toxin of prolonged loneliness.

Judging by the stray's tracks, Nate saw that the animal had picked up speed as it went along. Nate became more annoyed as time passed. Every minute spent pursuing the troublemaker was another minute's delay in reaching his family, and more than anything, he desired to see them again.

About half an hour after leaving the wallow, Nate spied several familiar objects lying less than a hundred feet ahead. He scowled. Mentally, he tongue-lashed the stray with every cuss word in his vocabulary. The errant animal had managed to buck off the packs Nate had so painstakingly arranged that very morning, scattering the contents over a wide area.

Dismounting, Nate collected every last item. Among them was the cow's hide, which had to be refolded and tied tight. The sun was perched on the western rim of the world when Nate rose and studied the pile.

Since the other packhorses were already laden with as much as they could safely carry, Nate had to leave the pile there until he reclaimed the troublemaker. He didn't like it one bit. A grizzly or wolves might happen by and make short work of the jerked meat he had spent hours drying in the hot sun—meat his loved ones were counting on him to bring.

In a bitter temper, Nate swung onto the big black and resumed riding. He had half a mind to trade the stray at the next rendezvous to a trapper known to be partial to horseflesh. It would serve the animal right for giving him such a hard time.

Brilliant pink, yellow, and orange hues flared above the distant snowcapped peaks as the blood-red sun relinquished its hold on the darkening vault of heaven to a rising sliver of pale moon in the east.

Nate King scanned the foothills bordering the Rockies for some sign of the stray without result. Free of the weight of the packs that would slow it down, he mused, the animal might be halfway to Mexico.

Twilight claimed the prairie. A few stars heralded the myriad yet to sparkle. As was customary at that time of day, the wind increased, ceaselessly rustling the grass. A wavering howl fluttered to Nate's ears, the first of many he would hear during the night, a signal that the wolf packs had commenced their nocturnal wanderings. Nor would they be alone. Nighttime was when the larger predators, the grizzlies and the cats, were abroad.

Nate wasn't worried. He had spent more nights than he cared to count alone in the wild. His trusty Hawken, crafted for him by brothers of the same name in St. Louis, could drop any animal—

provided he hit it in the right spot. In addition to the .60-caliber rifle, he sported a brace of pistols wedged under his wide brown leather belt. Both were smooth-bore, single-shot .55-caliber flintlocks. At close range, they had almost the same stopping power as the Hawken.

Slanted across Nate's wide chest were a powder horn and an ammunition pouch. As well as his possibles bag. In a beaded sheath crafted by his wife, slung on his left hip, snuggled a Bowie he had obtained at Bent's Fort. Tucked under his belt above his right hip was a Shoshone tomahawk, a gift from one of his wife's kin.

In short, Nate King was loaded for bear. He was supremely confident that he could hold his own against anything that came at him. Nor was his attitude unique. Those who made their living as trappers had to be as rugged as the mountains in which their quarry flourished. The Rockies tempered men much as a forge tempered metal, dissolving the weak into the dust from which they were spawned and molding the strong to the consistency of steel.

Survival of the fittest, some might say, and they would be right. It was the same way with the wild things. Nature was a cruel mistress, bestowing continued existence on those creatures that adapted to her harsh demands and denying it to those that failed to cope. It was a bitter lesson—one Nate King had learned well.

The mountain man's instincts told him that it was time to turn around. Wheeling the stallion, he hastened to where he had left the pile. By then it was so dark that anything more than a dozen yards away was a murky blur. He almost missed seeing the pile.

Rather than build a fire and advertise his presence, Nate opted for a cold camp. After stripping the packhorses and tethering them to picket pins to insure they would not imitate their wayward fellow, he unsaddled the stallion and gave it a thorough rubdown using handfuls of grass.

Jerked buffalo meat sufficed for supper. Tepid water from a half-full water skin quenched Nate's thirst. Then, spreading out his blankets next to his belongings, he reclined on his back, propped his head in his hands, and admired the dazzling celestial display.

Lulled by the deceptively serene surroundings, Nate dozed. He dreamed of Winona, his beloved, and of Zach and Evelyn, his son and daughter. In his dream, the four of them were by the lake near their cabin when they heard rustling in the brush. Growling broke out, the guttural snarls of unseen stalkers. In his dream, Nate had forgotten to bring a gun. He stepped in front of his family to protect them just as a horde of shadowy shapes hurtled out of the brush and pounced on them.

Abruptly, Nate King woke up. Clammy sweat plastered his forehead and neck. He raised a hand to wipe them, then tensed as an ominous growl issued from the grass.

Pushing up into a crouch, Nate grasped the Hawken. He did not need to see the beast that had made the sound to know what it was. Wolves were out there, ringing him, taking his measure.

They had caught the scent of the hide and the meat, and they were hungry. The stallion and the packhorses stood rigid, ears pricked. They had tangled with wolves before. They knew what to expect.

Nate detected a hint of movement and brought the rifle up. Usually wolves bolted at the sound of a shot. But not always. To be on the safe side, he wouldn't fire unless they left him no choice.

One of the pack animals whinnied. An inky form, slung low to the ground, had materialized out of the night, at the fringe of the cleared space in which Nate had made camp. He swiveled to cover the lupine intruder and the wolf promptly retreated into the grass.

The rustle of slinking bodies grew steadily closer. Made bold by the lack of resistance, the wolves were tightening the noose, closing in until they were near enough to converge on Nate and the horses in a concerted rush.

Nate could not let that happen. Cupping a hand to his mouth, he bellowed, "Light a shuck, you uppity varmints! Go pester someone else!"

Sometimes the mere sound of a human voice was enough to drive wild animals off, but not that time. The wolves continued to constrict the circle, their dark silhouettes distinct against the backdrop of lighter grass.

The moment of truth had arrived. Nate had no other option. Elevating the Hawken, he trained it on a particularly large wolf visible at the clearing's edge. There was always one wolf in every pack that was the leader. Drop the leader, the conventional wisdom went, and the rest would scatter.

Nate yelled again, giving the wolves every chance to get while the getting was good. The big wolf brazenly slunk into the open, creeping toward a packhorse. Another wolf appeared. Then a third. Aiming slightly behind the lead wolf's front shoulder, Nate pulled back the hammer, held his breath to steady his arms, then stroked the trigger.

At the crack of the shot, the big wolf leapt straight up into the air, spinning as it did, and vented a piercing howl that must have been heard a mile off. It hit the ground on its side with a pronounced thud, breaking into violent convulsions. The other two promptly turned tail.

Loud crackling in the grass assured Nate that the entire pack had taken to its heels. Rising, he marked their retreat until the noise dwindled in the distance. Satisfied they were indeed gone, he sat and hastily reloaded the rifle.

For over an hour Nate stayed awake, vigilant. It was highly unlikely the wolves would circle around to test his mettle again, but the shot might have been heard by unfriendly human ears. Only when he was convinced that no hostiles were sneaking up on him did Nate lie back down with the Hawken resting across his chest.

To the west, faint with distance, a grizzly coughed. To the south, coyotes erupted in an eerie chorus. Somewhere to the east, a bird shrieked in avian terror, its cry choked off to twitters and tweets that soon ended. All ordinary sounds.

Gradually, Nate felt the tension drain from his sinews. He drifted off. If he dreamed again, he did not remember the images when he awoke shortly before dawn. Rising, he stretched, then paced to warm himself. More jerky made a tangy breakfast. Packs went back on the pack animals, the saddle on the black stallion. The hide and extra packs Nate arranged in a low pile and covered with grass.

As the sun greeted the new day, Nate King forked leather and resumed his hunt for the stray. Were it not that he needed the troublemaker so badly, he would have let it traipse off to wherever it wanted and been gladly shy of the gadfly.

By the middle of the morning Nate reached the pine-covered foothills. There, he discovered the horse had turned due south. He did the same, angry because the contrary animal was leading him ever farther from home. Soon, though, Nate's anger evaporated, replaced by intense curiosity—and not a little anxiety.

The stray's trail bisected another. The new one had been made just the day before by three unshod horses heading northwest. It bothered Nate for two reasons. Unshod mounts usually meant Indians, and coming from the southeast as they were, the Indians were probably hostiles. Worse, they were heading in the general direction of the remote high valley that Nate called home. The addlepated stray had turned to the southeast.

Nate gazed out over the rippling prairie, thinking of the cache. It would have to wait. He was not going after the stray when his family might be in peril. Without another moment's hesitation the mountain man cut the black stallion to the northwest and trotted on into the foothills, giving a sharp tug on the lead rope to urge the pack animals along.

Nate paid close attention to the sign. Of the three horses, one was a big stallion like his, another a mare, and the third, based on the size of its hooves, a small horse, perhaps a mustang similar to those he had seen ridden by Comanches down in the Red River country. The three rode in single file, the stallion in the lead.

An hour later Nate found where the trio had stopped for the night, on a narrow shelf watered by a small spring. Moccasin prints bordered the soft earth rimming the water, those of a man larger than Nate. They were the only obvious tracks, and Nate did not linger to search for more, not once the style of the moccasins became apparent.

It was a little-known fact that no two tribes fashioned their moccasins exactly alike. The Pawnees, for instance, preferred footwear wider across the ball of the foot than anywhere else. Crows wore crescent-shaped moccasins. Kiowas liked theirs to have pointed tips.

The tracks at the spring had been made by a Comanche. There could be no mistake. It confirmed Nate's hunch about the mustang and filled him with keen dread.

Comanches were the scourge of north Texas.

Fiercely independent, they had resisted the inroads of the Mexicans for years; they were just as fiercely trying to drive the white man from their domain. Although generally stout of stature, they were sterling horsemen, widely considered to be the very best on the plains. For the life of him, the trapper could not imagine what the trio were doing so far from their established territory.

Of more immediate concern was the threat to his loved ones, and with that uppermost in mind, Nate raced ever higher, recklessly pushing the pack animals to go faster than was prudent. He was glad when a gap between two mountain ridges appeared above because it was the entrance to his family's haven. Spurring the stallion on, he came to the opening and beheld the large valley he knew as well as he did the backs of his own hands.

No sooner had Nate King set eyes on it than the crisp air was shattered by the blast of a rifle.

Chapter Two

No one knew when the practice started, but the hardy men who made their precarious living as trappers liked to refer to the lush high mountain valleys as parks. Having special names for things was a trademark of the mountain men. They called themselves mountaineers. They referred to beaver hides as plews and mountain lions as panthers. It was just another example of their colorful character, a rare blend of raw courage, unquenchable thirst for life, and, above all, the ability to adapt, that made them so unique.

Nathaniel King was a master at adapting. He had carved his own personal niche out of the wilderness in a spectacular park rimmed by snow-crowned mountains. A broad lake provided his family with crystal-clear drinking water as well as fish and fowl for their supper table. Deer, elk, and lesser game were in abundance. There were only three trails into the park, one from the southeast, one from the northeast, and a secret route to the west used only by Indians until Nate King came along. The southeast trail was the gentlest of the three, threading down a series of switchbacks and across the rolling valley floor.

Nate streaked down it, recklessly driving his horses in order to reach his cabin as quickly as possible. A thin tendril of smoke above the pines pinpointed its exact location close to the west shore of the lake. A second shot echoed off the surrounding peaks as Nate came to the bottom and lashed his reins like a man possessed. In his mind's eye he envisioned his wife and children being set upon by the three bloodthirsty Comanches and viciously slaughtered.

Figures moved along the lake. Nate let go of the lead rope and sped toward them. The packhorses would be all right alone until he could come back for them. His family was more important.

It had long been Nate's secret fear that one day he would return from a trapping trip or elsewhere to find his loved ones butchered or missing. He was no blind optimist. He knew the many dangers that might arise at any time, any one of which could snuff out the precious lives of those who meant more to him than life itself. Every free trapper had to live with the same ever-present possibility. It was an inevitable fact of life in the Rockies, the price paid for freedom.

Suddenly Nate glimpsed one of the figures moving swiftly through the brush toward him. He slowed and brought up the Hawken even as he anxiously scanned the shoreline for sign of his family.

The figure made no attempt to use stealth. Crashing through the underbrush like a bounding buck, it slanted toward the mountain man to head him off.

Nate rounded a knoll, skirted a thicket, and came to a small clearing. He reached it just as the figure dashed into the open on the other side. Elation coursed through Nate's veins and he sprang from the stallion.

"Pa! You're back!" young Zachary King cried. Dashing up, he threw his arms around his father and squeezed tight. He would never admit as much, but he always fretted terribly when his pa went off alone. "I was just fixing to do some target shooting and saw you coming."

A dozen questions were on the tip of Nate's tongue. Where were the boy's mother and sister? Had they seen any sign of Comanches? He forgot about them the next moment as a much larger form burst from the trees.

Nate's reaction was automatic. Pushing his son aside, he leveled the Hawken and began to curl back the hammer. Only then did he realize the newcomer had a bushy beard and could not possibly be an Indian. Belatedly, the man's features registered, and Nate blurted out in surprise, "Kendall?"

Scott Kendall was a fellow member of the elite mountain-man fraternity. His reddish beard creased in a warm smile as he said, "Howdy, hos.

It's been a spell, I reckon. This coon is glad to see you. Give me your paw."

Nate shook, noting the iron strength in the other's grip. As best as he could recollect, the last time he had run into Kendall had been at Bent's Fort several years earlier. "What brings you to my neck of the woods?"

"A business proposition," Kendall said. "Why not make yourself to home and I'll tell you all about it?"

Nate was eager to reach the cabin, but the safety of his family took priority. Surveying the lake, he said, "First things first. Have either of you seen any sign of Comanches hereabouts?"

"Comanches?" young Zach said, recalling the time they had traveled to Santa Fe and encountered a band along the way. Never in all his 12 years had he seen anyone who could ride like Comanches could. The warriors and their mounts had seemed as one, able to do feats he had never before witnessed.

"I came across some tracks," Nate said, stopping when Kendall chuckled heartily.

"Sheath your claws, friend. You and yours are safe. The only Comanches in these parts are the two on my feet."

Glancing down, Nate was flabbergasted to find that the other mountaineer wore a pair of genuine Comanche moccasins. "What the devil?"

Kendall lifted a leg to show the footwear off. "Comanches used to come to Bent's Fort now and then to trade. I was in need of new moccasins one day and took a shine to these. They shed water like a duck's back and are thick enough to last a coon's age."

Nate thought of the mare and the pony. "You brought your wife and daughter along?"

"Sure did," Kendall said. "They're up to the cabin, visiting with your missus."

Tension drained from Nate like water from a sieve. "Let's fetch my packhorses and we'll join them."

Zachary King fell into step between the two strapping men. He imitated their carefree swagger and cradled his Hawken in the crook of an elbow exactly as they did theirs. The men shared a hearty laugh over Nate's having been all upset for nothing, but Zach didn't see where the situation had been all that funny. What if it had been real Comanches? he asked himself. His ma, Evelyn, and he would have been in a fine stew.

Nate led the black stallion by the reins to give it a breather. He was intensely curious to learn why Kendall had paid him a visit, especially since they were no more than casual acquaintances, having met at the fort and a few times at the annual rendezvous.

As best as Nate could recollect, Kendall hailed from Massachusetts. So did the man's wife, a hardy pioneer woman who had braved the perils of mountains life for about a decade. Nate had to ponder a bit before he could recall her name. "How is Lisa faring?"

"Just fine," the bushy-bearded trapper responded in his booming voice. "She was as happy as a lark living at Bent's place, and she's even happier now that we might be going back to Boston."

"You're calling it quits?" Nate asked. It wouldn't surprise him, if so. Even though Kendall had struck him as the sort who loved living in the mountains, it was an all too true fact that few were able to bear up under the strain.

The actual numbers were sobering. Two out of every three who ventured to the Rockies perished within five years. Of those who survived, only one in ten stayed more than a half-dozen years. It took a rare soul to endure the unrelenting onslaught of the elements, savage beasts, and equally savage men.

"Not at all," Kendall said. "She's been after me to pay her kin back east a visit. I've put it off since we never have any money to spare. Now, thanks to Richard Ashworth, we have a chance to earn all we need for the trip and then some."

"Ashworth?" Nate said. "I don't believe I know the gent."

"You wouldn't," Kendall said. "He only showed up at Bent's Fort about a month ago, fresh from New York City."

"Does he aim to make his mark trapping?"

"You could say that," Kendall said, and smiled enigmatically.

For a while they hiked in silence, and presently they came to the south shore of the lake, which they followed around to the west. Ducks, geese, and brants frolicked on the water. Gulls wheeled and squawked above it. The birds raised a racket with their constant cries.

"Quite a hideaway you have here," Kendall

said, embracing the verdant park with a sweep of his brawny hand. "Your own personal Garden of Eden." He stared at the waterfowl, and sighed. "I wouldn't mind finding a little valley of my own like this somewhere. But I can't bring myself to put my wife and daughter at risk. That's why we've lived at the fort for so many years."

Nate sympathized. Planting roots there in the middle of nowhere had been one of the hardest decisions he'd ever made.

"I hear tell the Utes give you grief from time to time," the other mountain man mentioned.

"They used to," Nate said. The valley was located very close to territory the Utes claimed as their homeland, and for years after Nate settled there, the tribe had done all in their power to drive him off.

Several winters earlier, however, a dispute had broken out between the Utes and Nate's adopted people, the Shoshones, over a site both tribes regarded as sacred. Nate had wound up arranging a truce, and ever since, the Utes had left his family alone.

"What about the Blackfoot Confederacy?" Kendall asked. "Do they ever bother you?"

Nate shook his head. "They never come this far south." Which was a good thing. The Blackfeet were the most powerful tribe on the northern plains, and they hated whites. Together with the Bloods and the Piegans, they had formed a formidable alliance.

"Did you hear what they did to Art Bishop?"

"No. What?"

Young Zachary perked up. He loved to hear the latest news. Unfortunately, visitors to the homestead were few and far between, so his passion for gossip went largely unindulged.

Kendall frowned. "Bishop and two others weren't having much luck up Yellowstone way, so they sneaked on north into Blackfoot territory. Probably figured they could get in and out without being noticed if they stuck to the deep woods."

"What happened?" Nate knew Bishop fairly well and was surprised the man had been so foolhardy. But then, beaver were becoming scarce along the front range. Each season trappers had to foray farther and farther afield to find prime peltries.

"What else? A hunting party stumbled on them. Bishop and the others were scared hell west and cooked, but they didn't get far. The Blackfeet trapped them in a box canyon, then sent runners to a village. Before long a war party of two hundred had them hemmed in."

It was a story Nate had heard many times with only minor variation. Mountaineers who bucked the Blackfeet invariably bit off more than they could chew.

Zach listened in breathless anticipation. He had been a captive of the Blackfeet once for a short while and had grown to respect them, in spite of himself. How could he do otherwise when they had treated him so decently? A prominent warrior had even wanted to adopt him.

Kendall went on. "Bishop and his friends held

out for as long as their ammunition lasted. They saved three balls for themselves. But before they could do the deed, a bunch of Blackfeet sneaked up on them."

Nate glanced at his son, debating whether the boy should hear the rest. Blackfeet were fond of torturing captives—not out of any mean streak, but as a test of courage. Figuring that Zach shouldn't be sheltered from life's grimmer realities, he kept quiet.

"One of Bishop's friends had to run a gauntlet and was hacked to bits. The other was stripped, tied to a tree, and skinned alive. His eyeballs were gouged out, then forced down his throat." Kendall happened to look down at his side and gave a little start on seeing Zach. Coughing as if embarrassed, he said, "There was more, but you get the idea."

"How did you hear all this?"

"From Bishop. He showed up at Bent's Fort shortly before I left, on his way back to Ohio. He says that he's had enough of the wilderness to last him a lifetime."

Zach waited to hear how Bishop had escaped, and when a minute elapsed and their guest failed to elaborate, he said, "Tell the rest, Mr. Kendall. How did Bishop give those Blackfeet the slip?"

Kendall glanced at Nate, who snickered. "They saved him for the next day, son, and during the night he wriggled out of the ropes they had tied him with and helped himself to a war-horse. It raised a ruckus, so he had to light a shuck. Those

Blackfeet chased him clear to the Missouri River before they gave up."

"He was lucky to get away," Zach said.

"That he was." Nate said to impress on his son the folly of courting death. "Anyone with half a brain knows not to set foot in Blackfoot country." Out of the corner of his eye he noticed Kendall give him an odd glance.

"You have a point," the other mountaineer said. "But it's a crying shame that some of the best trapping grounds left happen to be north of the Missouri."

At that moment, they rounded a bend in the trail that linked the lake to the cabin and a childish squeal of glee drew their attention to a lively bundle of buckskins and curls that hurled herself into Kendall's arms.

"Pa! Pa! Evelyn has a doll almost the same as mine!"

"Does she, now?" the proud father said. "Imagine that. Girls with dolls. What will they think of next?"

Nate laughed, then turned as two women and another child emerged from the cabin. Tiny Evelyn tottered toward him, saying, "Papa! Papa!"

He swept her up and pecked her on the cheek. "How's my big girl?"

"Just fine, thank you," the woman with raven tresses who followed Evelyn said. Wi-no-na King was Shoshone. She favored buckskin dresses and beaded moccasins that were somehow all the more alluring for their simplicity. Radiating vitality, she molded herself to Nate and brushed his mouth with her warm lips. "We have missed you, husband."

"Good."

Winona's dark eyes sparkled. She never tried to hide her affection for her man, as some women were inclined to do. "I see by the pack animals that the mighty Grizzly Killer managed to find a buffalo, but lose a horse," she said in precise English born of long practice.

"The horse lost itself." Hooking the arm holding the Hawken in hers, Nate ambled toward their home.

Little Evelyn nuzzled his chin. "You itch me, Papa."

"I'll trim my beard in the morning." Nate's daughter never had taken a liking to it, and of late he had been half tempted to shave it off. Winona wouldn't mind, he was sure.

Scott Kendall had his own arms full with his daughter and wife. Lisa greeted Nate. Then the beaming parents introduced their pride and joy, Vail Marie, who surprised Nate with a blunt question.

"My pa says the Indians call you Grizzly Killer. Is that so?"

"It is," Nate said. The name had been bestowed on him on his initial trek west after he slew a grizzly using just a knife. It had been a once-in-a-lifetime event. But the name had stuck. Since then he'd had occasion to slay grizzlies, but never because he went looking for them. Sheer chance had repeatedly pitted him against the ferocious carnivores; sheer chance had enabled him to live through each conflict.

"Do you like that name?" Vail Marie asked with the typical innocence of a child.

"I never really gave it much thought," Nate said, "but I suppose I do. It's better than Silly Goose or Ornery Duckling."

The girl giggled. "You're poking fun! Indians don't have names like that."

"True. But they do have names like Big In The Center, Don't Know What It Is, and Made Himself Like The Man In The Moon. I'd rather be called Grizzly Killer."

Kendall and Zach gave Nate a hand stripping the packhorses and carting the packs into the cabin. Winona and Lisa busied themselves cooking while the girls sat in a corner and played with their dolls. Soon the tantalizing aroma of roasting buffalo haunch filled the single room, making Nate's stomach rumble with hunger.

No more was said about the reason for Scott Kendall's visit until after the meal, which consisted of sweet cakes, boiled roots, fresh bread, a pudding made from berries, and two pots of scalding hot coffee.

Nate ate with relish. He was an excellent cook in his own right, but in his humble opinion no one else on the entire planet could whip up meals as delicious as those his wife prepared. Treating himself to a second sweet cake and his sixth cup of black coffee, Nate leaned back in a chair he had built himself, and beamed. "This is the life."

"It doesn't get much better than this," Kendall

said. "The only thing that would beat it is having ten bales of prime plews ready to sell at the next rendezvous."

"Dream on, friend," Nate said. "No one has collected that many at one time in years. Jeb Smith was the last, I think, and he's long since gone on to his reward."

Kendall propped his hands on top of his beaver hat. "It could be done if a man knew where to find the beaver."

"Most of the streams in the central mountains are trapped out," Nate said.

"Who said anything about the central mountains?"

Nate paused in the act of taking a bite of sweet cake. "Why do I get the feeling that you're leading up to something?"

The man from Massachusetts chuckled. He had an easygoing way about him that Nate admired, a flair for taking life in stride. "Because I am, that's why." Kendall leaned forward. "Remember that coon from New York I told you about? Ashworth? Well, he might be as green as grass, but he has a plan to raise more plews in two seasons than anyone has raised in the past ten years."

"And you're throwing in with him?"

Kendall nodded with enthusiasm. "My wife and I have talked it over long and hard, and we think it's the right thing to do. Ashworth promises that every man who goes along with him will earn at least two thousand dollars, which is more money than my family has seen at one time in a long while."

Nate was intrigued. Winona and he had a tidy nest egg stashed away, but it was hardly enough to keep them in trade goods for the rest of their lives. "How many men is this Ashworth fellow taking along?"

"Sixty."

Unsure if he had heard correctly, Nate said, "Why, that's an entire fur brigade!"

Kendall took a swig of coffee and smacked his lips. "That it is, my friend. A brigade the likes of which no one has seen since old Jim Bridger and company roamed these mountains."

Fond memories of his first meeting with Bridger and the early efforts of the trapping fraternity washed over Nate. "Those were the days. Too bad they're gone for good."

"Who says they are?" Kendall asked. "Ashworth has invested thousands in outfitting a new brigade, and in two weeks, we leave for country where the beaver have never been trapped, where they're as thick as fleas on an old hound dog."

"I envy you," Nate said.

"Why not join us?"

The question brought instant quiet to the cabin. Zach King looked up from his chair by the fireplace where he was sharpening his butcher knife. His heart beat faster at the thought of going on an expedition to unknown country, of seeing new sights and meeting new people.

Winona King also glanced up, but her emotions were markedly different. She knew her man well enough to know that the prospect would tempt him, knew him well enough to worry that he might agree without taking time to think it over first.

Nate King rested his hands on the edge of the table. "Is that why you've come? To give me an invite?"

"From Richard Ashworth himself," Kendall said. "He needs a reliable man to be his second-in-command, and he's offering the job to you."

A feather could have floored Nate. "Me? Why not you or one of the other sixty?"

"The others are good men," Kendall said, "and I've done my share of trapping. But everyone knows that you're one of the two or three best trappers alive. The only one I can think of who might top you is Shakespeare McNair, who happens to be off visiting the Flatheads."

"I know," Nate said absently. McNair was his best friend and mentor, the man who had taught him everything he knew.

"So what do you say? Do you like Ashworth's proposal."

Nate did, but he was not about to commit himself unless he knew a lot more than he did at that moment. "Slow down, hoss. This is a big dose to take all at once. How do I know this Ashworth isn't a few cards shy of a full deck? Where in God's green creation does he think he'll find enough beaver to fill the pokes of every member of his brigade?"

"North of the Missouri."

"But that's Blackfoot country!"

Scott Kendall grinned. "Exactly."

Chapter Three

The early afternoon sun beat down relentlessly on the prairie. It was uncommonly hot. Beads of sweat dotted Nate King's brow as he reined the black stallion to a standstill and scanned the clear space in the high grass where he had left the cache of dried buffalo meat and the cow's hide.

"It's all gone," Scott Kendall said.

The two mountain men had ridden down from the cabin for the express purpose of retrieving the cache. In particular, Nate was desirous of reclaiming the hide, which Winona needed to make a new robe for herself. Letting the lead rope to the pack animal he had brought along drop, he slid from the saddle and sank to one knee to examine the ground.

Unshod hoofprints provided a clue to the culprits. Partial moccasin tracks and scuff marks showed where the packs and hide had been distributed among five mounted warriors. Another four had sat their horses nearby.

"A hunting party, you reckon?" Kendall said.

It was hard for Nate to say. The warriors might have been out after buffalo. Or it might have been a war party seeking to count coup on their enemies. None of the prints were clear enough to enable him to identify the tribe.

"You can head on back," Nate said as he climbed onto the stallion. "This isn't your affair."

Kendall snorted. "What sort of coon would I be if I turned tail at the prospect of getting in a racket with a few Indians?"

"Nine is more than a few," Nate said. "And I don't want you rubbed out on my account." Clucking to the black, he trotted off in the direction the band had taken, to the northeast. In moments Kendall was matching his pace alongside him. "I see you don't listen worth a hoot."

The bigger man showed teeth. "You know, my missus is always saying the same thing. She likes to tell everyone how she hitched up with the only man in all creation whose head is harder than a redwood."

"That's nothing," Nate said. "Winona claims my noggin was an anvil before someone stuck it on my shoulders."

The two trappers rode on in fine spirits for over an hour. Beside a ribbon of a creek that would be dry in another month they came on the camp site the Indians had used the night before.

"Well, lookee here," Kendall said, nodding at a

clear footprint at the water's edge. "Are they Pawnees?"

Nate took a look. "Cheyennes," he said, his brow knitting. He harbored no ill will toward the tribe. They had left him in peace over the years, even though they knew his family occupied the high valley. It must have been ten years since he had gone hunting one morning and happened on tracks left by a large party of Cheyennes who had spied on the cabin for at least half a day, yet never attacked. Ever since, Nate had made it a point to do nothing that would antagonize the tribe.

"Well, let's get after them," Kendall said, striding to his sorrel. "If we push real hard, by sunset tomorrow you should have your things back."

Nate reflected on whether going on was the right thing to do. By rights, he should forget about the stolen items and go on home. A few bundles of jerked meat were hardly worth their lives. But that hide was another matter. He had been promising one to Winona for weeks. He doubly hated to lose it after having put so much effort into hunting the small herd of buffalo down and carefully skinning the cow so as not to mar the hide in any respect. Somehow, Nate had to get that hide back without tangling with the warriors.

"Why the long face?" Kendall asked.

"There's something you should know," Nate said, then explained as they resumed riding. The other trapper didn't criticize his decision or mock him as being foolish. "If that's the way you want it, that's the way it'll be."

Twilight found them well out on the vast plain. In a basin that offered shelter from the wind and prying eyes, they made a cold camp. Until midnight, they talked about their respective pasts, Nate telling about the father who had ruled him with an iron fist and later despised him for becoming, as he saw it, a worthless vagabond.

Kendall's childhood had been tame by comparison. Reared by loving, religious parents, he had almost become a minister. The lure of adventure had drawn him to the mountains, and once there, he had never wanted to go back.

A pack of coyotes on a nearby knoll was competing with another pack far to the north to see which could howl the loudest—or so it seemed to Nate as he rose and went to the packhorse. Agitated by the din, it pranced and tugged at the picket pin. He stroked its neck and spoke softly until it quieted down. By then, the howling had tapered to a few plaintive cries.

Scott Kendall was asleep when Nate stretched out on his blankets. So only Nate witnessed the spectacular descent of a flaming meteor that disappeared over the horizon in the same direction Nate and his companion happened to be traveling.

Most Indians, Nate knew, would have taken the sight as an omen. A meteor was considered bad medicine, a sign that something awful was going to happen. Nate hoped that they were wrong as he closed his eyes and slipped into a fitful sleep.

At first light the two mountaineers were in the saddle. The band had made no attempt to hide their trail, so Nate had no problem tracking them to a tributary of the South Platte River. The moment the winding belt of cottonwoods and willows hove into sight, Nate drew rein. A thin column of smoke rose from among the trees.

"We did it," Kendall said. "But what now? How do we snatch your effects without being snatched ourselves?"

It was a good question. Retreating to a gully where they secreted their mounts, Nate and Kendall snaked through the tall grass to a vantage point several hundred feet from the smoke.

The Cheyennes were in a wide clearing, their horses grazing a stone's throw away. Immediately it was apparent that there were more than nine warriors. Nate counted 21 and a corresponding number of horses.

"Where the dickens did those others come from?" Kendall whispered.

Shrugging, Nate slanted to the left, toward some willows. He slowly parted the blades in front of him with the barrel of his rifle, then slid between them without rustling the grass. At length a patch of shade shrouded him and he rose onto his knees.

Nate's plan was to wait until dark, then sneak in as close as they dared. He twisted to say as much to Kendall. Low voices coming closer changed his mind. Instantly he flattened, as did his friend.

Nate could not understand a word being said. He assumed the warriors were speaking in the Cheyenne tongue until two strapping men appeared, both armed with bows. Unlike Cheyennes, who usually wore their hair parted in the middle and braided, the pair wore theirs swept back at the front, with only two tiny braids hanging on either side. They were Arapahoes.

Nate watched as the two warriors moved off along the stream, apparently to hunt. It was no surprise to find Cheyennes and Arapahoes mingling. The two tribes had long been staunch allies. They met regularly in grand councils. They traded horses and guns.

It didn't take a genius to figure out that two hunting parties had bumped into one another and were going to spend the night feasting and swapping tales. In that respect, as in so many others, the red men were no different than the whites they so often despised.

Nate did not move until confident the hunters were long gone. Nudging Kendall with an elbow, he crawled forward, relying on every bit of available cover, until he could see the camp clearly. The Indians were clustered in several small groups. Those who did not know the other's tongue relied on the universal language of the Plains tribes, sign language, in which Nate was fluent.

A burly Cheyenne was telling several Arapahoes about the time he ran up against a wounded grizzly. Another warrior was relating his prowess in battle against the Dakotas. Still a third was praising the merits of a certain Cheyenne chief.

A light touch on Nate's shoulder drew his attention to Scott Kendall, who pointed across the clearing at the base of an oak tree. Piled there were Nate's packs and the folded buffalo hide. The tree was close to the stream and could not possibly be reached without arousing every warrior in the camp. For Nate to reclaim his property, strategy was called for.

Nate mulled over his options as the afternoon waned. The Indians got two small fires going. From parfleches an assortment of pemmican and jerked meat was passed out. Shortly before sunset, the pair of Arapahoes showed up bearing a buck slung on a pole. In no time, the deer had been skinned and the meat carved into portions. The hunting parties settled in for the night.

When the sky was deep blue and dominated by stars, Nate backed away from the camp. Kendall imitated him. They covered 60 yards before Nate stood and pumped his left leg to relieve a cramp.

"Do you still aim to go through with this?" Scott Kendall said.

"I do," Nate said, feeling slightly sheepish for being so stubborn but unwilling to give up after having come so far. "Once they fall asleep, I'm going in."

"They're bound to post a guard."

"Can't be helped." Nate sat on a log, drew his Bowie, and proceeded to cut enough whangs from the sleeves of his buckskin shirt and leggings to craft a rawhide rope several feet long.

Nate tied one end around the barrel of his Hawken just below the front bead sight and the other end on the narrow neck of the stock. It made a dandy makeshift sling he used to drape the rifle over his back.

Kendall leaned against a trunk. "Wouldn't it be easier to just go out and find yourself another buffalo? What's so blamed special about the hide they took anyhow?"

The gruff question hid obvious worry for Nate's safety. He slid the Bowie into his sheath, saying softly, "Think about it. The Cheyennes know that my valley isn't all that far from where they found the cache. They might put two and two together and figure out that the hide and the packs are mine. Once word spreads how easily they skunked me, some of the younger warriors are bound to take it into their noggins to pay my place a visit. I don't want that to happen."

"Never thought of it like that," Kendall said. "I guess you have to teach them who's boss or they'll be swiping your stock and whatever else strikes their fancy any time they see fit. All right, then. What do you want me to do, pard?"

"Wait by our horses."

"And let you take all the risk? No, sir."

"They're my packs. Since one of us has to be ready to light a shuck, you're elected."

Kendall protested, but Nate held firm. The husky mountain man grew somber as the hours went by. Toward midnight, Nate nodded and said, "Off you go. Keep your eyes skinned. I'll likely be in a hurry."

"Shoot sharps the word," Kendall said. Then he was gone, melting into the vegetation as if part of it.

Nate crept to the stream. It was no more than eight feet wide, the banks steep, the current sluggish. Sliding down to the water, he paused before entering to take both his pistols from under his belt. A flintlock in either hand, he entered the stream in a crouch. The level quickly rose as high as his knees. In the middle, where the current had worn a shallow trench, the water was still only as high as his waist.

Bending so low over the surface that his cheek nearly brushed it, Nate waded downstream. He held the pistols against his chest to keep them from getting wet. A misfire, a flash in the pan at just the wrong moment, might mean the difference between life and death.

The hubbub of voices had died down. Only one of the fires still crackled. Around it were seated three older warriors, two Cheyennes and an Arapahoe. The rest had all curled up and gone to sleep right where they had been sitting when fatigue overcame them.

Nate noticed that the horses had been rounded up and were enclosed in a rope corral, an unusual precaution for Indians to take. He didn't give it a second thought though, and that shortly proved to be a mistake.

Moving his legs at a snail's pace, Nate drew abreast of the clearing. The flames were so low that none illuminated the stream. Thanks to a moonless sky, he was virtually invisible. He paralleled a third of the open space with none of the Indians being any the wiser. When a sleeping Arapahoe snorted and started to sit up, he froze until the man settled back down. When one of the older warriors by the fire glanced his way, he again stopped, counting on his silhouette to blend into the background. The man betrayed no alarm and went on talking.

Nate waded a few more feet, then went rigid for a third time, but not because of anything the Cheyennes or Arapahoes did. It was a sound behind him that glued him in place; the stealthy pad of human feet. For a few nerve-racking moments Nate believed that he had erred, that one of the Indians must have crossed the stream earlier and was returning. But a rapid count of those in the camp accounted for all twenty-one. Yet if none of them were behind him, who was?

Swiveling only his neck, Nate saw furtive forms approaching the stream. Seven, eight, nine at least, and possibly more lurking in the vegetation. Had a third hunting party spotted the fires and come to join their friends? If so, why were they moving so quietly, as enemies would?

It hit him then with the force of a physical blow. His stupidity made him want to slam his head against a tree. The shadows nearing the stream were acting just as enemies would because they were enemies of either the Cheyennes or the Arapahoes or both. And there he was, caught between the factions with nowhere to run, nowhere to hide. Damn his luck!

The nearest newcomers slowed. Nate distinguished that they wore their hair in an odd style, shaving it except for a strip from the middle of the forehead to the back of the neck. They had on thigh-high moccasins and what could only be described as short buckskin skirts that ended just above their moccasins. Most carried thick war clubs decorated with brass tacks, clubs that sported wicked sunken blades able to slice a man open as easily as a sharp knife would a ripe melon.

Nate's mouth went dry. Only one tribe wore their hair in that distinctive style. Only one tribe was partial to clubs just like those the warriors carried. The newcomers were Pawnees. Their hatred of the Cheyennes and Arapahoes was well known. Some might say they had a valid excuse since the latter two tribes had settled in land once claimed by the former and held it even though the Pawnees had tried time and again to drive them off.

Nate had to get out of there before the Pawnees spotted him. Staying low to the water, he sidled toward the tree where his packs were piled.

The Pawnees had huddled, perhaps for a last palaver before attacking. More had materialized out of the night and others were arriving every few seconds.

The Cheyennes and their allies were severely outnumbered. They wouldn't stand a prayer if caught unawares.

Nate tried telling himself that he didn't owe the Cheyennes a blessed thing. They had stolen his effects, and no doubt would have taken him captive if they had the chance. But they had never tried to make wolf meat of him and his family, as the Utes and Blackfeet and others had done. They had never given him a lick of trouble in all the years he had lived in the cabin. So how could he stand idly by while they were massacred? The answer, of course, was that he couldn't.

Nate went faster. A few of the Pawnees had glided to the water's edge and were about to cross. They were 20 feet away, but they had eyes only for the Arapahoes and Cheyennes. As yet they had no inkling that he was there.

A few more yards and Nate could climb out. He would duck behind the oak tree, then let out with a holler that would bring the Cheyennes and the Arapahoes to their feet before the Pawnees swooped down on them. It would give the two hunting parties a fighting chance. And while all the Indians were embroiled in battle, he would retrieve what was rightfully his and get out of there while the getting was good.

Nate had it all figured out. He grinned as he reached the bank and slid out onto a gradual grassy incline that in turn brought him to level ground only a couple of feet from the oak. He could see his packs and the hide lying there just waiting for him to reclaim them.

The mountain man moved soundlessly toward the trunk. He threw back his head to give the yell that would bring on the bloodbath. Inadvertently, the movement saved his life. For as he tossed his head, a nasty metal spike imbedded in the end of a Pawnee war club hissed past his face, missing him by the width of a whisker.

Instinctively, Nate let go of the twin flintlocks

to grab the club before it could spear at him again. He nearly had his arms wrenched from their sockets as whoever held the other end yanked with all his might. Tottering, he stumbled to one knee behind the oak and glanced up into the hate-filled visage of a towering Pawnee.

How the warrior got there was irrelevant. Maybe he had been sent on ahead to keep an eye on the camp until the war party was ready to close in. Maybe he had been impatient and had crossed ahead of the others so he could count first coup. Whatever the case, it was unimportant.

Of sole consequence to Nate King was the fact that the Pawnee was there. The warrior was trying to kill him. A knee as hard as granite slammed into Nate's chest, knocking him onto his back. The breath whooshed from his lungs as the man pounced, straddling him, pinning him to the ground.

A viperish hiss fluttered from the Pawnee. Bending, he forced the club against the base of Nate's neck. It was all Nate could do to keep his throat from being crushed. Straining with every sinew in his body, sputtering for breath, he tried to push the club away.

The Pawnee was built like a bull. Eyes wide with a craving to kill, the warrior threw his full weight into bearing down on his weapon. Leverage and over 190 pounds of solid muscle and bones were in his favor.

To Nate's dismay, he could feel the warrior prevailing, the club gouging into his yielding flesh a fraction at a time. As if that were not enough, at that very moment the night was pierced by a series of fierce war whoops. It could only mean one thing. The Pawnees were attacking.

Chapter Four

All hell broke loose. Loud splashing was punctuated by shrieks and yells. A gun cracked, then another. Bow strings twanged. There was the thunk of arrows hitting home, the sickening squish of clubs rending flesh, the heavy thud of bodies striking the ground. All of which registered in the back of Nate King's mind as he struggled for his life against the Pawnee, who was slowly but surely choking him. The pain was excruciating. Nate tried to take a breath, but couldn't.

The Pawnee's features were aglow with brutal glee. Grunting, he shifted to throw more of his weight against the long club. Unless Nate did something quickly, he was going to die. The stark thought spurred him into throwing his body from side to side in a frenzied attempt to dislodge the warrior. It was like trying to throw off a clinging vine.

A feral smirk creased the Pawnee's face. He knew that he had Nate dead to rights. Another few moments and it would all be over.

Nate's lungs screamed for air. His body was racked by pain, and it was all he could do to think straight. In a last desperate bid, he bucked upward. He failed to throw the Pawnee off, but he tilted the warrior backward, within reach of his own legs. With all the strength Nate had left, he rammed his knees into the Pawnee's spine, not once but three times in swift succession.

The warrior arched his back and involuntarily cried out. His grip on the club loosened, enabling Nate to shove it to one side and twist out from under it. Simultaneously, he drove one fist into the Pawnee's gut. His other punched the man's cheek, splitting it and sending the Pawnee sprawling.

Scrambling to his feet, Nate dropped a hand to his Bowie. As the knife cleared the sheath, the warrior's club lanced at Nate's left eye. Ducking, Nate slashed at the warrior's midsection, but the Pawnee backpedaled.

For a few moments, the two of them regarded one another, each taking the other's measure, while not ten feet away men were locked in bloody combat or dying in pools of blood.

The Pawnee renewed the clash by swinging the club at Nate's temple. Again Nate dodged. Again he tried to sink his blade into his adversary. The warrior had the greater reach, though, and blocked the blade easily with his own weapon.

Circling, both sought an opening. Nate stayed in a crouch, balanced on the balls of his feet. He parried a thrust, ignored a feint, and skipped to the left when the Pawnee sprang and swung a blow that would have caved his skull in.

Suddenly, as if in a fit of frustration, the Pawnee arced the club at Nate again and again. Nate skipped backward, staying just out of reach. So intent was he on avoiding the club that he didn't pay attention to where he was until, without warning, his left foot slipped out from under him and he began to topple to the rear.

In a flash of jarring insight, Nate realized the wily Pawnee had driven him clear back to the brink of the bank. Frantically, he tried to gain purchase, but gravity would not be denied. He fell, landing on his shoulders, the Hawken's hammer poking deep into his shoulder blade. Momentum carried him to the bottom. Propping his hands on the slick grass, Nate pushed to his feet.

The mountain man was not quite erect when a bloodcurdling screech alerted him to the human hawk diving on him. Nate glanced up; then he was bowled over by the Pawnee, and they were both propelled into the stream.

Nate was on the bottom again. The water closed over him, seeping into his nose and parted mouth. Pushing upright, he sucked in air while staggering to the right.

The Pawnee was rising, the water lending his rippling muscles a damp sheen. He said something in the Pawnee tongue, then snapped the club overhead and bore down like a runaway steam engine.

Nate retreated, wishing he had a gun he could use. But his pistols were somewhere near the oak tree and his rifle had been drenched and would probably not fire. He had to rely on his knife, which gave the Pawnee a decided edge.

A jolting blow to the shoulder rocked Nate onto his heels. He threw himself out of the way of another swing, then bent low over the water. Flipping the Bowie from his right hand to his left, he jabbed at the Pawnee, who grinned at the futility of the act.

The warrior raised the club one more time and slowly advanced. Nate backed away, wagging the knife to keep the Pawnee focused on it and not on his right hand, which had slipped to his side.

Above them, the battle still raged. War whoops, strident yells, grunts, and bellows mingled with the pounding of feet and the constant flurry of personal combat.

Nate turned his left side to the Pawnee as if to present a smaller target. It hid his ulterior motive. His right hand found what it sought. The Pawnee feinted several times, playing with him, drawing out the inevitable. Nate connected with the club, but the blade did nothing more than nick the wood.

The Pawnee paused to set himself. He was going for the kill, leaving nothing to chance. Holding his weapon so that the imbedded spike pointed at Nate's chest, he stepped to the left, pretended to shift back to the right to throw Nate off guard, and continued left even as he streaked the spike at Nate's heart.

It was the moment Nate had been waiting for. Pivoting so the club missed him, he brought his right hand up and around. In it was clenched his Shoshone tomahawk. The keen edge caught the Pawnee in the center of the forehead and sheared through flesh and bone into the brain. A dark spray shot from the gash, spattering the water.

Nate jerked the tomahawk out and drew it back for another blow. None was needed. The Pawnee was dead on his feet, his eyelids fluttering. Nate placed a finger against the warrior and pushed. Arms outflung, the Pawnee toppled.

Losing no time, Nate dashed to the bank. Clambering out, he replaced the knife and tomahawk, then scrambled to the top and peeked over the edge.

It was a scene straight from a madman's worst nightmare. Bodies were everywhere. Arrows jutted from some. Others bore gaping wounds. Still others had skulls that resembled pulp. Blood drenched the soil, forming puddles. One man lay in a pool inches deep.

The Cheyennes and Arapahoes had lost fully half their number. Those still alive were holding their own and were retreating into the trees on the other side of the clearing, fighting every step of the way. Many were locked in grim struggles with Pawnee foes.

Confident that the Indians were too occupied to notice him, Nate rose up from concealment and ran toward the oak. Slowing when he spotted one of his flintlocks, he grabbed it up. The other pistol was close by. He took a step to retrieve it. Suddenly a feeling deep within him caused him to glance toward the conflict.

Three Pawnees had seen him. Surprise lining their painted faces, they glanced at once another. At a word from the stockiest, all three charged. Two held clubs, the stocky one a lance that he poised to cast.

Nate fired from the hip. The flintlock boomed and bucked and the heavy lead ball lifted the warrior clean off his feet and flung him a half-dozen feet to sprawl in a disjointed heap. The other two vented howls of outrage and leapt forward, their clubs upraised.

Dropping to one knee, Nate palmed the second flintlock. In a blur, he swiveled the piece out, clicked back the hammer, and stroked the trigger. The muzzle belched smoke and lead. The foremost Pawnee lost an eye in an explosion of gore and fell to the earth. That still left one very mad warrior who roared like a beast and aimed a hasty blow at the mountain man's head.

Tucking at the waist, Nate executed a shoulder roll. The club glanced off his arm, inflicting a sharp pang, but nothing worse. Nate swept up onto his feet next to the warrior. Before the man could strike again, Nate bashed him across the nose with a pistol. The Pawnee teetered, blood spraying into his eyes. Nate struck with the other flintlock. Stunned, the man tried to bring up the club; so Nate waded in, battering the warrior senseless, reducing the Pawnee's face to a shattered wreck. Only when the warrior groaned and pitched over did Nate relent.

Meanwhile, the fight raged on. Most of the Indians were in the cottonwoods, the Cheyennes and Arapahoes giving ground grudgingly, the Pawnees strung out in a crescent, trying to encircle their enemies without success.

Nate seized the moment. Wedging the pistols under his belt, he darted to the pile. He no longer cared about the packs of jerked meat. Getting out of there alive with the hide would be enough to suit him.

Stooping, Nate wrapped both arms around it, rose, and turned. It wasn't all that heavy, but it was bulky. He couldn't carry it with just one arm. Making sure that no other Pawnees had spotted him, he sprinted toward the high grass. Two minutes were all he needed to reach the gully; then all he had to do was throw the hide over the packhorse, tie it down, and head for the hills.

A wolfish yip was Nate's first inkling that things were not going to go as he wanted. Two Pawnees had spotted him. He plunged into the grass just as they gave chase. Hunched over, he zigzagged over 20 feet, then hunkered down to see if the Pawnees had given up. They hadn't. Spaced mere yards apart, they were heading straight toward him, looking right and left.

Like an antelope fleeing a pair of predators, he bounded deeper into the grass. He deliberately angled away from the gully in order not to lead them straight to Kendall. Retrieving the hide had been his brainstorm. He had to deal with the situation himself and not endanger his friend.

One of the Pawnees bayed and the couple came after him, their supple forms flowing over the ground like copper-skinned bloodhounds.

Nate ran as fast as he could. The smart thing to do was to drop the heavy hide so he could go even faster, but he refused to abandon the blasted thing after all he had gone through to recover it. Weaving wildly to try and throw his pursuers off, he covered approximately a hundred yards, then abruptly dived onto his side.

The drum of moccasins let him know the pair were much too close. Nate made no noise. Provided all went well, they would run right past him and not realize he had given them the slip until he was long gone. Once again, Fate thwarted him. The pair halted so close that he could hear them pant from their exertion.

Nate craned his neck. Their dusky figures were framed by the paler tapestry of stars and sky. They whispered urgently back and forth; then one pointed to the south and they hurried off.

At last something had gone Nate's way. Once their footsteps faded, he rose and headed for the gully. Whoops and shouts rose from the belt of vegetation, a testament to the sustained savagery of the battle.

A large shape unexpectedly loomed before Nate. He drew up short, sighing in relief when it nickered and galloped westward. Jogging onward, he presently came to the gully and scanned the bottom for Kendall and their horses. They were nowhere to be seen.

Wondering if maybe he had misjudged the spot where he had left them, Nate moved along the gully rim. He only had to go 50 feet to verify that he had been right. Since he couldn't see the man from Massachusetts deserting him, there was only one logical explanation. Kendall had heard the uproar and gone to help him.

Dreading that the other trapper had paid the supreme price for his own pigheadedness, Nate raced toward the trees. His arms were growing weary from toting the hide, but he held on anyway.

A fire still flickered in the clearing, casting an eerie glow over the corpses. The swirl of combat had gravitated dozens of yards from its point of origin and none of the principals were visible, although Nate did catch sight of a few warriors as they darted from cover to cover.

Kendall was another story. Halting, Nate rotated on the heel of his right foot a full 360 degrees. He surveyed the clearing, the wall of vegetation, and the plain. It was as if the earth had swallowed his friend and their mounts, not leaving a trace.

Nate was leery of lingering for fear the battle would spill into the prairie and engulf him. Yet he couldn't leave without Kendall. He slanted to the right, thinking that maybe the other trapper had circled the clearing and he would do the same.

Where the Pawnees came from, Nate never knew. One second he was working silently along, his senses primed, certain that no one else was within 50 yards of him. The next, a shrieking banshee rose up out of the grass and a club rained down. Nate would have died then and there if not for the hide absorbing the brunt of the blow. The impact pushed him backward, but he was unharmed.

The second Pawnee was only a few steps behind the first. He lunged, overextending himself, and missed. In a twinkling Nate grabbed the club, pivoted, and pulled. It was the same as if he had shot the warrior from a slingshot. The Pawnee flew headlong into the grass, tumbling end over end.

It was a momentary respite. Like a cat hurled through the air, the warrior bounced back onto his feet. Side by side, the two stalked Nate, who gave ground, matching them stride for stride.

The mountain man was upset with himself for not reloading his guns when he had had the opportunity. He had drawn the tomahawk, but it would do little good him if both Pawnees pounced at once, which they were girding to do. Sharing sly looks, they separated so that they could come at Nate from two directions. Nate kept glancing from one to the other, trying to tell by their body posture when they would spring.

It was not Nate's night. As he took another step, his heel hooked on a clump of grass. He tugged to free himself, and in so doing he nearly lost his balance when the clump pulled up out of the ground.

Yowling like coyotes, the Pawnees were on him. Nate looked up as they began to arc their clubs up and around. He was in no position to defend himself.

"Try me on for size, you murderous devils!"

From out of the night galloped Scott Kendall. The mountain man had his Hawken tucked to his shoulder. It spat flame and one of the warriors dropped like a poled ox. The other spun. Kendall clubbed him full in the face, felling him where he stood. Wheeling the sorrel on the head of a pin, he beamed at Nate. "So here you are! I was about to light a bonfire to get your attention."

"My horses!" Nate said, anxious to get out of there before more Pawnees appeared.

"Yonder," Kendall said, nodding to the northwest. "I left them there when I saw you were in trouble."

Nate saw the stallion and the packhorse close to the clearing. Picking up the buffalo hide, he was off in a flash.

Kendall rode alongside him, reloading the Hawken. "Tell me something, friend. Do you make it a habit of getting into scrapes like this over something as silly as a buff hide?"

"Not as a rule, no."

"Good. Because between you and me, hoss, you had me worried. Shakespeare McNair once told me that you have the darnedest luck of any man he's ever known, and I'm beginning to see what he meant."

Whether that was a compliment or not, Nate never got to ask. In the trees, a death scream rose above the general uproar. Nate was glad when he reached his horses. Heaving the hide onto the pack animal, he started to lash it in place.

"What about your jerky?" Scott asked.

"No time," Nate said, tying furiously.

"Are you sure? It won't take but a minute—"

Whatever else Kendall was going to say was lost in the commotion caused by a group of Indians who exploded from the cottonwoods into the clearing. Five Cheyennes and two Arapahoes were locked in a fierce struggle with at least ten Pawnees.

"Do we take sides?" Kendall asked.

"We do nothing except get out of here," Nate replied. He wasn't finished tying, but it would have to do. Grasping the lead rope, he boosted himself into the saddle and turned to depart. He should have known it would not be that simple.

"Pards of yours?" Kendall said, pointing.

How the man could joke at a time like that was beyond Nate—especially since four Pawnees were bearing down on them like a pack of rabid dogs. And Nate still hadn't reloaded. "Damn!" he fumed, reaching for his Bowie.

Quick as thought, Kendall drew one of his pistols and tossed it over. "Here, catch. And if we get out of this with our scalps where they should be, remind me to take your advice the next time you tell me I don't need to go somewhere with you." The big trapper slapped his legs against his sorrel and charged straight into the Pawnees, firing the Hawken on the fly.

Nate was right behind him. He saw a warrior go down with a hole the size of a walnut in his neck. The sorrel trampled another. Then Kendall was in the clear, swinging wide to skirt the knot of clashing men beyond.

A tall Pawnee barred Nate's path. He was notching an arrow to the string when Nate's shot penetrated his jaw. Deflected by the bone, the lead tore up through the neck and blew off the lower half of an ear as it exited.

At a full gallop Nate, thundered past the Pawnees and the battling warriors. He lit out across the prairie, thankful to be alive, and he did not slow up for over a mile. The first thing he did was give the pistol back to Kendall and commence reloading his own.

"It's too bad you don't want to go on Ashworth's expedition," the other mountaineer remarked wistfully. "We work well together."

"I almost got you killed."

"True. But lucky for you, I don't hold grudges. Besides, now I have a tale to tell at the next rendezvous that will top them all."

It was no secret that the trapping fraternity was fond of swapping stories that most outsiders branded as outright lies. Jim Bridger, for instance, liked to tell about the time he visited a petrified forest where petrified birds sang petrified songs. Another trapper by the name of Baker claimed that he once had come on a hairy giant over eight feet tall who smelled like a passel of skunks holding a contest to see which one could stink up the landscape the worst.

"Just so you don't mention my buffalo hide," Nate said. "I don't care to be the laughingstock of the rendezvous."

They were in good spirits since they were safe. Nate treated himself to pemmican that Winona had packed and passed out some to Kendall. "I hope you won't hold it against me that I don't want to go with Ashworth," he said. "But that greenhorn is liable to learn the hard way that most people fight shy of the Blackfeet for a reason."

"I'll agree that a small group of trappers wouldn't last as long as a frog in a snake den," Kendall said. "But sixty well-armed men can hold their own against any number of warriors."

Nate had his doubts, and he hated to see his newfound friend go off and get himself killed. "Remember the Missouri Legion?" he asked, referring to an attempt by an army colonel to punish the Arikara for an attack on another trapping expedition. The good colonel had sallied forth from the settlements with over 200 men of the U.S. Sixth Infantry, several swivel guns, and two cannons. En route, he added over 700 Sioux to his force. Yet the wily Arikaras outfoxed him and fled unscathed.

The ill-fated effort had done more to hurt white prestige among the warlike Plains tribes than any other single event in the short history of the untamed frontier.

"That was different. Their leader was an idiot," Kendall said. "Ashworth is made of sterner stuff. If you'd only meet him, you'd see for yourself that he's not afraid of man or beast."

Courage was commendable, Nate mused, if it

wasn't taken to an extreme. "I just hope you won't regret your decision."

Kendall had pulled a few yards ahead. Glancing back, he was going to respond, when from the grass in front of his horse rose a sound that sent a chill through both trappers and caused the sorrel to rear in panic. Nate's stallion also shied, while the pack animal whinnied and attempted to run off.

The sinister, hollow clatter of a rattlesnake's tail always had that effect on horses.

Chapter Five

As the black stallion snorted and plunged to one side, Nate King firmed his grip on the reins and applied more leg pressure to bring his mount under control. The big black pranced a few feet, then calmed enough for Nate to turn to the packhorse, which was kicking its hind legs so hard that the buffalo hide had started to slide off. Nate hauled on the lead rope with both hands, taking up the slack. The animal tried to toss its head and rear, but couldn't. Stymied, it stood stock-still, its flanks quivering. Nate was fortunate. No real harm had been done by the fleeting panic.

But Scott Kendall did not fare as well. His sorrel shot straight up into the air and came back down with all four legs as rigid as boards. Kendall had been twisted around, facing Nate, and before he could get a better hold, he pitched to the left and was nearly unhorsed. Through sheer grit he held on, and he might have scrambled back up into the saddle had the rattler not slithered off into the grass right under the sorrel's nose. The horse launched itself skyward again. When it hit, the jolt sent Kendall sprawling.

Nate saw the sorrel vault upward a third time. "Look out!"

Scott Kendall tried to roll out of the way. He almost made it. His left leg, though, was under the horse when those four heavy hooves thudded onto the ground, and one of them caught him on between the knee and the ankle. The resultant crack was like a gunshot. Kendall arched his spine, his mouth wide, but he did not scream in anguish as most would have.

Swiftly, Nate moved in. Goading the stallion up next to the sorrel, he bent and gripped its dangling reins. Tugging, he guided the sorrel away from his prone friend. Once Kendall was safe, he hopped down and ran over. He was going to ask how bad it was, but there was no need. He could see for himself.

The hoof had split the legging, sheared through flesh as if it were so much paper, and snapped the bone like a dry twig. A jagged section of tibia, glistening dull white in the starlight, jutted from the ruptured skin. Surprisingly, there was very little blood.

"Oh, Lord!" Kendall said, his hands clasped to his leg above the break. "I haven't hurt this bad since the time I fell off a cliff."

Kneeling, Nate gingerly probed with his fingertips. "I'll have to set this right away." If he didn't, infection might set in. Once that happened, Kendall stood a very real risk of losing the leg.

"Do what you have to, hoss," the other mountain man said through clenched teeth.

There was only one problem. Nate scanned the prairie but there wasn't a tree in sight. It might be hours before they spied one, and they couldn't afford to wait. Sliding his tomahawk from under his belt, he placed it beside Kendall, then did the same with Kendall's Hawken.

As he drew his Bowie and stepped to the pack animal, Kendall said, "After all we went through, you aim to use that? There must be something else."

"There isn't," Nate said flatly. Untying the robe, he set it flat and unfolded it halfway. He inserted the tip of the Bowie at one end, four inches from the edge, and sliced upward until he had a length of hide over three feet long. Cutting it off, he added it to his growing collection. "That was the easy part."

"I know," Kendall said. Flat on his back, he was caked with perspiration and barely able to keep his eyes open. "You'd better hurry or I'm liable to pass out on you, and then it will be that much harder."

Nate fetched their water skin. At last he was ready. Seating himself facing Kendall's left foot, he lightly wrapped his fingers around the man's ankle. "You might want to bite on something."

Kendall drew his own knife, stuck the hilt between his teeth, and nodded. "Ready when you are," he said, the words slurred.

Bracing his feet against Kendall's upper leg, Nate steeled himself, then yanked sharply with all the power in his shoulders and arms. Kendall stiffened, his head quaking, his veins bulging, his face flushing. The leg popped straight. The broken bone slid back under the skin. Nate kept on pulling, knowing he had to get it just right or Kendall would spend the rest of his days a cripple.

When his arms tired, Nate eased off, squatted, and moved to the break. Since he couldn't build a fire out there in the open with a Pawnee war party on the prowl, he slid his fingers into the wound, probing to determine if the bone had realigned properly.

It hadn't. The bottom section was slightly higher than it should be. Nate worked his palm into position, then pressed. It gave reluctantly, rubbing down over the upper section until the two halves were locked together.

A tiny spur of bone poked at an angle above the break. Nate pried it back and forth with his fingernail until it came off. "That should be the worst of it."

Kendall had passed out, the knife still clenched in his mouth. Nate cleaned the wound as best he was able. Next he placed the Hawken, barrel up, against the leg. His tomahawk went against the other side, at the break. It took some doing to wrap the hide without disturbing the set bone, but at length he tied a bulky knot and sat back to inspect his handiwork.

It would do, Nate decided, until he could make

a proper splint. Rather than wake Kendall and go on, he let the man enjoy badly needed rest. His rifle across his lap, he sat up the remainder of the night, keeping watch.

A band of bright pink highlighted the eastern horizon when Scott Kendall moaned and opened his eyes. Wincing, he began to rise.

"I'd take it easy, were I you," Nate said. "If any dirt gets in that break, you'll be sorry."

"It's morning already?" Kendall said sluggishly. Holding onto the barrel of his Hawken to steady his leg, he sat up and examined the improvised splint. "I'm obliged. You did a right fine job."

"Care for some jerky?"

"Don't mind if I do."

From his possibles bag, Nate took several pieces and passed them over. Helping himself to a sizable chunk, he hungrily took a bite. "I'm real sorry it had to come to this."

"Wasn't your fault," Kendall said with his mouth full.

Nate felt differently, but said nothing. It never would have happened if he hadn't been so pig-headed about recovering the damn hide.

"I won't be able to go on Ashworth's expedition, but at least I'm alive," Kendall said. "Somehow or other, I'll scrape up enough money for Lisa and me to pay her folks a visit. The good Lord will provide. He always does."

The knot of guilt that had formed in Nate swelled. He had completely forgotten about the funds the Kendalls needed to go back east. Now they were stuck in the mountains, and all on account of him. A germ of an idea took root. He mulled it over as he helped Kendall to stand and gave him a hand mounting.

Kendall gnashed his teeth and huffed and puffed, but he accomplished it on the first try. Holding fast to the saddle, he grinned weakly and said, "Good thing for you, friend, that I only weigh about two hundred and forty. Imagine if I was really heavy!"

Despite himself, Nate chuckled. He rigged the lead rope so that the sorrel would follow his stallion and the packhorse brought up the rear.

For the better part of the morning the two trappers traveled to the southwest. Nate watched Kendall closely. The man from Massachusetts dozed several times, but always managed to stay upright.

Noon found them in the shade of a cleft knoll. Nate allowed himself a few sips from the water skin, then let Kendall drink to his heart's content. He examined the leg. It had swollen to twice its normal size and was mildly discolored above the broken bone. Nate picked at the flesh to insure it wasn't gangrenous.

Kendall tried to make light of his predicament. "Maybe you want to stomp on it a few times to see how it holds up?"

Nate was eager to reach his cabin as quickly as possible. He pushed the horses, but not so fast as to cause Kendall undue suffering. Even after the sun went down, he rode on, refusing to rest until almost midnight.

"By tomorrow at this time you'll be snug in a

bed," Nate said as they turned in. Since there had been no hint of pursuit, he judged it safe to catch some sleep himself.

"I wouldn't want to put you out on my account," Kendall said. "We'll make a lean-to near your cabin and make do."

"Try a harebrained stunt like that and I'll bust your other leg."

Kendall cocked a bushy eyebrow. "You're not related to my missus by any chance, are you?"

"No, why?"

"Just wondered."

The next morning Kendall's forced levity was absent. Overnight the leg had swollen even more and the discoloration had spread a few inches. Nate mimicked a marble statue as he removed the strip of soiled hide and replaced it with a new one. He did not want his worry to be apparent.

The wound was infected—not seriously yet, but Nate had to reach Winona before another day went by. She was skilled with herbal treatments—remedies unknown to white doctors, yet every bit as effective.

Kendall did all right until the middle of the morning. Nate happened to look back and saw that he had dozed off for the ninth or tenth time and was slowly sliding to the right. Another few seconds and the man would fall. Wheeling, Nate came alongside just in time. He looped an arm around the trapper's midsection.

"What?" Kendall said, awakening.

"You were about to try to stand on your head," Nate said.

"Maybe you should have let me. In my condition, it'd be easier to walk on my ears than my legs."

The afternoon turned out to be extremely hot. Nate held the horses to a walk, never more than arm's reach from his companion. His earlier estimate turned out to be wrong. There was no way they would reach the valley by midnight. His best guess was that they would arrive by the next afternoon. That meant another night without treatment for poor Kendall.

A dry wash offered a safe haven. Nate discovered that his friend had a fever, and he stayed up as long as his body held out, placing one wet cloth after another on Kendall's hot brow. By morning, the fever was worse and Kendall was so weak that Nate had to tie him on the sorrel.

More hours of plodding across the shimmering grassland went by. Nate was glad when the foothills framed the plain in the distance, even gladder when he made out Long's Peak. Named for an army lieutenant by the same name, the highest peak in the central Rockies was located due south of his hidden valley. Whenever Nate saw it, he knew that home and hearth were not far off.

The climb was grueling. Nate had to go slow because Kendall was too weak to ride unassisted, even tied on. They made painstaking progress. It was late afternoon when they cleared the gap that brought them down to the valley floor within sight of the lake.

Kendall swayed with every step the sorrel took. Nate had to ride next to him and hold onto Kendall's shoulder. When still a hundred yards out, he hollered, "Hello, the cabin!"

The door opened within moments. Winona and Lisa Kendall came out. One look was all it took to bring the pair on the run. Zach was not far behind, and he helped Nate get the stricken mountain man down.

From then on, the women took over. Winona shooed Nate and Zach out and told them to be handy in case they were needed. Nate made for the lake to get a drink, but stopped when his wife reappeared.

"Husband," Winona said urgently, wishing they had a few quiet moments they could spend together, "we need *pannonzia*." That was the Shoshone word for yarrow. Her people boiled the whole plant for use as a poultice.

"I know where to get it," Nate said, and jogged off. Her tone inflamed him with urgency. Evidently, Kendall was at death's door.

"What about me, Ma?" young Zach asked, eager to be helpful. "Is there anything I can do?"

"*Dabi segaw*," Winona said.

"I will fly like the wind," Zach promised in the Shoshone tongue and raced northward.

Winona went back in. Lisa Kendall, as pale as the sheet on which her husband lay, stood by the bed, gripping his hand. Vail Marie was against the wall, petrified with fear for her father. Winona would have liked to have told them that Scott Kendall would be fine, but she had never told a lie in her life and it was far from certain that he would pull through. So she said, "I have treated broken bones before. Most are nothing to worry about."

Neither wife nor daughter responded. To take their minds off Kendall, Winona said, "We will need hot water. A lot of it. And I am low on wood."

"Leave it to us." Lisa beckoned to her offspring, then hastened through the doorway.

From a wooden peg, Winona took a beaded parfleche and set it on the table. She removed a small clay bowl, an egg-shaped rock she used to grind leaves and sometimes entire plants into a fine powder, and packets of herbs she had collected.

The family's coffeepot rested on the coals in the stone fireplace Nate had constructed many winters past. Winona emptied the grounds and swished the pot clean with a slender brush fashioned from porcupine quills.

It wasn't long afterward that Lisa and Vail Marie returned bearing a full water skin and busted branches. Lisa started a fire. In short order the coffeepot was boiling over.

Winona was about to go see what was keeping her husband when Nate showed up with the yarrow. Not knowing exactly how much she would need, he'd brought enough to treat the entire Shoshone tribe. He handed it over without comment and stepped to the bed where Kendall's wife and child held the brawny trapper's calloused hand.

"Don't fret none. My wife can mend him if anyone can."

They didn't say anything. They didn't have to. The anxiety their faces mirrored was eloquent evidence of their innermost feelings.

It was another half hour before Zach arrived. He'd had to venture farther afield to find the plant his mother wanted. No one noticed him, at first. They were crowded close to the bed, observing his ma. He went over to see what she was doing and had to choke down bitter bile.

Winona had removed the crude bandage, exposing a hideous wound. More black and blue than the normal hue of human flesh, it gave off a rank odor. Pockets of pus rimmed the edge. In one spot, the bone was exposed, and around it the flesh had festered to where it was downright putrid. Winona was cleaning the wound with a thin knife, cutting away strips of decayed skin and puncturing the pus bubbles.

Zach feared he would be sick. Placing the plant on the table, he hurried outdoors and greedily gulped fresh air. A hand fell on his shoulder, causing him to nearly jump clean out of his moccasins.

It was Nate. Since his wife knew ten times more about doctoring than he did, and Lisa and Vail Marie were ready to render any aid Winona might need, he had left everything in their capable hands. "Are you all right?"

"Sure," Zach said, adopting a casual air. "Why wouldn't I be, Pa?"

"You tell me. You're the one who is as green as one of those caterpillars you like to catch and squish."

"I am not, am I?" Zach rubbed his throat and averted his face to hide his embarrassment.

"Being a mite squeamish is nothing to be ashamed of," Nate said. "It's when your heart turns so hard that the sight of blood no longer bothers you that you have to worry."

Father and son strode to a large log at the border of the clearing that fronted the cabin. Nate sank down with a sigh, wearily rubbed his eyes, and somberly contemplated Long's Peak. "I did that man wrong, son," he said.

"Pa?"

"Mr. Kendall wouldn't be lying in there at death's door if I hadn't been as cocky as a bantam rooster." Nate plucked a blade of grass and stuck it between his teeth.

Zach could tell his father was upset but he was not quite sure why. "His horse stepped on him. How can you be to blame for an accident?"

"Because the man was doing me a kindness and he wound up paying dearly," Nate said. "I owe him, son. And there's only one way I can think of to pay him back."

"How's that?"

Nate changed the subject. "If I was to go away for a spell, would you do me a favor and look after your ma and sis?"

Disappointment and worry stabbed deep into the boy. "Where are you going? And for how long?"

"North a ways. I can't rightly say when I'll be back. It all depends on how things go."

"Can't I come too?" Zach asked. "I'd behave myself, honest. And I'd do whatever chores needed doing with no complaints."

Regret tore into Nate's heart like a two-edged sword. He removed the stem and crumpled it. "I'd like nothing better, son. But your ma is going to need your help more than me. The Kendalls will be here for quite a while. Winona will need for you to keep food on the table and your eyes skinned for hostile Indians."

Zach had a strong suspicion where his father was off to, and he would rather have been bitten by a rabid raccoon than miss out. But he had been raised to cherish his family above all else, to always put their best interests before his own. "You can count on me, Pa," he said dutifully.

"I knew I could," Nate said, affectionately ruffling his son's long hair. "Now what say we go catch some fish for supper?"

A flame-red sun roosted on the majestic western peaks when they tramped up the trail to the cabin. Zach carried six large fish; Nate had their poles. On a stump near the corral, the boy sat and palmed his butcher knife. "I'll have these cleaned in no time."

Nate walked to the window to peek in. As he passed the door, a shadow filled the entrance.

Winona King wiped her hands on a cloth and answered her husband's questioning gaze with a shrug. Kendall's health was out of her hands. She had done all she could, thoroughly cleaning the wound and applying a poultice. Whether Scott Kendall survived the night depended on his will to live.

Winona glanced over a shoulder. Lisa and Vail Marie were perched on chairs beside the bed.

They were not about to go anywhere until assured that Kendall would be all right.

"Can you take a break?" Nate asked.

After 12 years of living with Grizzly Killer, Winona could read her man easily. It was obvious that he had an important matter on his mind. "I have done all I can. What troubles you?"

Taking her by the elbow, Nate moved to the northeast corner of the cabin so that their son would not overhear. "How soon before Kendall will be back on his feet?"

"If he heals with no problem, he will be able to stand in about one moon. But he will not be able to run or ride or trap for at least two moons. The bone was almost shattered." Winona's lovely eyes narrowed. "Why?"

"I have to make good for what happened."

It took a few seconds for his full meaning to sink in. Winona's breath caught in her throat. "You do not owe him your life."

"It's an entire brigade. Sixty men. I'll be as safe as if I were home with you."

"I know of two brigades that were wiped out almost to the last man," Winona said. "And even if all goes well, you will not be back for a whole year. No, husband, I will not stand by and let you do this."

"I have to."

"Then I will go with you."

"Someone has to look after Kendall, and you're the only one who has doctored folks before."

"I will teach Lisa how to use my herbs. It is not difficult." Winona folded her arms. "There is no changing my mind on this. Besides, I know something you don't. You must take me whether you want to or not."

"How so?" Nate said, his confidence shaken by her smug attitude.

"Scott Kendall was not the only one Ashworth hired. Lisa and several other women are to cook for the men and handle other chores." Winona traced the outline of his square jaw with a finger and smiled. "So you see, husband, where you go, I go—even into the heart of Blackfoot country."

Chapter Six

If there was one lesson married life had taught Nate King, it was that a woman always got her way in the end. A man could argue and cajole, he could reason and plead, he could even rant and rave if he didn't mind making a complete yack of himself. But in the end, the wife's will invariably won out. Any jasper who claimed to the contrary was only fooling himself.

In this instance, Nate fervently wished he had been able to prevail on Winona to stay behind. As they wound down a game trail toward the Green River Valley, he twisted in his saddle to soberly regard his wife. She grinned merrily, as if they were on a pleasant family outing instead of on the verge of committing themselves to a venture that might well result in all their deaths. Strapped in a cradleboard on her back was little Evelyn. Behind them rode Zach, who looked as happy as a bear in a berry patch.

"Quit pouting, husband," Winona said in her precise English. "We have made up our minds. Now we must live with our decision. What will be will be."

That was another thing about women that got Nate's goat. They could be as logical as a college professor when it suited their purpose, and they were always right even when they were wrong. A man could argue until he was blue in the face and never get them to admit as much. They'd close their ears and go on about their business not hearing a word he said. It was downright irritating.

Sighing, Nate faced around. It would do no good to bring up the subject again, so he might as well bow to the inevitable and make the best of a bad situation.

They had left the cabin several days ago. Descending to the foothills, they had traveled north to the Sweetwater River and across South Pass, then to the northwest to the Green River Valley.

It was vast and fertile, the site of more annual rendezvous than any other spot in the mountains. About six years earlier, a man by the name of Bonneville had built a fort at the confluence of Green River and Horse Creek. Dubbed Fort Nonsense by the mountaineers because it was too cold in those parts in the winter to maintain a garrison, it had since been abandoned and was mainly used as a storage site during rendezvous.

From a bare spine overlooking the river, Nate

could see the bench on which the old fort stood. North of it a new structure had been erected, a small stockade around which bustling activity was taking place. Near the stockade were over two dozen Indian lodges.

"Absarokas," Winona said, making no attempt to keep her dislike of them from her tone.

Nate promptly reined up. No one had said anything to him about Crows being involved with the Ashworth expedition. The Shoshones and the Crows had long been bitter enemies. Often, they attacked one another on sight. He was not about to expose his wife and children by taking them down there until he knew exactly what was going on.

Veering into a stand of saplings, Nate halted in a clearing wide enough to contain them and their two packhorses. "Stay here and keep out of sight until I see whether it's safe."

Zach straightened up. He had a hankering to go down too. But he never voiced it. He knew why his pa would rather have him stay with his ma and sister.

"Be careful," Winona advised. Since Nate was white, she doubted the Absarokas would try to harm him. But he was also an adopted Shoshone, and that made him fair game, as he might say. She was worried.

"Always," Nate assured her.

The trail was in deep shadow until near the bottom. Nate reached the valley floor without being seen and rode slowly toward the stockade. He loosened both flintlocks under his belt and adjusted his Bowie so that the hilt angled forward.

Whites and Crows mingled outside the enclosure. It all seemed peaceful enough, but it never paid to take the Crows at face value. They had a reputation for being as crafty as the day was long, and while they were friendly when they wanted to be, they had killed their share of trappers over the years.

A Crow woman digging roots at the edge of the encampment was the first to spy Nate. At a yell from her, a number of warriors clustered close to a lodge advanced to meet him.

Nate drew rein when still 40 yards from the stockade. He saw a white man dash into it while others gathered at the gate. Then he confronted the Crows, his hands flowing fluently in sign language, saying, in effect, "Come no closer."

The five warriors halted. All wore knives, several had slung bows, and one man, the smallest, carried a lance. This last jabbed the butt of his spear into the ground and leaned it against his shoulder to free his hands. "Why do you treat us as if you can not trust us, cap wearer?"

Cap wearer was a sign equivalent for white man. There wasn't a mountaineer alive who didn't favor a hat or cap of some sort, and Nate was no exception. He was partial to a beaver hat that he adorned with a single eagle feather. "I know the Crows," he responded. "I know that you like to speak with two tongues."

It was the same as calling the tribe a pack of liars. The small man darkened and several of the others muttered in their own tongue.

The warrior with the lance surprised Nate by saying in passable English, "You mistake, white man. Absarokas like whites. Absarokas good friends."

"Then you won't mind keeping your distance," Nate said. "I don't want the same thing that happened to Ike Webster to happen to me."

Webster, a free trapper, had been on his way to Fort Laramie and had happened on a Crow village. He had agreed to stay the night after a warrior offered his wife in exchange for a point blanket and a few trinkets. The next morning, Webster's gutted body had been found in nearby bushes. No one was ever held to account, and his possessions were never recovered.

"I not hurt you," the small warrior declared. "I friend. Called Little Soldier. Maybe you hear my name, eh? Many know of me."

The name was indeed familiar. Of all the Crow leaders, Little Soldier had a reputation for being the most devious. Joe Meek liked to say that a mountaineer could trust Little Soldier about as far as he could fling a moose.

"I know of you," Nate signed.

The Crow swelled his chest. "I count thirty-one coup," he declared matter-of-factly. "One day I be high chief of all Absarokas."

Nate resorted to English. "Then you will need to count a lot more coup, and none of them will be at my expense."

It was common knowledge throughout the Rockies that the warrior who ranked as the supreme leader of all the Crows had counted over

60 coup. His name was Long Hair, and it was said that he had seen at least 80 winters. Not once in all that time had a blade touched his head. As a result, his hair was over 11 feet long, and he wore it in an enormous queue. Perhaps his age had something to do with it, but Long Hair was one of the few tribal leaders the whites could trust.

"Again I say you mistake, white man," Little Soldier said. "I not count coup on you. Who you be, friend? I think maybe I see you at a rendezvous."

This time Nate employed sign. "The Shoshones, the Flatheads, the Cheyennes, the Dakotas—they all know me as Grizzly Killer."

Little Soldier's expression was almost comical. Hatred and canny intent waged a fleeting war. Then an oily smile creased the Crow's thin lips. "I have heard of you," he signed. "I have heard you have a Shoshone wife. I have also heard that her people adopted you into their tribe. Is all this true?"

Switching to English again, Nate responded, "Since when are my personal affairs any of your business?" He gestured sharply. "Stop badgering me and move aside."

Nate lifted the reins. He was fixing to ride right on through them whether they liked it or not.

Suddenly four white men arrived. Two wore buckskins. The third was a veritable giant in a wool shirt and pants of the type in style in St. Louis. But it was the fourth man who interested Nate the most. He was tall and dapper and dressed in the height of New York fashion. He wore an immaculate black suit complete with a dress beaver hat and a black cape. He even carried a polished black cane, which he twirled as if it were a baton. Around his slim waist were strapped a pair of matching pistols with inlaid ivory designs in the shape of flowers.

"What's the meaning of this, Little Soldier?" the man in black asked. "I can't have you accosting every white man who pays us a visit. If this keeps up, I'm afraid I'll have to ask you to have your people move their lodges. You gave me your word that you would behave yourself, and I intend to hold you to it." The man wagged his cane in reproach at the Crow. "Gentleman's honor and all that."

Nate King was stupefied. How any white man in his right mind could expect an Absaroka to know anything about a code of conduct peculiar to the upper crust of white society was beyond him.

"I sorry," Little Soldier said. "I only want be friend. Crows good people. Crows help you."

"So you keep saying," the man in black said. Tucking the cane under an arm with a flourish, he smiled evenly up at the mountain man. "Welcome, stranger. Have you come to enlist in our grand expedition?"

"Let me guess," Nate said. "You're Ashworth?"

Ashworth tapped the brim of his hat. "That I am, sir."

The truth was Richard Ashworth happened to be in extraordinarily fine spirits. And why not?

Everything had gone superbly since he had left New York City.

Traveling westward via the Erie Canal, Ashworth and his constant companion, Emilio, were conducted by boat the entire 363 miles of the waterway's length. After buying horses, they rode south to the Cumberland Road. More commonly known as the Great National Pike, it had been built mainly with federal funds to facilitate the westward exodus.

On arriving at St. Louis, Ashworth had made no secret of his intentions. Within days over 40 trappers down from the high country for the summer had hired on, and others would do so over the course of the next several weeks. By the time the expedition departed for the frontier, Ashworth had 51 men under him.

At Bent's Fort, Ashworth had picked up another nine mountaineers. One of them, Scott Kendall, had so impressed him that he had offered to make Kendall his second-in-command. To his amazement, Kendall had recommended someone else.

All that Ashworth needed was for Kendall to return and he could be on his way. He couldn't wait to get started. The heady intoxication of adventure, the thrill of triumph over insurmountable odds, and the promise of great wealth charged him with vitality. They inspired him with a lust for life he had never experienced before.

At that moment, gazing up into the piercing emerald-green eyes of the stranger on the black stallion, Ashworth was happier than he had been in years. "Who are you, sir? And how might I and my company of fine fellows be of assistance?"

"I'm Nate King." Nate would have gone on had the man from New York City not stepped up and clasped his leg as if he were long-lost kin.

"King! As I live and breathe!" Ashworth declared. At last he could get underway for the north country! It made him giddy with joy until he noticed that someone was missing. "Wait a minute! Where are Scott Kendall and his charming wife and daughter?"

Briefly, Nate told about the mishap. He didn't emphasize that it was his fault or explain that he was there to atone. "I told them that they're welcome to stay at my cabin for as long as they need to."

"How very decent of you," Ashworth said sincerely. He had heard a lot of stories about this solitary mountain man, and he could not help but wonder how many of them were true. More Shoshone than white, it was claimed. Responsible for slaying 20 grizzlies in half as many years. Next to Jim Bridger and Shakespeare McNair, King was more widely respected by his peers than any other trapper.

"Is your offer still good?" Nate asked, secretly hoping that perhaps Ashworth had changed his mind and no longer needed his services.

"It is," Ashworth answered. "I would be grateful if you would agree to be my second-in-command. I assume Scott filled you in on all the details?"

Nate nodded. "I still have some questions." He gazed at the stockade, where a considerable number of mountain men had gathered. Among them was a sprinkling of females. Most were Indian women from various tribes, although two or three whites were also present.

"Certainly," Ashworth said. "Come to my quarters for refreshments and I'll explain everything to your satisfaction."

"I have to fetch my family first," Nate said. Out of one eye, he saw Little Soldier perk up. "My wife is interested in hiring on in place of Lisa Kendall."

"She's more than welcome to," Ashworth stated. While he was sorry to lose the Kendalls, he was ecstatic to have everything else falling so neatly into place. "I'll tell you what. It's almost time for my evening repast. Why not bring your family in and be my supper guests?" As an added inducement, since he had learned the mountain men were fond of it, he added, "We're having roast elk with all the trimmings."

"In about half an hour be all right with you?" Nate asked.

"Perfect."

Nate reined the stallion around to depart, but paused when someone hailed him. From out of the throng of trappers strolled a lanky frontiersmen with greasy black hair well past his shoulders and an equally greasy mustache. His skin was tanned bronze from spending almost all his time outdoors. Lively brown eyes sparkled with amusement. "As I live and breathe!" Nate exclaimed. "Henry Allen!"

"It's been a while, ain't it, Nate?"

The two trappers shook hands. As best as Nate could recollect, he had last seen the feisty Tennessean over five years ago when they had tangled with the Blackfeet. "I thought you were heading back to the States to take up farming?"

Allen chuckled. "Hell, I tried. I must have been set to leave twenty times or better, but I could never bring myself to do it." He made a show of sniffing the air. "Blame the scent of freedom. It gets in a man's blood and won't let go."

"Do you have a horse handy? You can ride on back with me and let me know exactly what I'm letting myself in for," Nate proposed. "I know Winona and Zach will be glad to see you again."

"My dun is in the stockade," Allen said with a jerk of his thumb. "Give me two shakes of a lamb's tail and I'll fetch it."

"Go ahead." Nate sat back to wait while his good friend ran off. Ashworth and his entourage were filing back inside, but the Crows lingered.

"Grizzly Killer," Little Soldier called out. "Maybe you come my lodge, eh? Maybe you smoke pipe."

"I'll keep it in mind," Nate said flatly. The Absarokas were all smiles as they left, but Nate wasn't deceived for a minute. As Allen had once noted, a Crow could claim to be the best friend a man ever had one minute and stab him in the back the next.

Soon the lean man from Tennessee trotted out on a splendid dun. As they headed for the game trail, Nate posed the question that would determine whether he went through with the insane scheme. "What's your opinion of Ashworth?"

Allen was one of the few people Nate would

trust to give him a reliable assessment. The Tennessean had been in the mountains almost as long as he had and knew the ways of the different tribes and the wildlife as well as Nate himself, if not better in some respects.

"You want to know if we can count on him to lead us halfway decent? Judging by how he's behaved so far, I'd have to say he'll do right fine."

"He's done that well, has he?"

The Tennessean removed his blue cap to scratch his hair. "Oh, sure, he's as green as grass and as full of himself as a balloon, but he tries hard. He listens to those who know better than he does, and he takes their advice. That stockade, for example. When we first got here, some of us took him aside and told him that, for all our sakes, we needed one to make sure our throats weren't slit in the middle of the night."

It was a definite plus in Ashworth's favor. Many a booshway, as the trappers referred to leaders of expeditions, acted as if he was the only one who had a lick of common sense and knew how to get things done right. Some, in their arrogance, had wound up leading a lot of decent men to their deaths.

"Ashworth is a rare coon," Allen continued. "He knows he's as ignorant as a rock and he's not ashamed to ask for advice when he needs it."

"Does he have any notion of what he's letting himself in for?" Nate wondered. "Does he know how fierce the Blackfeet can be?"

"He has as good an idea as any man who hasn't actually locked horns with them. In his opinion, sixty men are more than enough to hold off a small army of those devils."

"I don't know—" Nate began. The Blackfeet were hardly cowards.

"There's a method to his madness," Allen interrupted. "He's brought two rifles and four pistols for every man." The Tennessean patted one of his. "He likes to go on about how it's not the number of men that's important. It's our firepower."

"Firepower?" Nate repeated quizzically. The word was a new one on him.

"Near as I can tell, it boils down to how much lead we can throw at the Blackfeet at any one time," Allen detailed.

"What about the men who are with him? Are they all as up to bear as you are?"

Allen was plainly flattered by the compliment. "This child thanks you. And, yes, I'd have to say most of them are good men. There are a few flashes in the pan and some coffee coolers, but that's to be expected in an outfit the size of ours."

They came to the game trail and Nate took the lead. "Is it true he has money to spare?"

"The man must be rolling in it, going by how fast he spent it back in St. Louis and at Bent's Fort. Honestly, Nate. He's got enough provisions to last us five years. And north of the stockade, guarded by twenty-five men day and night, is a herd of four hundred horses."

It boggled Nate's brain. "That's almost as many as Bridger had the time he got into a racket with The Bold over Joe Meek."

Meek, by common consensus, was the champion tall-tale teller of all time. Whenever trappers gathered to spin yarns, Meek beat them all, hands down.

Four years previous, Meek had been taken captive by a war party of Crows led by a warrior called The Bold. In typical flamboyant fashion, Meek outfoxed the bloodthirsty warrior by tricking The Bold into taking him to Bridger's camp. Meek had convinced the Crows that Bridger only had a few men with him and could be easily wiped out. But the truth was that at the time over 250 were in Bridger's party. Their horse herd had numbered twice that many. Needless to say, Bridger had forced The Bold to hand Meek over.

And Joe Meek? His former captors bestowed a new name on him, *Shiam Shaspusia*, or He Who Can Outlie Crows.

The memory spurred Nate to ask, "Why is Little Soldier's band staying so close to the stockade? What is he up to ?"

Allen was silent a few seconds. "It's the only mistake Ashworth has made."

"What is?"

"He went and signed on Little Soldier to be his Indian guide."

Nate whipped around. "The hell, you say!"

"Afraid so. Some of us convinced Ashworth that it would be wise to have a few Indians along who knew the lay of the land. We had in mind a couple of Delawares, but Ashworth took it into his noggin to hire Little Soldier."

"Can't you talk him out of it? That reptile will

sink his fangs into us the first time we turn our backs on him."

The Tennessean sighed. "You know that, and I know that, and pretty near every coon fit to wear buckskins knows that. But Little Soldier has been licking Ashworth's boots from the day they first met. Ashworth thinks he's plumb harmless."

Above them appeared the stand of saplings. Nate peered deep into the slender boles, but did not catch sight of his loved ones. "I'll have a palaver with Ashworth. If the man doesn't have the gumption to tell the Crows to go stand in front of a herd of stampeding buffalo, I don't want anything to do with him."

At the same point where Nate had entered the stand before, he did so again, trotting swiftly back to the clearing. As the stallion passed the last of the trees and the open space unfolded before them, Nate's heart jumped in his chest and he reined up short in alarm.

"Something the matter?" Henry Allen inquired.

"My family!" Nate exclaimed, stunned.

The Tennessean looked all around. "What about them?"

"They're gone!"

Chapter Seven

Nate King vaulted off the black stallion and scoured the ground, reading the tracks as readily as most Easterners could read the print in a book. He saw where Winona had ground-hitched the horses, where she had carried Evelyn to a grassy spot and sat down. Zach had come over, and apparently they had been talking for a while.

Scuff marks showed where a struggle had broken out. Moccasin tracks indicated four warriors had sneaked up on Winona and Zach, leapt out of the undergrowth, and overpowered them before they could get off a shot. The type of moccasins worn by the quartet revealed their identity just as effectively as if they were standing there before Nate. "Crows!"

"They went this way," Allen said. He had climbed down and roved the perimeter of the clearing. Hunkered over a gap between saplings at the southwest border, he pointed at a jumbled trail of human and horse tracks that led into the forest.

"Away from the stockade," Nate noted, hurrying to the stallion.

"They can't have gotten far," Henry Allen said. "You weren't gone that long."

"Long enough," Nate said bitterly. Certainly long enough for the Crows to have had their way with Winona and to have slain her and the children. Lashing the black, he trotted into the trees. The path the Crows had taken widened, allowing him to ride at a gallop. He avoided logs and ducked under low limbs.

At the bottom of a slope the trees thinned even more. Nate climbed swiftly, the stallion's iron hooves gouging into the soil to keep it from slipping.

The Crows had ridden in single file, one leading Winona's mare, another Zach's bay, each of the others a pack animal. Fresh grooves revealed where a packhorse had slipped and nearly gone down.

At the crown, Nate didn't even pause. He swept up and over and down the other side, a quick glance enough to confirm there was no trace of the warriors up ahead. His heels jabbed hard into the stallion. He feared that at any moment he might stumble on a crumpled, lifeless form. Just thinking about it made him shudder. To lose any of those he cared for so dearly would tear his very soul apart.

Another hill fell behind them, then yet one more. The clever Crows were crossing them on purpose so that on top of each they could check their back trail.

Nate could only pray that he spotted them before they spied him. Odds were that the warriors were more interested in the horses and plunder they had stolen than in Winona and the children. If pressed, the Crows might kill them in order to make good their escape.

Allen had the same notion, for he called out just loud enough to be heard, "Maybe we should find us some cover, Nate. We don't want anything to happen to your lady and the sprouts before we catch up, do we?"

Nate knew that his friend feared he was letting his dread over their welfare get the better of him. Truth to tell, he was somewhat, or he would have realized their mistake sooner. Angling into pines on his left, he paralleled the trail, only letting it out of his sight for more than a few seconds when he went around trees and thickets and such.

Meanwhile, the sun steadily arced toward the western horizon. Should night descend before Nate and the Tennessean overtook the Crows, there was a very real chance that the Crows would elude them.

The warriors had changed direction and were traveling due south, hugging the hills that flanked the Green River Valley. It occurred to Nate that if they continued on as they were doing for another two to three days, they would be in the very heart of Crow country.

The blazing sun settled on the brink of the earth. The shadows lengthened. Scared to the bone that they would lose their quarry, Nate pushed the stallion as he had never pushed it before. Allen called for him to wait up but he was not about to slow down, not with all that gave his life meaning at stake.

One more hill rose before him. Nate leaned forward to better distribute his weight and make it easier for the stallion to gain the crest. He was all set to plunge down the opposite slope when movement below brought him to a sliding stop.

A broad valley bisected that of the Green River. A tributary wound eastward, looping like an oversize serpent for mile after mile, forming a series of fertile benches separated by belts of trees, primarily cottonwoods. Halfway across were six riders and two packhorses. Second in line was a woman with long raven tresses.

"Winona!" Nate said softly to himself. A glance back revealed that the Tennessean had fallen hundreds of yards behind, and Nate was not about to sit there and wait for Allen to catch up.

Never leaving the sanctuary of the pines, Nate descended rapidly. Once on flat ground, he was hidden from the Crows by the intervening cottonwoods. At a trot he shadowed them, narrowing the gap minute by minute.

The sun was gone when Nate saw them again. They had slowed, and the warrior in the lead seemed to be searching for a spot to stop for the night. Zach's hands had been bound behind him. Winona's were free, but her ankles had been looped together under the mare, and she had Evelyn in her lap.

Nate yearned to charge the Crows with his flintlocks blazing. Were it not that his family might be caught in the crossfire, he would have. Swinging wide to the east, he drew within 40 yards of the warriors without being discovered.

Under a spreading willow, the lead Crow drew rein. He barked instructions. A husky warrior yanked Zach off the bay and shoved him over by the wide trunk. Winona's ankles were untied and she was accorded the same rough treatment. When she tried to push the man's arm aside, she was slapped for her effort.

Nate dismounted. Securing the reins to a low branch, he padded in a wide half circle that brought him up on the willow tree from the rear. The Crows were busy setting up their camp, all except for one man who stared back the way they had come. Going to ground, Nate made like an eel, wending through a maze of high weeds without rustling one.

A few feet from the willow, low voices were audible.

"—a little more work I can slip my hands out, Ma. Then I'll grab one of our guns those varmints took and—"

"You will do no such thing, Stalking Coyote," Winona chided, using Zach's Shoshone name. "Not until I say to."

"But, Ma—."

"Heed me, son," Winona said sternly. "Would you have your sister or me suffer because of your impatience? Wait, and when the time is right, we will show these Absarokas that they are no match for Shoshones."

Nate crawled closer to the tree. He couldn't see his family, but he did observe a Crow unload a parfleche from one of the packhorses and open it to see what was inside. The man removed a handful of pemmican and stuffed some into his mouth.

Mighty glad the Crows were being so careless, Nate came to the trunk. A low limb six feet overhead invited him to rise, grab hold, and swing up before anyone was the wiser. Keeping the tree between himself and the warriors, he climbed several feet higher.

Nate clasped the Hawken under his left arm, removed his beaver hat, and inched an eyeball far enough out to see all the Crows. The one still rummaged through packs. Another had just tethered the last of the horses. A third gathered dead wood for a fire, while the last man, the lookout, moved toward a knoll that would give him a better view of the surrounding countryside. Henry Alley had yet to appear.

Taking a gamble, Nate eased out farther and saw those he cared for more than life itself. Winona's ankles had been retied so that she couldn't run off. Evelyn dozed on her shoulder. Zach had his back to the tree and was furiously rubbing his wrists back and forth.

Nate was tempted to whisper, to let them know he was there and that all would soon be well. But at that moment the warrior who had taken care of the horses came toward them. Ducking from sight, Nate replaced his hat and gripped the rifle to keep it from falling. The crunch of footsteps neared. A gruff voice addressed Winona in slurred English.

"You cook for us, woman. Give Thunder Heart girl."

"I will not," Winona responded.

There was a thud, then the sound of a scuffle and of little Evelyn crying out.

"Leave them be, you polecat!" Zach fumed. "I'll bust your knees for you!"

Another thud, and the sound of someone striking the tree. Nate wanted to peek out but he was afraid the other Crows would be watching and see him.

The scuffle subsided. "I will do as you say!" Winona declared. "Only do not hit him again!"

"You learn, Shoshone dog," Thunder Heart growled. "You do as I say or you suffer. All suffer."

"What manner of man are you that you would harm a child?" Winona demanded.

The taunt was wasted. "Shut mouth. Cook food," Thunder Heart commanded. "Be quick, or maybe I cut out boy's tongue to teach you to listen."

Nate heard an armload of branches clatter to the ground and another Crow speak in the Absaroka tongue. Thunder Heart replied in kind. Their tones implied that the other warrior was upset about something and Thunder Heart was annoyed that the man would complain.

The twilight darkened. Nate felt safe in climbing down. He hung from the lowest limb until he stopped swaying, then dropped lightly and pressed flat against the willow.

Several of the Crows were talking. Nate sank to his knees, rolled onto his side, and wriggled to the edge for a look.

Winona was starting a fire. Seated near her, sporting a bloody lip, was Zach. Three of the four Crows were beyond them. The last was 70 feet off on the knoll, barely visible in the encroaching darkness.

Nate's eyes grew as flinty as steel when he beheld his daughter being held by the Crow named Thunder Heart. The man had her by an arm and half dangled her as if she were a sack of potatoes. Evelyn was gritting her teeth, her features lined with pain.

Winona broke in on their parley. "You are not as smart as you think that you are, Thunder Heart. Soon my man and many other whites will arrive and punish you for stealing us."

The burly Crow spun. In doing so, he jerked Evelyn as if she were a doll. She moaned and clamped her eyes shut.

"I not warn you again, Shoshone. Your man not find us at night. Two sleeps we be at village. Never see man again."

Nate fingered a pistol. Tears had formed at the corners of his daughter's eyes. It tore him apart to see her abused. But if he jumped up and started shooting, he wouldn't put it past Thunder Heart to use her as a shield.

Unexpectedly, the Crow on the knoll let out

with a wavering yip in perfect imitation of a coyote. He bolted toward the camp, speaking urgently as he drew near. Thunder Heart threw Evelyn to the grass, clamped a hand on Winona's rifle, and stalked forward, flanked by the others. Winona scooped her daughter up.

Nate had no idea what was happening. He couldn't imagine his friend being to blame. The Tennessean could move like a ghost when the need arose. So Nate was all the more shocked when a rider materialized at the edge of the clearing, and it was none other than Henry Allen.

The Crows halted in midstride. None resorted to a weapon although they were all as tense as wolves facing a riled griz. Thunder Heart raised the rifle to his waist but no higher. He greeted the man from Tennessee in his own language.

Only when the Crow dialect spilled from Allen's mouth as glibly as if Allen were a Crow born and bred did Nate recollect that Allen had taken a Crow woman for his wife.

The Tennessean had his long Kentucky rifle resting across his saddle. He had also aligned his pistols close to his belt buckle. Jabbing a finger at the Crows, he reverted to English. "I won't honor your tongue, you skulking devils, by using it. For what you did to me and mine, Thunder Heart, and for what you plan on doing with the wife of Grizzly Killer, I aim to make worm food of you and your pards."

Thunder Heart took a step to the right and sneered. "How many times we say same words,

Cloud Rider? Piegans kill your woman and boy. Not me."

"You lying sack of manure," Allen countered. "I didn't believe you back then, and I sure as hell haven't changed my mind since." The Tennessean nudged the dun forward. "Too bad for you that Little Soldier and his bunch aren't here to back your play. It's just me and you four vermin."

Nate rose and eased around the willow. Thanks to Allen, the Crows were not paying any attention to his family. But he fretted that, if a fight broke out, they might be hit before he could get them out of there. Hunched low, he crept closer. Winona and Zach were riveted on the Tennessean and had not noticed him yet.

The Crows began to spread out. One held Zach's rifle, another a bow. The lookout was armed with a fusee, a trade gun dispensed by the Hudson's Bay Company for prime plews.

Henry Allen didn't seem to care that he was outnumbered. It didn't seem to matter to him that he was riding straight into the jaws of death. Making no move to raise either his Kentucky or a pistol, he spoke in his pronounced Southern drawl.

"You seemed to think that I'd let what you did go. You took it for granted that I'd never try to take revenge. But you were wrong, Thunder Heart. And you, too, Feather Earring. I've just been biding my time, knowing that sooner or later I'd get my chance. And here it is."

Nate was almost to Winona. He had a hunch that Allen was jawing partly to keep the Crows from realizing what he was up to. He knew Allen had seen him, but the Tennessean betrayed no reaction.

"Fetches the Man meant everything to me," Allen went on. "She was a fine, decent woman who deserved better than to have her brains splattered over the ground by the filthy likes of you, Thunder Heart."

The Crow did not reply. His countenance was that of a bird of prey about to swoop in for the kill.

"She loved me," Allen said harshly. "And because I was white, and you hate all white-eyes, you sneaked up on her when she was washing clothes at the river and you bashed her over the head with that bloody rock. Oh, I know you claimed that you were in your lodge, gambling with your pards when she was killed, and I know most of the other Crows took you at your word, but I never did."

"Like all your kind, you be fool, Cloud Rider," Thunder Heart spat.

"For falling in love with a Crow woman?" the man from Tennessee retorted. "Or for not seeing sooner that your hatred of whites would cost Fetches The Man her life and the life of our sprout?"

Nate finally reached his wife. Touching her on the shoulder, he pressed a finger to his lips as she started and whirled. Nate drew his Bowie and slashed the three-foot cord linking her ankles.

No words could describe Winona King's joy. She had been worried that the Crows were right: that it would be dark before Nate discovered they were missing and that the Crows would be far into the mountains before Nate could catch them. Pressing her hand to his to convey her affection, she then lifted Evelyn and backed toward the willow tree.

Zach was just as thrilled to see his pa. Beaming like an idiot, he motioned for his father to cut the cord binding his wrists.

Nate shook his head and motioned for his son to follow Winona. They had to get out of there while they could. The fire crackled noisily. Bathed in its glare, they were ideal targets if any of the Crows turned.

Henry Allen had reined up a dozen feet out but he was still distracting the warriors. "Scum like you don't deserve to go on breathing, Thunder Heart. You hate for the sake of hating. You kill for the sake of killing. It wouldn't matter if you were red or white or black or yellow or pink. You'd still be the worthless trash you are. You're a mad wolf, long overdue to be planted. And I'm just the coon to do it."

Thunder Heart's contempt was thick enough to be cut with a razor. "Why your kind talk so much? This day you die, white dog." So saying, Thunder Heart whipped the rifle to his shoulder.

It was the cue for all the Crows to bring their weapons to bear.

It was also the cue for Henry Allen, whose right hand materialized as if out of thin air in front of him, holding a cocked flintlock. He fired a heartbeat before Thunder Heart, and both men recoiled to the impact of searing lead. Thunder

Heart fell to one knee, losing his grip on the rifle. Allen wrenched to one side, then recovered and drew his second pistol.

The other three warriors were about to let fly or stroke a trigger.

Nate would have preferred it if his loved ones were safely behind the willow before the affray commenced, but since it had, he promptly sprang to the Tennessean's aid by rushing up to the warrior with the fusee, jamming the Hawken's muzzle against the man's ribs, and firing at point-blank range.

The Crow jolted forward, sprawling onto his hands and knees. Blood spurted from a cavity in his chest, but still he was able to shift and extended his fusee at Nate.

With the speed of a striking rattler, the mountain man produced a pistol and fired before the Crow could. The ball splatted into the warrior's forehead above the nose and blew out the rear of his skull in a spectacular scarlet spray.

As the man toppled, Nate turned toward the remaining pair. The Crow holding Winona's rifle was swiveling toward him, while the one with the bow loosed a shaft at Henry Allen. Nate was unable to see whether it scored or not. He had to dart in close and slam his pistol across the temple of the Crow about to shoot him. The warrior staggered but did not go down, so Nate hit him again.

As the Crow crumpled, nearly senseless, Winona saw the warrior with the bow swing it toward her husband while nocking an arrow. Nate could not possibly evade the shaft. To save him, she did the only thing she could think of: She threw back her head and screeched at the top of her lungs. The bowman, distracted, glanced around at her in that crucial instant before he let go of the arrow.

Nate also started to pivot and awakened to his peril. He leapt, swatting the bow with his Hawken as the Crow zinged the shaft at his belly. The arrow was deflected into the earth between them. Then Nate was on the man, ramming his rifle stock into the warrior's midsection, doubling the Crow over. He hiked the rifle to deliver the blow that would render the warrior unconscious, but the man was lightning fast and came at him first, a knife glinting dully as it sheared at Nate's chest.

By happenstance, the Hawken got in the way. The blade scraped the barrel, sending sparks flying. Nate backed up, dropped the rifle, and brought his Bowie into play. The Crow performed a dizzying blend of thrusts and slashes that he barely countered.

Meanwhile, young Zach, his back to the willow, had succeeded in fraying the cord that bound him by rubbing it on the bark. The moment the cord parted, he dashed toward the men who had slapped him and mocked him and made him watch as his mother was treated as if she were garbage.

Winona, guessing his intent, shouted, "Stalking Coyote! No! You do not have a weapon!"

Zach remedied that easily enough. At the fire he bent and seized a burning brand. Brandishing it, he rushed at the Crow his father had smashed with a pistol. The warrior was already rising, shaking his head to clear it. Zach never gave him the opportunity. In three swift bounds, he was close enough to shove the brand into the man's face.

A scream tore from the Crow's throat as his eyes, nose, and mouth were engulfed in flame. Flailing at the branch, he flung himself backward.

Zach pressed his advantage. Shoving the burning end at the Crow's eyes, he was more amazed than the warrior when the man's oily hair caught fire. Like dry grass, it flared brightly.

The Absaroka vented a cry more animal than human and slapped in vain at his head. Throwing himself flat, he attempted to smother the flames by rolling in the grass. To an extent, he was successful, but the effort cost him dearly. Gurgling like a furious bull, he went to stand; but collapsed.

Overjoyed at his victory, Nate turned to see how his father had fared. Nate was flat on his back, the Crow astraddle his chest, his Bowie the only thing that kept the warrior's long knife from slicing into his neck.

"Pa!" Zach cried.

The Crow suddenly reversed his grip, slid his knife clear, and stroked downward.

Chapter Eight

Reflexes are a lot like a knife blade. They can be honed as sharp as steel that can split a hair, or they can be left to atrophy, to waste away to the point where they are next to useless. Any man or woman who has lived in the wilderness for any length of time, who has had to deal daily with wild beasts and other dangers, inevitably develops their reflexes to an amazing degree, to a state equal to that of the beasts with which they must deal.

Nathaniel King was no exception. Years of living in the wild had endowed him with a quickness rivaling that of a mountain lion or bobcat. It was not a conscious effort on his part. He merely thought about doing something and did it simultaneous with the thought.

In this instance, as the Crow reversed his grip

on the long hunting knife, Nate reversed his own on the Bowie. As the knife slashed toward him, he slashed the Bowie upward. The blades pinged off one another. The Crow's was deflected harmlessly aside. The Bowie, however, speared straight up, impaling the warrior in the base of the throat.

Stiffening, the warrior hurled himself back onto his knees and clutched at the hilt. He pulled the Bowie out, took a ragged breath, and swayed as blood spouted from the rupture. Mewing like a kitten, he futilely sought to stem the flow by placing a hand over the hole. The blood squished through his fingers and sprayed from around the edges of his hand.

Nate warily regarded the Crow as he slowly rose. He was taking no chances. On many an occasion, a mortally stricken enemy had rallied and made a final defiant attempt to rub him out.

The Crow, weakening, slumped over, dropping the Bowie. Nate bent to retrieve it. Fortunately, he never took his eyes off the warrior because the man shot up at him with the hunting knife thirsting for a vein. A swift step to the right spared him from the lethal thrust, and once again the Crow pitched forward, this time to lie lifeless, blank eyes fixed on the crackling fire.

Nate spun to check on the other Crows. The one he had shot would never rise again. Another warrior, badly burned about the face and head, was unconscious. Of Thunder Heart there was no sign.

Zach stepped up. "Are you all right, Pa?" he

asked. For a moment there it had seemed his father was a goner, and his heart had been in his throat.

"Fine, son," Nate said, wiping the Bowie on the leggings of a dead Absaroka. He rotated on a heel as Winona ran into his arms, Evelyn gripping her as if for dear life. "How is Blue Flower?" he asked, using their daughter's Shoshone name.

"Unhurt," Winona said gratefully. "I saw Thunder Heart run off and wanted to stop him, but Evelyn would not let go of me."

Zach, hearing a tread behind him, pivoted. "Pa!" he exclaimed at sight of a scarecrow apparition.

It was Henry Allen, uncommonly pale, shuffling toward them with his left hand tucked against a dark stain on his buckskin shirt and a pistol in his right hand. In tremendous pain, he glared about him and growled, "Where is he? Where is that murdering bastard? I vowed to see him made wolf meat, and by God, I will!"

"He got away," Nate said.

The Tennessean scowled. "Damn his bones! But he can't have gone far. I'm going after him."

"Not in your condition, you're not," Nate said.

"I have it to do," Allen insisted. He turned toward his dun. He took no more than a few steps when his legs buckled.

Nate was there to catch him. He steered Allen to a spot by the fire. The lanky frontiersman did not resist. As Allen sat, he mustered a wan grin and said, "I reckon you're right. It'll have to wait. But I'll make him pay. Mark my words."

"Let me look at that wound," Nate said.

"Never mind about it. I'll be fine in no time."

Winona would hear no more nonsense. "Men!" she snorted, and knelt beside the Tennessean. "Why do you always pretend you are made of stone when you are flesh and bone like everyone else?" Before Allen could stop her, she tugged his shirt high enough to expose the wound. "You must excuse me, Henry. There is only so much silliness a woman will abide."

Zach was astounded at how his mother treated the trapper. He half expected Allen to give her a piece of his mind, but instead the man smiled.

"Hello, Mrs. King. It's been a spell, hasn't it?" The Tennessean coughed self-consciously. "Actually, I'm the one who should be begging your forgiveness. I had no call to use improper language with a lady present. And you're right. I shouldn't act the fool. It's just that—" He had to stop, his voice breaking.

"I am sorry to hear about Fetches The Man and your son," Winona said. She had never met the woman, but she had heard about her from Allen on several visits to the cabin. She felt profoundly sorry for the man. She knew how it would devastate her if she were to lose Grizzly Killer, Stalking Coyote, or Blue Flower.

"Thank you," Allen said huskily.

Winona had always liked the lanky trapper. Unlike some moutaineers, he didn't look down his nose at Indians and their way of life. One of the few to be friendly with the Absarokas, he had been very much in love with the maiden he took as his wife.

Nate, busy reloading his guns and keeping his eyes skinned for Thunder Heart, wanted to learn more about Fetches The Woman's death, but he didn't pry. His friend was upset enough without having to relate the loss.

Young Zach, having reloaded his rifle, nodded at the dun and said, "I'll fetch his horse, Pa, if you want."

Nate's first reaction was to tell the boy that it was too risky with Thunder Heart lurking in the area. But he hesitated, reminded that his son was at an age when Shoshone boys were sometimes allowed to accompany warriors on raids, at an age when most Indians were eager to prove their bravery and count their first coup. His son already had that distinction, so it would be unwarranted of him to deny permission.

"Go ahead," Nate said, "but stay alert."

Nodding, Zach scooted toward the horse. It pleased him that his pa was treating him the way he deserved and not like a kid who couldn't tie a knot without help.

The dun stood with head hung low, the reins snagged in a bush near its front legs. Zach spoke softly in order not to spook it as he reached out. The dun snorted and bobbed its head. Zach assumed he was to blame, but then he saw that the animal was staring into a strip of woodland to the east. He looked, too.

A large shadow detached itself from a tree and was promptly screened by foliage. Zach brought up his Hawken, but the shadow did not reappear. His glimpse had been too fleeting to tell whether it had been the Crow or something else.

Snatching the reins, Zach backed toward his father and mother. "I saw something, Pa. Yonder. Should we go have a look?"

Nate didn't hesitate. Under no circumstances would he leave his wife and daughter alone. "No."

Winona was gently probing the furrow left by the lead ball in Henry Allen's side. She could insert a finger as far as the first joint. It had bled considerably although the shot had missed a vital organ. Allen would be sore for months but he would live. She informed him as much.

"That's nice to hear," the Tennessean said. "I wouldn't want to go under before I settle accounts with Thunder Heart."

To dress the wound, Winona needed to stop the bleeding. Asking Allen to hold his shirt up, she sidled to the fire and selected a suitably fiery brand, one long and slender so she could hold it without being burned.

Allen knew what she was going to do. "Hold on a second," he said, and stuffed the hem of his shirt into his mouth. Clamping his teeth tight, he nodded.

Zachary King's stomach churned when his mother pressed the brand against the trapper's side. Dizziness assailed him, and for a few seconds he feared he would embarrass himself by fainting. A sizzling hiss filled the air, along with a peculiar odor.

The man from Tennessee shuddered and gave

a tiny grunt. That was all.

Winona lowered the brand. It had seared the flesh, cauterizing the furrow. "We should bandage you."

"For a tiny scratch like this? That won't be necessary, ma'am," Allen said, lowering his shirt. "By morning I'll be as spry as a jackrabbit."

A muffled groan caused all of them to turn to the unconscious Crow. "I'll deal with him," Nate said. Collecting the lengths of cords that had been used to tie his wife's ankles, he bound the warrior's wrists and feet. The man's face was charred black in spots, his hair burnt to the scalp here and there. "Do you know this one?" he asked the other trapper.

"His name is Tall Bear," Allen said. "He never thought much of me and I never thought much of him. Let me load my pistol and I'll save you the trouble of carting him back."

"I want him alive," Nate said.

Tall Bear's eyes snapped wide. He promptly tried to sit up, discovered he was bound, and glared at his captors. Snarling like a caged bear, he yanked on the cord, but to no effect.

Nate employed sign language. "You will do as we say or you will suffer. Do you understand?"

Incredibly, the Crow snarled louder and pushed himself toward Nate. Bending, he snapped at Nate's leg, his teeth gnashing shy of their mark.

"You should learn to do as you are told," Nate signed, and kicked the man full in the face. Tall Bear was flung onto his back, his lips pulped, his mouth welling with blood. To Allen, Nate said, "Let him know that I will only tell him to do something once. Every time he doesn't listen, I'll chop off a finger. When I run out, I'll start in on his toes."

The lean mountain man did as he was bid. The Absaroka responded, and Allen snickered. "He says that your father was the hind end of a buffalo and your mother mated with snakes."

Nate kicked the man again, in the gut this time, doubling the warrior over. "Convince him that if he puts his mouth on me again, I'll stomp his teeth in."

Apparently this time the warrior believed that Nate was not bluffing. After the Tennessean translated, he lay there as sullen as a lynx with its leg caught in a trap.

"If looks could kill, you'd be a pile of bones," Allen remarked. "Don't turn your back on him or he's liable to try to stomp you to death."

Zach had been scanning the woods. He was bothered by a persistent feeling of being watched by unseen eyes. Tending to shrug it off as just raw nerves, he recollected words of his wisdom his father had once imparted. "Always trust your instincts, son. I can't count the number of times mine have saved my hide. When they act up, when they tell you that something is wrong even though everything seems just fine, believe them. You'll live longer that way."

"Pa," the boy now said, "I think Thunder Heart is still out there."

"Probably waiting for us to ride on out so he

can jump us," Allen speculated.

"Then he'll have a long wait," Nate said. "We're not leaving until daylight."

"What about Ashworth's supper invite?" Allen asked.

Nate motioned at the star-dotted heavens. "It's a little late for that. Maybe he'll treat us to breakfast."

The Kings and the Tennessean spent the next half hour bedding down. The horses were gathered and picketed close to the fire, which was allowed to blaze high so the glow reached the trees. All weapons were loaded. It was agreed that two of them would stay awake at all times. Only Blue Flower enjoyed uninterrupted slumber.

Winona and Zach kept watch just before daylight. She added wood to the fire and busied herself making coffee so it would be ready when the men woke up.

Zach sat close to the fire. Lulled by its warmth and the quiet that always preceded the dawn, his eyelids grew heavy. Try as he might, he couldn't stay awake. His chin drooped and he dozed.

When Winona noticed, she grinned. She was more amused than annoyed. Since the sun would rise in another half an hour or so, she let her son sleep. He needed the rest.

Not a minute later, several of the horses lifted their heads and fidgeted, among them Nate's black stallion. Wary, Winona stood with her rifle in hand. She made a circuit of the string, surveying the shadows under the trees. Nothing moved, not even a bird. The horses calmed down. Even the stallion cropped grass, no longer concerned.

Convinced that whatever had been out there was gone, Winona turned to finish with the coffee. She took a few steps. Suddenly the black and her mare looked up again just as a whisper of air forewarned her that she had made a grave mistake. An arm as strong as granite encircled her waist, a hand clamped over her mouth. She was lifted bodily and hauled toward the forest.

Winona did not need to see her attacker to know who it was. In her ear hissed Thunder Heart's voice in broken English.

"Make no sound, Shoshone bitch, or you die!"

Winona still held her rifle but she deliberately released it so the Absaroka would not get his hands on it. He started to lunge to catch the barrel, but evidently decided not to release her and continued to drag her into the trees. Once they were under cover, Winona's knife was snatched from its sheath and the edge placed roughly against her neck.

"You not move, Shoshone," Thunder Heart warned.

Winona dared not resist as he relieved her of her pistols, which he wedged under his breechcloth.

The warrior wasn't content. He patted her buckskin dress, seeking hidden weapons, and when done, he seized her by the wrist to propel her northward.

"We go now."

"Go where?" Winona asked much louder than she needed to in the hope her son or one of the men would hear. She never saw the hand that smacked her cheek with such force she was driven to her knees.

"Try again, I cut you from chin to stomach," Thunder Heart said. To emphasize his point, he entwined his fingers in her hair and shoved her so that she stumbled forward. "Keep mouth closed until I say."

Through a gap in the trees Winona could see the camp. Zach still dozed; the men were sound asleep. Only Evelyn, snuggled next to Nate, was awake, but she was staring off into the distance with no idea of the fate that had befallen her mother.

The Crow was in a hurry. If she so much as lagged an instant, she was pushed and prodded. Winona did not understand why he was in a rush. Whenever she glanced at him, he wore a sly smile, as if he up were to something that betokened ill for those she cared for most in the world.

The trees ended at the base of a low bluff that merged into the foothills to the northeast. Thunder Heart jabbed Winona with the knife. A gesture indicated she should bear eastward. In 40 yards they came to a deer trail that wound to the top. Again the Crow jabbed her. This time he wanted her to go up. His crafty smile broadened.

Winona did as he demanded. By this time a golden celestial crown framed the horizon. She knew that Nate would be up; he always woke up before first light, a habit born of his many months spent working trap lines, when it was essential that the traps be checked first thing every morning.

Presently they climbed above treetop level and Winona sought a glimpse of her family. Pinpointing the willow, she saw them scurrying about the clearing. They were seeking sign and soon would be on her trail. It wouldn't be long before she was rescued.

"Go faster!" the Absaroka growled. "We must be ready."

Ready for what? Winona wondered. Then she had to devote all her attention to the last leg of their ascent. A steep incline, nearly sheer in parts. Scaling it taxed her ability. Frequently she had to dig in her fingers and toes and cling to the side of the bluff with nothing to stop her from falling to her death if she lost her grip.

Thunder Heart glanced repeatedly into the trees. He grew more and more impatient with her. If she slowed a shade too much to suit him, he pricked her with the knife. Twice he drew drops of blood from her leg, once from her arm.

Finally, every muscle in her arms sore, her shoulders aching terribly, Winona reached the summit. Broad and flat, it was covered with brush, mostly sage.

"That way!" Thunder Heart barked, pushing her toward the west end.

For the life of her, Winona still could not guess what he was up to. She doubted he would attempt to ambush Nate and Allen, not when he had pistols and they had rifles. The outcome would be a foregone conclusion.

It occurred to Winona that the Absaroka might shove large boulders down on the others, but when they came to the spot that suited him, only rocks the size of melons were handy. Hardly a threat.

The Crow grasped her wrist and twisted it. "Sit!" he directed, nodding at a flat rock a few yards back from the edge. After she complied, he paced, smacking the flat of the blade against one palm.

Winona plotted to add to his nervousness. "You will die, you know. My husband is Grizzly Killer. He has counted more coup than any ten Absarokas."

Thunder Heart sniffed as if at a foul odor. "You man is white. Whites are weak. I kill him as I have others."

This was news to Winona. Adopting a casual air, she probed, "You have rubbed out other trappers? Henry Allen never mentioned it."

"Would I tell him?" Thunder Heart said. "Many times we find trappers alone. Many times we kill and take all they have."

"It is men like you who give all your people a bad name," Winona declared. "You are a coward who strikes only when you and your friends outnumber those you prey on. How many had their backs to you when you killed them? No doubt all of them."

The Crow's features twisted in anger. His hands flew in sign language. "The Absarokas are not Shoshones. We do not grovel at the feet of the whites! We do not want them taking all our beaver! We do not want them killing all our buffalo! I will never rest so long as a single white man defiles our land."

His vehemence bordered on blind hatred. Winona had struck a nerve and rattled him to the point where he might not think straight when the time came for him to spring his trap, which was exactly what she wanted.

To the south a horse nickered. Thunder Heart gestured for her to be silent and stepped to the edge. Squatting, he surveyed the woodland.

Winona saw her chance. His back was to her. All it would take was a single push and he would hurtle over the brink to the boulders 60 feet below. Rising soundlessly into a crouch, she edged toward him, her arms outstretched for the fatal shove. She covered half the space between them. Three-fourths of it. Her fingertips were the span of a single hand from his spine.

Thunder Heart spun. Lightning bolts seemed to flicker in his eyes as he drew one of the pistols, pointed it at her face, and cocked the trigger. "Did you think I be that easy?" he rasped.

Winona waited for the hammer to fall. Instead, he made her sit back down, then slid her knife under the thin leather strap that supported his own knife sheath around his waist.

"Not try that again, woman," the warrior said.

Off in the forest, a twig snapped. It was loud enough to tell Winona that her husband was very close. Soon he would be within pistol range. Would Thunder Heart really be brash enough to fire, even though it would take someone with great skill to hit anyone at that range with a flintlock? Surely not, she assured herself.

"This way, Nate! I found their tracks!"

Winona tensed. It had been Henry Allen who yelled. She heard hooves pound and muted voices. They had to be near the tree line. Coiling her legs, she prepared to sell her own life if need be to preserve the life of her mate and her children.

The Absaroka grinned from ear to ear. "The great Grizzly Killer not smart, eh?" he whispered. "Him care too much for you. Him do what I want."

A hoof pinged off stone. Winona could wait no longer. She was going to warn Nate even if it meant the warrior killed her. An outcry was on the tip of her tongue when once more the Crow swiveled and grabbed her by the left wrist. His strength was overpowering. She was wrenched erect, her arm twisted behind her back. Then she was herded to the lip of the bluff in plain sight were her family and Allen. They immediately drew rein.

Thunder Heart, shielding himself with her body, jammed the pistol's muzzle against Winona's temple. His taunting laugh rolled off across the valley. "We meet again, Grizzly Killer!" he cried. "This time, you die!"

Chapter Nine

Richard Ashworth started off the morning in a good mood. He awoke at the crack of dawn, invigorated from an undisturbed night's sleep. He was raring to face the new day and whatever challenges it might offer.

Birds filled the surrounding woodland with a sensational chorus of varied cries as Ashworth stepped from his tent and inhaled the crisp air. He had never felt so alive before, never been so inspired by a heartfelt zest for life.

Back in New York City, Ashworth had invariably slept in until 11 every day. He'd had to drag himself from under the sheets, pour a gallon of black coffee down his throat, and take a hot bath before he even began to feel vaguely human.

The long nights were to blame, Ashworth felt. Practically every night of the week he had stayed up until all hours, making the rounds of the theaters, visiting the best clubs, eating at only the best of restaurants.

Small wonder, Ashworth mused, that the family fortune had dwindled to its pathetic state. But that would all change. His plan was all coming together. Within two years he would have enough money to go on living in the lap of luxury for a long time to come. Invested wisely, the funds might even be sufficient to last his lifetime. What more could a man ask for?

Ashworth adjusted his cape, then tilted his high beaver hat at a rakish angle. Not far off a trapper was tending to the stock, and Ashworth noted how different the grungy man's beaver hat was from his own.

Beaver hats sold in the States were regarded as the height of fashion. They were treated and trimmed until they were as smooth and soft as a baby's bottom. The favored shape was much like a stovepipe, with a circular brim. At ten dollars a hat they were quite expensive, but no gentleman of means would be seen without one. They were a mark of status, of culture and breeding.

The mountain men, on the other hand, stitched their beaver hats together from freshly skinned hides. They left the hair on, and they preferred a a shape that reminded Ashworth of the hats worn by Russian cossacks. Crude beyond belief, the hats nevertheless kept the wearer's head warm and dry in the worst of weather. Ashworth would never be caught dead in one.

A footfall behind him brought the New Yorker

around to find his second shadow had once again attached itself to him. As usual, he made an effort to be civil. "Good morning, Emilio. Another fine morning, is it not?"

The hulking giant did not answer. Over the course of the nine weeks they had been together, Emilio had not grown to like Ashworth any better than he had that first day they met. If anything, his contempt had grown. Ashworth reminded Emilio of the landed gentry back in the old country, of the simpering aristocrats who believed they had a God-given right to trod everyone else underfoot.

The lack of a response mildly ruffled Richard Ashworth's feathers. He told himself that he should be accustomed to it by now, that the watchdog was as refined as a lump of coal and marginally more intelligent than a turnip. "Don't answer me then," he scolded. "Exhibit your lack of social grace for all the world to see."

Emilio smirked. He cared no more for the niceties of society than he did for those who practiced them.

Ashworth hid his irritation and strode toward the closed gate. Tendrils of smoke rising skyward west of the compound confirmed the Crow encampment was still there. The Indians were not allowed in at any time, a precaution suggested by Scott Kendall and Henry Allen. All business with the Crows and other bands who showed up was conducted outside.

The two trappers on guard duty were scruffy sorts with greasy beards and buckskins. Ashworth knew that he should know their names, but although he tried his best, he couldn't recall what they were. Truth was, one mountain man pretty much looked like every other one to him.

"Morning, gentlemen," Ashworth said. "Would either of you happen to know if Mr. King showed up during the night?"

"As far as this hoss knows, booshway," said a gnarled specimen of manhood, "no. If'n you ask me, them Crows made buzzard bait of the Kings. Little Soldier and his bunch are no account any ways you lay your sights."

"I beg your pardon?" Ashworth said. Trying to comprehend trapper jargon vexed him greatly. Most of them had an appalling grasp of grammar and mispronounced words with careless abandon.

"Maybe the Crows rubbed them out," the man clarified.

"Why would they want to do that?" Ashworth asked. "Little Soldier gave me his word of honor that he would be on his best behavior the whole time he's camped near us."

From behind the New Yorker a new voice intruded. Reminiscent of gravel being poured over a tin plate, it at least had the distinction of clear diction. "When are you going to learn, sir, that you can't trust those Crows any farther than you can heave a griz? Little Soldier is only being friendly because it suits his purpose."

Ashworth turned. Of the 60 men under him, three stood out as eminiently reliable. One was Kendall, another Allen. The third was Clive Jenks, a fellow New Yorker who had left a farm upstate to seek his fortune west of the broad Mississippi. "And how many times must I tell you, Mr. Jenks, that so long as Little Soldier behaves himself we must give him the benefit of the doubt?"

Clive Jenks was a short, rawboned man whose buckskins were nearly worn out at the elbows and knees. He was so fond of snuff that he always had a wad in his mouth, bulging one cheek or the other. Spitting brown juice at his feet, he cocked a blue eye at Ashworth. "Any coon that goes around giving Injuns the benefit of the doubt is just asking to spend the rest of his days bald, if you take my meaning."

"My intellect is up to the challenge, thank you very much," Ashworth said dryly. It bothered him a little that, after all he had done to meet the trappers halfway, after he had accepted their advice on every matter under the sun, they still saw fit to question his judgment on this one trivial affair.

Ashworth had always rated himself an excellent judge of character, and in his opinion, Little Soldier was as dependable as any savage could be and more so than most. The Crow had bent over backward to comply with every demand made of him, and was tickled silly at being picked to help guide the expedition into Blackfoot country.

Why couldn't the mountain men just accept that? Ashworth mused. Why did they persist with their unfounded suspicion? It was no wonder the trappers and several tribes were on such bad terms, when the whites refused to offer an open hand of friendship.

Ashworth would change all that. He would make them see that the Crows could be trusted. He would teach them that the proper way to conduct themselves was as perfect gentlemen. And who knew? Once he had proven it worked with Little Soldier, maybe he would do the same with the Blackfeet.

As his father had always said, a little breeding went a long way.

Nate King started to raise his Hawken, but stopped at the sight of his wife perched precariously on the very brink of the bluff. A fall from that height would cripple or kill her. "Don't shoot," he said as Henry Alley began to lift the Kentucky.

"Did you really think I would?" the man from Tennessee responded.

Zach King made no attempt to use his rifle. He had his hands full with Evelyn, who had been entrusted to his care. She sat in front of him, always squirming and fidgeting in the saddle, a regular armful. On spying their mother, Evelyn bawled, "Ma! Leave her be, bad man!" She tried to scramble down off the bay but Zach held on tight.

"Be still, Blue Flower," Nate said, and she instantly obeyed. Both children had learned at an early age not to sass their parents. Indian children were brought up the same way. Their lives too often hung in the balance for them to get into the nasty habit of rebelling. Not so back in the States, where pampered offspring of immature parents were frequently permitted to do and say whatever they wanted, when they wanted, including talking back to their own folks.

Nate saw that the Crow had one of Winona's flintlocks pressed to her temple, and his blood ran cold. "You can't hope to kill us all!" he shouted up. "Let her go, and I give you my word that you'll be free to leave. You can even take one of our horses."

Thunder Heart gouged the muzzle deeper into Winona's skin. "Drop guns, white dog, or I shoot!" He pushed Winona a trifle farther out and dirt cascaded from under her moccasins. "You shoot me, she fall!"

Winona knew her husband would do as the Absaroka wanted. Nate would do anything to spare her from harm, even put himself at the mercy of a warrior who had none. She tried to twist and grapple with Thunder Heart but he held her too firmly.

Only Winona's heels rested on the rim. Another fraction more and she would topple onto the boulders below. Glancing down, she observed a long, thin ledge. No more than a couple of inches wide, it was too narrow to support a person—or was it?

Nate slowly lowered his Hawken to the ground, saying out of the corner of his mouth, "Sorry I got you into this, Henry. It was my fight, not yours."

"What else are friends for?" the Tennessean said, bending low so his Kentucky would not hit the ground hard when he let go. "But if you think I'm giving up my pistols, too, you have another think coming. Once he disarms us, he'll torture us a spell. No matter what he claims, he wants to see us suffer."

"Now the pistols!" Thunder Heart called down.

Nate needed to stall, to have time to ponder. "Let my wife back away from the edge and we'll do as you want."

Laughing, Thunder Heart shook Winona so violently that she nearly went over. "Drop your pistols!" he repeated. "I not say it again!"

Nate reluctantly put a hand on each flintlock. He wished that Winona could somehow take a short step to either side to give him a clear shot.

Zach was thinking that, if he could slip a hand behind his sister's back, he could draw his flintlock without being seen. The only drawback was that, if the Crow spotted him and fired, Evelyn might take a ball meant for him.

"Be quick!" Thunder Heart warned. "Or I shoot Shoshone!"

Winona's arm was close to being torn from its socket. She could feel the Absaroka's knuckles digging into her spine between her shoulder blades. He had such an unbreakable grip that it was just possible he would be unable to let go quickly enough if she could take him by surprise.

Nate put a hand on his right pistol. He had been backed into a corner. He had to draw swiftly and fire and pray that Winona did not fall when the Crow did. His hand tensed, his thumb hooked the hammer.

Up on the bluff, Thunder Heart gloated in Winona's ear. "See, Shoshone? The great Grizzly Killer not so mighty! You make him weak! Because of you, he lose life!"

"That's what you think," Winona said. Suddenly she flung her heels over the brink. She dropped like a rock, tearing loose from her captor. As she fell, she twisted around to face the bluff. The ledge flashed up to meet her and she flung both arms out, her fingers digging into the soil. For a dreadful moment, she feared the earth would give way and she would plunge to the bottom, but the ledge held. Her arms lanced with torment, she hung on.

Nate's breath had caught in his throat. He almost screamed his wife's name, then saw her catch hold. At the same time, Thunder Heart, who had toppled forward and nearly gone over the rim, was on his hands and knees, taking aim at her. Nate drew and his flintlock thundered. The crack of his pistol was echoed by the blast of Allen's, who in turn was echoed a split second later by the boom of Zach's.

Like a punctured water skin, the Crow deflated. Three new holes had sprouted into existence on his face, two above his eyes, one below them. The pistol slipped from his nerveless fingers.

Winona flinched when a hard object struck her shoulder. The flintlock appeared below her, tumbling end over end. She saw it smash down at the bottom and the butt shatter. Glancing up, she discovered that the Absaroka was slowly sliding over the rim—directly toward her.

"Ma!" Zach cried.

Nate was in motion, galloping along the bluff in search of a way to reach the crest. A game trail bearing scuff marks and partial prints revealed how his wife and the Crow had gained the summit. Vaulting from the saddle, he flew upward, legs pumping. He tried not to think of Winona slipping, tried not to imagine the result should she be dashed onto those jagged boulders. Just climb! his mind screeched.

Winona had seen her man ride off. It would not take him long to find the trail, but reaching the top would be another matter. Could she hold on that long when her shoulders were aflame with agony and the dirt under her fingernails was slowly but steadily crumbling away? She heard her children calling her name and marshalled her strength to reply.

"Do not fear! I will be all right! Your father will save me!"

Zach wanted to believe her. But the sight of wisps of dust swirling from under her hands alarmed him. Even he could see that her grip was being lost bit by gradual bit and that eventually she would do as the pistol had done. "There must be something we can do!"

"If only there were, boy," Allen said. "If only there were."

Winona overheard. It occurred to her that, if she fell, her son and daughter would witness every grisly detail. "Stalking Coyote!" she hollered. "Take Blue Flower into the trees!"

For the first time in his entire life, Zachary King balked at doing something his folks wanted him to do. "I'm staying right here, Ma!" he responded, at a loss to understand why she wanted them to leave.

"Please, son!" Winona said. Her fingers were losing their purchase, especially her left hand, where her little finger no longer had a grip. The ledge under it had dissolved.

"I should stay with you!" Zach insisted.

The Tennessean leaned toward him and said, barely above a whisper, "Think, boy! She doesn't want your sister to have to live with the memory."

"The memory of what?" Zach asked. No sooner did he phrase the words than he knew. The trapper's expression was his clue. He glanced at his mother, then at Evelyn, who gaped upward in undisguised terror. "Oh, I reckon I savvy now. Sorry."

Zach started to rein his bay around to trot into the woods when a rain of dirt and pebbles snapped his gaze on high. More of the ledge had crumbled. His ma's left hand clung to the bluff by a fingernail. "Hang on!" he yelled. "Please, Ma! Don't let anything happen to you!"

Winona was doing her best. She held herself as still as was humanly possible and breathed shallow. She also had propped her knees against the bluff to take some of the strain off her arms. But there was nothing she could do about the ledge. It continued to fall apart, small clumps of earth at a time.

The biggest clod yet broke off. Winona's left hand clawed empty air. Dangling by one arm, she groped the sheer wall, seeking in vain for a solid handhold that wasn't there. Her legs swung from side to side. The muscles in her right shoulder were aflame with anguish. It wouldn't be long.

A rain of dust heaped onto Winona's head from much higher up. Tilting her head back, she saw that the Absaroka was about to pitch over the edge. Hoping to swing out of the way, she tried to place her left hand next to her right, but she couldn't clamp her fingers tight enough to get a solid grip.

The rattle of dirt increased. Winona looked up again. A tingle ran down her spine as Thunder Heart's body began to slide toward her. There was no escape. It would smash into her, tear her from her roost, and together they would crash onto the boulders.

It was not the end Winona had envisioned. She would rather have died in her cabin with her family by her side or in battle next to her mate.

The Absaroka's corpse slid faster, pouring more dirt and dust down on Winona's head, so much that it choked her. She broke into a fit of coughing that threatened to tear her right hand loose.

"Ma!" Zach and Evelyn screamed in unison.

Thunder Heart was almost on top of her. Winona braced for the impact. It was then that the bluff rocked to the clap of a heavy-caliber rifle. Above her there was the familiar squishy thud of a lead ball ripping into human flesh.

In a twinkling, Winona took it all in. Henry Allen had fired his Hawken at Thunder Heart's head, blowing off the top of the Absaroka's skull. It seemed a silly thing to do. But the Tennessean knew what he was about. The jolt of the ball bounced the body against the bluff and kicked it outward, flipping it into the air so that it narrowly missed her on its descent.

Winona would have thanked Allen if she had had the breath. He had bought her a few more seconds of precious life. She hung there as limp as a wet rag, caked with dust from head to waist, on the verge of exhaustion. She'd had a good life. Her parents had treated her kindly, and even though both had fallen to a war party of Blackfeet, they had lived rich lives.

About the same time, Nate King had claimed her heart. Of all the men she had ever known, both Indian and white, he was the one who had stirred her soul in ways she had never imagined any man ever could. He was the one who had kindled a passion so overpowering that the only way she could deal with it was to take him as her man. And wonder of wonders, since then that passion had grown, not tapered. It was safe to say that she loved him more now than she had when they first met.

A new shower of dirt appraised Winona of the fact her time had run out. This one came from under her own fingers. The ledge was giving way entirely. Some of the dirt brushed her wrist. More did the same.

"Grab hold!"

Belatedly, Winona realized it wasn't dirt that had touched her wrist. It was a shirtsleeve.

Nate had arrived. Since he couldn't reach his wife by leaning down, he had stripped off his shirt, gone prone, and dipped the shirt low enough for her to seize. "Hurry!" he goaded, aware of how little was left of the ledge.

Winona did not need prodding. Impulsively, she snatched the sleeve with both hands and promptly dropped. For a few heartbeats she thought that she had torn Nate off the bluff. Jerking up short, she swung wildly, banging her right knee. She had to crane her neck to see her man. His face was as red as raw meat and he had his teeth clenched. "Are you all right?" she shouted.

"Fine," Nate lied. He thought that he had been firmly planted, but the abrupt weight of her body had yanked him forward over two feet and he was balanced on his belt buckle on the very lip. A sneeze was all it would take to send them both hurtling to their deaths.

Some men would have lain there paralyzed with fright. Some would have hesitated, unsure of what to do. Some would have told their wives to try to climb to them rather than do that which Nate King did, which was to suddenly rear back onto his knees and haul upward with all the power in his broad shoulders.

It was a bold gambit. If the shirt tore, or Winona threw him off balance, or he couldn't pull her up, one or both would perish.

Every sinew in Nate's torso bulged as he raised her inch by laborious inch. He wasn't all that worried about the shirt ripping. Winona had sewn it herself, double stitching the seams and sleeves so it would hold up under the roughest of wear. No, he was more afraid that she would lose her grip or that he would. And he couldn't bear that last notion, couldn't abide the thought of being responsible for her passing. He'd rather die himself.

For her part, Winona did nothing that would make his task harder. She didn't kick or try to climb. As motionless as could be, she let him do all the work. She had every confidence that he would save her. He was Nate. Her man.

Below, Zach watched breathlessly as his ma hiked higher and higher. He could see his pa heaving, see the muscles on his pa's neck stand out like bands of iron.

Nate was tiring. The climb up the bluff had taxed him terribly. His mad dash to the west end had tired him even more. Now his body was being called on to go beyond any limit it had ever reached. Hand over hand, he pulled, pulled, pulled.

All went well until Winona reached the rim. She couldn't get up over it on her own. Nate had to exert himself an extra degree. A moment she hung there, her sweaty palms starting to slip. Their eyes locked.

With a monumental heave, Nate yanked his wife onto the bluff and into his waiting arms. She molded herself to him and for the longest while they stood there, silent except for their heavy breathing and the fluttering in their chests.

Then Winona kissed him. "You did it," she said huskily. "It is over."

"Not by a long sight," Nate said.

"What do you mean?"

Fire danced in the mountain man's eye's. "I have a hunch that someone put Thunder Heart up to what he did. And that someone is going to pay."

Chapter Ten

It was the middle of the afternoon. Richard Ashworth had repaired to his tent to rest on his cot and take leisurely swigs from a silver flask that had once belonged to his father. He liked to let the Scotch slowly burn its way down his throat into his stomach.

Ashworth could no more get through the day without a few nips than he could without breathing. At the age of 16 he had picked up the habit and he'd never been able to shake it. Not that he tried. His ability to handle liquor was a source of personal pride. Never yet had he met anyone who could drink him under the table.

In a corner of the tent were stacked two unmarked crates filled with carefully packed bottles of Ashworth's favorite brand. The mountain men knew nothing about the crates, nor was he about to tell them. Even though Kendall and Allen had maintained that those who signed on were an honest outfit, Ashworth doubted some of them would be able to resist temptation if they should learn of his secret stash.

At the moment, Ashworth was mulling over when to break camp and head north. It annoyed him that King and Henry Allen had seen fit to wander off without so much as a word of explanation. Allen, in particular, knew that he was eager to get underway.

Earlier that day Ashworth had sent Jenks and five competent trackers to go find the pair. Jenks had returned to report that they had tracked the two men in a clearing on a nearby hill, and that from the sign, it appeared King's wife and a boy had been taken against their will by Crow Indians and that King and Allen had gone after them.

Ashworth suspected that the mountaineers, for all their vaunted prowess, had been mistaken. He'd confronted Little Soldier about it, and the chief had assured him in no uncertain terms that the Crows would never commit so vile an atrocity.

A shadow loomed on the flap of Ashworth's tent.

Involuntarily, he tensed, hoping it wasn't Emilio. The watchdog was getting on his nerves. Every time he ventured out, there Emilio was. The man dogged his footsteps from the moment he woke up in the morning until he went to bed at night. It was aggravating beyond belief. Yet there was nothing Ashworth could do about it. He had given his word to the Brothers, and a proper gentleman never broke a promise.

"Mr. Ashworth, sir!"

The tension evaporated. It was Jenks, not the giant brute. Ashworth capped his flask. "What is it?"

"You'd better come quick. There's trouble at the gate."

Ashworth sighed. When it rained, it poured. Rising, he picked up his cape and shrugged it over his shoulders. "What sort of trouble, my good man?"

"Nate King is back, and he's looking to lift some locks."

The news that King had finally shown up thrilled Ashworth."What do you mean by lift some locks?" he inquired as he slipped the flask into a pocket.

"He's fixing to kill Little Soldier," Clive Jenks clarified.

Ashworth was out the tent in a rush and flying toward the stockade entrance. For once, he wasn't peeved when a monstrous form appeared at his side. If trouble was brewing, he wanted Emilio on hand to deal with it. The Crows, he knew, were in awe of the swarthy Sicilian, and had dubbed Emilio Man-Bear in their language. Even the mountain men were treating Emilio with respect after one of their rowdier fellows challenged the giant to wrestle and had been soundly defeated.

Ashworth had seen the match. It had taken place during the supper hour, over a week ago, while the expedition members were lounging around the stockade. The mountain man who issued the challenge, Ren Weaver, was himself the size of a tree, or so it seemed. From the lusty cheers and whoops that had gone up, it had been apparent he was highly regarded.

Emilio had refused, at first. Only when Ashworth, for amusement's sake, had told the giant that he could indulge himself unless he was afraid, had Emilio waded into the mountaineer and disposed of him so swiftly, the bout was over before it had really begun.

Ashworth was still not sure what Emilio had done. He'd seen Emilio's hands flick out, twice, and Weaver had oozed to the ground as if made of putty.

A tremendous commotion brought an end to Ashworth's reflection. Fully half the trappers were congregated just inside the gate and the rest appeared to be gathered outside.

Shouts and cries filled the air. Ashworth couldn't see what was happening for the press of mountaineers.

"Let us through!" Clive Jenks yelled, but few paid him any heed.

Ashworth, thwarted, glanced at the watchdog. "If you would be so kind, Mr. Barzini?"

Emilio plowed into the mass of excited men with all the power and impact of a tidal wave. They parted before him like chaff before a storm, those who didn't scatter being effortlessly shouldered aside as if they were so many rag dolls.

Emilio's face showed no emotion, but secretly he was immensely pleased. Until he beat their champion, Weaver, the mountain men had not thought much of him. He could tell. To have them recoil like sheep before a wolf gave him that feeling he often had in New York City when people on the streets of Little Italy, as the district was called, would cower in his mere presence, knowing that he worked for the Brothers.

Emilio liked that feeling.

In the Old Country, a man had earned respect two ways, either by being born into the aristocracy, or by belonging to La Cosa Nostra. The former bestowed wealth and prestige. The latter gave one a sense of power, power that stemmed from the raw fear La Cosa Nostra instilled in rich and poor alike.

Since Emilio had not been born in the lap of luxury, and since he had not liked the idea of spending all his days toiling in a field under a burning sun, he had gone to the Brothers and offered to enter their service. They had gladly accepted him on the basis of his imposing size alone, and in no time he had risen through the ranks to become one of their trusted lieutenants.

If Emilio had known that one day they would sail for America, he would never have gone to work for them. He loved the Old Country, loved it almost as much as he did the real reason he had come on Ashworth's stupid expedition. Duty had little to do with it.

Just then, Emilio plowed through the last row of trappers, and halted. In a cleared space in front of him were the Crow, Little Soldier, and the mountain man he had heard so much about, Nate

King. They had knives in their hands and were circling one another.

Emilio found this interesting. He preferred to kill with his bare hands, although on occasion he had used knives. And he knew other members of La Cosa Nostra who were masters with a blade. He was curious to see how well Nate King did, to measure King's skill against theirs.

Richard Ashworth, a few steps behind the giant, was appalled. He couldn't believe what he was seeing, couldn't imagine what had gotten into King. By all accounts the man was one of the most reliable frontiersmen, yet there he was, trying to kill an Indian Ashworth rated an ally.

The object of Emilio and Ashworth's attention was unaware they had arrived on the scene.

Nate held his Bowie low, the blade angled upward. He feinted, and had to admire the agility with which Little Soldier skipped to the left.

The Crow's face blazed hatred. On his right cheek was a large red puffy welt, courtesy of a stinging backhand.

Nate had not minced words. He had not demanded an explanation. He had not given Little Soldier time to concoct an excuse. On spying the Crow outside the stockade, he had dismounted, walked up, said, "Thunder Heart sends his regards," and hit Little Soldier across the face.

Since no Crow warrior worthy of the name would allow himself to be struck with impunity, Little Soldier had promptly resorted to his knife, which suited Nate just fine.

Taking a step to the right, Nate suddenly reversed direction, spearing the Bowie at the warrior's chest. Little Soldier deftly parried, shifted, and tried to repay the favor. Nate ducked under the blow, slashing upward as he did. The edge of his blade bit into the Crow's forearm. Not far, but deep enough to produce a trickle of blood.

"You die!" Little Soldier hissed as he weaved a glittering pattern with his weapon. Every swing was countered, every stroke blocked.

Nate skipped backward, away from an especially vicious thrust, one that would have deprived him of his manhood. He heard his son cry out.

"Watch out, Pa! Behind you!"

Among those watching the fight was a knot of Crows. They had been with Little Soldier when Nate and his family arrived, and several had made as if to intervene after Little Soldier was hit. Now Winona, Zach, and Allen covered them, keeping them at bay.

Inadvertently, Nate had nearly bumped into one. The warrior's hand rested on the handle of a tomahawk but the man made no attempt to use it. Not with Henry Allen standing five feet away, his Hawken leveled.

It was Nate's intention to kill Little Soldier. To that end, he pressed his attack, his Bowie constantly in motion.

As weapons went, the big knife was a newcomer to the frontier. In 1827, the man widely credited as its inventor, James Bowie, had killed Major Norris Wright with one in the notorious

Sandbar Duel, a fight written up in newspapers all across the country.

As word spread of the knife's size and reliability in tight situations, more and more frontiersmen wanted to get their hands on a Bowie. Cutlers and blacksmiths could hardly keep up with the demand.

Just four years previous, Bowie himself had died at the Alamo, but the legacy of his famous knife lived on. Bowies were regularly sold at Bent's Fort and other outposts, while back in St. Louis they were the knife of choice for any man venturing into the untamed wilderness.

Nate had owned his only a few short months. For years a long butcher knife had sufficed. But on a recent trip to Bent's Fort he had seen the shining Bowie in a glass case, and it had been love at first sight. He'd had to have it.

Now that knife served Nate in good stead as the wide blade deflected a cut that would have opened his throat wide open. Pivoting, he kicked out with his right leg, tripping Little Soldier, who sprawled onto his back. Raising the Bowie for a fatal stab, Nate closed in.

Richard Ashworth had seen enough. He would not stand idly by while the Crow leader was slain, not when he had given his word that so long as the Crows behaved, they were welcome to stay in the vicinity of the stockade with no fear of being harmed. "Emilio," he said loudly to be heard above the throaty roar of the unruly mountaineers.

Emilio did not need to be told what to do. A

single step brought him up behind Nate King. He grabbed King's knife arm in one hand, the scruff of King's neck in the other.

Nate had no idea who had jumped him. Thinking it must be a Crow about to kill him, he reacted automatically. He swept his left elbow back and around, catching someone in the ribs, and used his own momentum to rotate on the heel of his right foot and slam his right fist into the square jaw of his attacker.

It all happened in the blink of an eye. To the onlookers, Nate's swing was an incredible blur. Even more astonishing was the result.

Emilio had never been hit so hard in his life. His bones were jarred clear to his feet. The punch lifted him off the ground, something no punch had ever done before. More shocked than hurt, he landed sitting upright and sat there numb with disbelief.

A hush fell over the throng. The only person to move was Little Soldier, who took advantage of the respite to spring to his feet and back away from Grizzly Killer.

Richard Ashworth was stupefied. Never in his wildest dreams would he have thought any man capable of knocking Barzini down. He saw the Sicilian flush scarlet, saw those massive hands bunch into fists the size of hams, and guessing what would happen next, he sprang between the two men. Flapping his arms, he ordered, "Enough! Enough! There will be no more fighting! Is that understood!"

Nate, wary of getting a knife in the back,

whirled to face Little Soldier and was surprised to discover the warrior had moved over next to the other Crows. His natural inclination was to finish the fight, but the warrior had lowered his weapon.

Ashworth, worried that King was about to disobey him, moved around in front of the mountain man and planted himself broadside. "Didn't you hear me, sir? Haven't I made it clear that these Indians are under my protection? That being the case, I can hardly permit you to indulge in whimsical mayhem."

"What?" Nate said, growing less impressed with the New Yorker by the second. Allen's praise notwithstanding, the man had to be a simpleton to interfere in someone else's business.

"Give me your knife," Ashworth said, pointing at the Bowie.

"Like hell." Straightening up; Nate let the blade droop. He sensed rather than saw a new threat on his right, and twisted. A fist missed his cheek by a whisker.

"No man lays a hand on me!" Emilio stated, cocking his arm for a second punch. Now that the shock had worn off, all he felt was outrage that another man had gotten the better of him. It had never happened, not once in all the years of his violent life.

Young Zachary King had also been covering the Crows. Now he advanced and trained his Hawken on the mountain of muscle who had jumped his father. "Attack my pa again when he isn't looking, you varmint, and I'll splatter your brains from here to kingdom come."

Emilio looked at the boy. Were it not for the rifle trained on his midsection, he would have dismissed the threat as the boast of a mere child. He debated snatching the gun, then realized that both the boy's mother and the trapper named Allen also had rifles fixed on him.

Ashworth didn't notice. He had turned to the Crows. "Please accept my apology for King's behavior," he said. "There is no excuse for the way he acted."

Nate had about reached the limits of his patience. "Oh? What do you call having my wife and children abducted by Little Soldier's friends?"

Unruffled, Ashworth said, "So Clive Jenks claimed. But what proof do you offer?"

"My word should be more than enough."

"Hardly enough to satisfy a court of law, and certainly not enough to justify your barbaric behavior," Ashworth pointed out. He was severely disappointed. After hearing so many flattering remarks about King, he'd expected the trapper to hold to a higher standard of conduct than the majority of uncouth mountain men.

To Nate, the implied insult was enough to rate a sound throttling, but he held his temper. "You want proof, greenhorn?" he shot back. "We'll give you proof." Nate gestured. "Henry, would you do the honors?"

All eyes settled on the Tennessean as he walked to the string of horses beyond the crowd and led a pack animal over. Lying across it, bound and gagged, was Tall Bear.

"What is the meaning of this outrage?" Ashworth wanted to know. The Indian's face looked as if someone had held it over an open fire until the flesh was nicely done and then pounded on to tenderize it. In addition, one eye had swollen shut.

"He's a Crow," Nate said. "Him and four of his friends snatched my family and were heading for Crow country when I caught up with them." He gestured curtly at Little Soldier. "Why don't you ask your good pard here about it? Or do you just naturally side with polecats?"

Ashworth suddenly became aware that the ring of trappers had grown openly hostile toward him. He could see it on their faces. King had put him on the spot. The only way out was to get to the bottom of the dispute. "Little Soldier," he said, "I want to hear your side."

"I not know anything about taking of woman and brats," the Crow answered in much better English than he had used to date. "Tall Bear and others do it on their own."

Ashworth nervously grinned at King. "There, see. You assaulted an innocent man."

"And I was born yesterday," Nate said, eliciting snickers from some of the mountaineers. "Do you really believe, mister, that it was purely by chance that those warriors took my wife and kids? Do you really believe that any warrior in Little Soldier's band would risk turning every white man in these mountains against them without Little Soldier's say-so?"

"I don't quite follow you," Ashworth conceded.

Nate jabbed a thumb at the Crow leader. "Then I'll spell it for you. Did you, or did you not, let Little Soldier know that you sent Kendall to fetch me?"

Ashworth had to think a moment. "I believe I did, yes."

"How did Little Soldier take the news?"

Again Ashworth had to jog his memory. They had been over by the Green River at the time. Ashworth had been on one of his twice-daily strolls to get some exercise and several Crows had appeared. "He was very quiet for a while, as I recall."

"He didn't say anything?"

"Yes, as a matter of fact," Ashworth remembered. "He told me that I didn't need your help, that I already had more than enough men to get safely into Blackfoot country and out again."

Nate nodded. "He didn't want me to show up because he knew I'd make damn sure you got rid of him. So my guess is that he sent warriors to watch the trails leading in from the east and four of them spotted us coming. When I rode on down, they took my family captive to draw me off."

Ashworth glanced at Little Soldier and was horrified by a fleeting crafty gleam that confirmed everything King alleged.

"Your pard knew that I wouldn't rest until I found them," Nate went on. "He figured that you'd tire of waiting and head on out without me."

"Little Soldier?" Ashworth said. "What do you have to say for yourself?"

The Crow hesitated, and Nate stepped closer. "He'll never admit it. But you can take it as gospel that he wanted me out of the way so he could help himself to your supplies and stock."

"Aren't you exaggerating?" Ashworth said. "He'd have to kill every last man here to do that."

"Exactly."

Ashworth stared hard at the Indian he had formerly trusted and a cold chill passed through him. Could it really be, he mused, that King was right? Had he nearly made the biggest and perhaps last mistake he ever would? Allen and Scott Kendall had tried to warn him, but he wouldn't listen. "I'm still not one hundred percent convinced," he said, "but I'll bow to your judgment. What do you propose we do?"

Nate walked up to Little Soldier. "You have until tomorrow when the sun is straight overhead to break camp and leave. I'd make you go sooner, but you have women and children along."

"And if we do not go?" the Crow snapped.

It was Henry Allen who answered, first in English for the benefit of the mountaineers, then in the Absaroka tongue. "If you haven't taken down your lodges and made yourselves scarce by then, you'd best be prepared to tangle with the whole pack of us. Remember, I know your treacherous, thieving ways better than most. If you pester or molest us in any way, we'll smear the grass with your guts and turn it red with your blood."

Little Soldier and the Crows could not hide their resentment. As one, they wheeled and marched off to their camp.

"I'll sleep a whole lot easier once we're shy of them," Allen commented to no one in particular.

Nate agreed. He was sorely disappointed that he had not given Little Soldier his due, but there was every likelihood their paths would cross again one day. Still holding his Bowie, he strode to the packhorse. Tall Bear glared at him as he grabbed the Crow by the hair and dumped him on the ground. Bending, he cut the warrior loose. "You're free to go," he said and stepped back to say the same thing in sign language.

Tall Bear slowly rose and departed, rubbing his mouth. If looks could kill, he would have withered Nate to a blackened husk on the spot.

Richard Ashworth hardly gave the warrior a glance. To atone for his blunder, he warmly clasped King's hand and pumped it. "I'm glad we've worked that out. And now I need to know. Are you with us or not?"

"There's still a lot I need to learn about your expedition," Nate answered. "And there are conditions we must both agree on before I can say yes."

Ashworth frowned. There was that word again. Conditions. First the Brothers, now the mountain man. "Such as?"

"If I'm to be your second-in-command, you're to do as I say when it comes to trapping and dealing with Indians. Not to hurt your feelings, but as you've just shown us you're about as savvy as a Chinaman about life out here."

"That's all?" Ashworth said, pleased.

"Not quite. My wife is to take the place of Lisa Kendall. Half of the money she and I make will go to them after we get back."

Richard Ashworth waited for additional demands. When none were forthcoming, he smiled smugly and placed his arm on the mountaineer's wide shoulders. "Mr. King, I can see that working with you is going to be a real pleasure. If you handle the Blackfeet like you just did the Crows, we won't have a thing to worry about."

"You hope," Nate said, and prayed to high heaven they would all get out alive.

Chapter Eleven

Two days later, as the sun crested the far eastern horizon, the Ashworth expedition began its long trek northward. Riding well ahead of the main column were six heavily armed mountaineers who would scout the terrain ahead and keep their eyes peeled for hostiles. Six others rode about the same distance to the rear, just in case.

The main body was strung out over hundreds of yards, some of the men riding four and five abreast, others riding alone. Immediately behind them came the horse herd tended by twenty trappers, ten strung out on either flank to prevent any of the animals from straying.

All precautions that could be taken were taken. By and large the mountain men stuck to open ground. When that wasn't possible, a dozen would fan out wide to either side to insure no nasty surprises were sprung by unfriendly tribes or savage beasts.

The first day passed uneventfully. Richard Ashworth was in tremendous spirits when camp was made that night. They had covered 17 miles. If they duplicated that every day, they would arrive at their destination in three weeks, perhaps less. It would give them time to spare before the next trapping season began.

Ashworth had been perturbed to learn that the mountain men did not lay traps 12 months of the year. There were two seasons, the first starting in early fall and lasting until winter set in, while the second began in the spring and came to an end about the middle of the summer, when hot weather induced the beaver to shed a lot of hair and rendered their hides next to valueless.

Ashworth had counted on trapping all year long. The lost time meant he had to stay longer in the wilderness than he had bargained on in order to acquire as many pelts as he needed. It would delay his return to New York. It also increased the odds of being discovered by the Blackfeet or their allies.

Even so, Ashworth was not about to call the expedition off. He had invested all the funds he had plus most of the money loaned to him by the Brothers. He had to succeed or else lose everything.

Ashworth shrugged off such disturbing thoughts as he rose to greet his supper guests. A table with swivel legs occupied the center of his tent. Around it had been placed seven collapsible stools. "Greetings, fine people!" he declared happily. "Welcome to my humble abode."

Nate held the tent flap open for Winona and the children. As he entered, he glanced back to find Emilio giving him the same sort of a look a grizzly might give prey it was sizing up for the slaughter. No one needed to tell him that the giant harbored a grudge over being knocked down the day before. Sooner or later they would lock horns again.

Winona matched their host's smile and stepped to the table. Among her people, women always bore to the left when going into a lodge and sat apart from the men. She had never given the practice much thought since it had been the accepted Shoshone way since the dawn of time. After meeting Nate and learning how his kind did things, she had to admit that she much preferred the white custom of men and women mingling as they so desired."Thank you for inviting us, Mr. Ashworth," she said.

"My pleasure," Ashworth replied, marveling at her impeccable English. He hastened to pull out a chair for her.

Winona did not know what the man was doing. Nate always let her seat herself. She wondered if perhaps Ashworth were being forward with her, as Nate would say, and whether she should slap him for the affront. But then she decided that he would hardly be stupid enough to insult her with her husband present.

Puzzled by her perplexed expression, Ashworth glanced at the mountain man. "You can assure your wife that I don't bite, Mr. King. It's safe to sit."

Nate turned from the flap. "He's just being polite," he told Winona. "Holding a chair for a lady is considered the proper thing to do."

"Then why have you never done it for me?" Winona asked.

"It's done in public, at restaurants and such," Nate explained. "A man doesn't do it in his own house." He snickered at the quaint notion. "Heavens, he'd never get to relax."

Young Zach listened with half an ear. They hadn't been there two minutes and already he was bored enough to cry. He'd begged his folks to be allowed to stay with the mountain men around one of the campfires, but they had insisted that he come. "The invite is for all of us," his pa had said. "It would be rude if only three of us showed."

Zach was resigned to several hours of dull talk. He didn't think much of the expedition leader. The man reminded him of an oversize chipmunk, always chattering and never able to sit still for more than a few seconds at a time. Besides that, Ashworth's handshake was clammy and weak, a sure sign of a puny nature.

The Kings sat, Winona holding Blue Flower in her lap. Nate leaned his Hawken against the table within easy reach. No sooner did he do so than a shadow fell across him. Someone had opened the tent. He grabbed for the rifle, expecting it to be the man called Emilio, but it was only Henry Allen and Clive Jenks.

"Come in! Come in!" Ashworth hailed them.

"Pull up a chair and we can start."

Nate exchanged nods with the two lieutenants. He didn't know if Ashworth intended to make supper together a daily ritual. If so, the man was in for a disappointment. His place was out with his fellow mountaineers, sharing the work. Not to mention overseeing the hundred and one tasks that needed to be done.

Ashworth surveyed his guests and had to suppress a smirk. At his last supper party before leaving New York City, a city council member, a state senator, and one of the richest men on Long Island had attended. Contrasting their expensive clothes with the rustic buckskins of the bumpkins before him was outright comical.

Clapping his hands, Ashworth yelled, "Lester! You can serve the first dish now!"

Nate's brow knit. He'd seen a scrawny trapper named Lester Maddox hovering around Ashworth like a hummingbird around honey water throughout the day, but he hadn't really given it much thought until now. Into the tent came the man in question, awkwardly trying to carry five small platters at once.

"Careful! Careful!" Ashworth warned. Those plates were the finest china money could buy. They had belonged to his grandmother. He rubbed his hands in anticipation as one was set in front of him. His smiled died. Aghast, he raised his fork and picked at five charred lumps.

Nate was flabbergasted. He hadn't set eyes on a set of china in more years than he cared to recollect. His nose crinkled at the burnt odor but he picked up one of the lumps and plopped it into his mouth. He had to chew a bit before he recognized it for what it was. "Roasted mushrooms. Now that's something we don't see out here every day. They're quite tasty," he said to compliment their host.

Ashworth could feel the blood drain from his face. He was so embarrassed, he wanted to shrivel into a ball and die. "You're too kind," he said lamely.

Rising, Ashworth watched Lester fumble with a plate and place it with a thump in front of Winona King. He cleared his throat. "Mr. Maddox, when I agreed to take you on as my manservant, I knew I couldn't count on you to do as sterling a job as my butler and chef back in New York. But I did think you would be able to cook a pot of mushrooms without burning them to a crisp!"

"Sorry, hoss," Maddox said. "But this coon ain't never et no rabbit food before. So I cooked 'em the same way I like my meat. Tough as shoe leather."

Ashworth was apoplectic. "You did what?" he said. "After I went to all the trouble of having some of the men pick them for me just for this occasion? I'm sorry, Mr. Maddox, but you really won't do. I know you wanted the extra pay, but I'll have to find someone else to fill the position."

Nate had heard enough. "I'm sorry, too," he said, "because no one else is going to bother."

"What?" Ashworth said blankly, unable to come to terms with his supper being ruined.

Folding his arms, Nate did not mince words.

"You're not in the States any longer," he began. "Out here, no one has the right to lord it over anyone else. There are no servants. We're all free men. Equals."

"Equals?" Ashworth repeated, dazed by the concept. How could a bunch of ragtag ruffians rate themselves on a par with the cream of high society?

"You've hired eleven women to do our cooking," Nate continued. "It's only fair that you eat whatever they fix, just like the rest of us."

"Now see here," Ashworth broke in. "Never forget who is the leader of this expedition and who is the second-in-command! I have every right to demand special treatment. Without me, none of this would be possible."

Nate glanced at Allen, who rolled his eyes. "You're missing the point, Ashworth," he said. "It has nothing to do with you. It's us. Mountaineers don't take kindly to anyone putting on airs around them."

"Well, I never!"

"You won't catch a trapper having a servant," Nate detailed. "It's just another word for a slave, as far as we're concerned. Out here, when a man wants something done, he does it himself."

Richard Ashworth blinked. "But that's preposterous! What good is having money if a man can't use it to make life's burdens easier to bear? Why, I've never had to cook a meal in my life!"

"Not once?" Winona found it unbelievable that any person could have been so pampered. "What about your clothes?"

"What about them?"

"Did you make them yourself?"

"Oh, my dear woman, be sensible!" Ashworth sat back down, his chin in his hand. Having to stoop to sharing the common meal was too depressing for words. "Surely there must be some way around this? Some compromise we can reach?"

"No," Nate said bluntly. "It's in the best interests of everyone for you not to act as if you're our lord and master."

Ashworth sulked. He was beginning to regret bringing King along. "Any other changes you'd like to make?" he sarcastically quipped.

Taking the New Yorker seriously, Nate said, "If it were up to me, we wouldn't have any women or kids along. But it's too late to send them packing."

"Where's the equality in that?" Ashworth said. "Aren't you saying the women can't hold their own? That they're inferior to all you trappers?"

"Don't put words in my mouth," Nate said. "The women shouldn't be here because the Blackfeet won't hesitate to wipe them out along with the men. And the men won't be able to put up a good fight if they're worried about their women."

Ashworth, rankled at being made to submit to conditions fit only for primitives, groused, "You're assuming that the Blackfeet will find us, of course. Which they won't. The route I've plotted will see us safely into their territory and out again."

Nate was not going to bandy words. He was

content to remark, "On a map, all routes look safe." He let it go at that for the time being.

Two more days went by. The expedition headed northwest across Bridger Basin, as the mountaineers called it, to the foothills of the Wyoming Range, which they hugged as they traveled northward. They never ventured too far out onto the plain, where they would be exposed to hostiles, nor did they cross arid tracts where they were liable to raise dust clouds that could be seen for miles.

Nate was kept busy every minute. Before first light he was up to see that the cook fires were lit and pots of coffee brewed. The stock had to be watered and counted. Scouts had to be sent out. Then the expedition would get under way, the women and children at the center where they could be protected.

Until noon the column would wend along through the rolling hills, stopping at whatever source of water happened to be convenient, whether a spring or a stream. Half an hour of rest was all they were allowed. Jerky and pemmican sufficed to fill the empty bellies of those who couldn't wait until evening.

During the afternoons, Nate always pushed their animals to cover as much ground as possible before sunset. Twilight would find them in camp, the horses being bedded down, the women and a few trappers at the cook pots, married men erecting lean-tos for some privacy.

A third day came and almost went. Nate made it a point to rove the line from front to rear several times a day. They weren't in Blackfoot country yet, but the Blackfeet were known to roam far afield.

On this occasion, Nate had just left the horse herd and was riding back to check on the rear guard. His son and the Tennessean were along.

Zach had a question he was burning to ask. "Pa?" he began. "Do you really think we can get out of Blackfoot land without having our hair lifted?"

"We'll try our best," Nate said, rising in the stirrups to scour the woods for the men supposed to be dogging their steps.

"But will that be good enough?" Zach gnawed on his lower lip. "I heard some of the men jawing last night. They seem to think none of us will see the Green River again. But they came anyway. They say it's the last chance they'll ever have to raise enough beaver to fill their pokes."

Henry Allen swiveled. "Shucks, son, most of us feel the same way. It's nothing to fret about. If anyone can get us through this, it's your pa."

Zach had every confidence in his father. But the talk he'd overheard had upset him intensely. He'd been so thrilled to join a fur brigade that he hadn't given the threat posed by the Blackfeet much thought. Now he knew why his pa had balked at taking the job.

Nate rose in the saddle again. His orders called for six mountain men to ride one hundred yards behind the horse herd at all times. Yet there was no sign of them. "Something is wrong," he announced, jabbing his heels into the stallion.

Holding the Hawken across his waist, Nate hunted for sign. It wasn't hard to find. Hoofprints revealed the six men had wheeled their mounts and trotted off to the south for some reason. He did likewise, but only at a brisk walk to avoid riding into an ambush.

"Yonder they are," Henry Allen declared, pointing.

Coming through the pines were the six buckskin-clad trappers. In their lead was a lean man known as Wild Tom for his habit of getting so drunk at the rendezvous that he made a spectacle of himself. Seldom did he remember his antics, either. The man hollered and angled to meet them.

"What drew you off?" Nate inquired.

"Injuns," Wild Tom answered. "Jud spotted four of them on that crest." His rifle extended toward an adjacent ridge. "We went for a look but they had lit a shuck by the time we got there."

"Tracks tell you anything?"

"Unshod horses is all," Wild Tom said. "They were too far off for us to tell which tribe. Could have been Flatheads or Shoshones."

Nate doubted it. The Shoshones and the Flatheads were the two friendliest tribes in the Rockies. Warriors from either tribe who spotted the expedition were bound to ride on down for a parley and to smoke a pipe. The fact that the Indians had sped off before the rear guard could reach them did not bode well.

"Keep your eyes skinned," Nate advised. "I doubt they had our best interests at heart."

"Maybe so," Wild Tom allowed, "but at least we know they weren't Blackfeet."

The horses were the reason. Although practically every other tribe from Canada to Mexico relied heavily on the four-legged critters introduced by the Spanish, the Blackfeet still liked to go on raids on foot, just as their fathers had done, and their fathers' fathers before them.

"The Dakotas roam this far west," Nate noted.

"Or it might have been Utes," suggested one of the mountaineers beside Wild Tom. His idea was greeted with a few guffaws.

"Utes never come this far north," another man stated. "Don't you know anything?"

Henry Allen had the final say. "Which tribe doesn't matter if they're hostile. One knife is as good as another when it comes to scalping a man."

The group made for the horse herd. By the position of the sun, Nate calculated they had an hour of travel time left. He left the rear guard, skirted the herd to keep from swallowing enough dust to choke a moose, and came abreast of the knot of women.

Winona was one of those in the lead, Blue Flower nestled in a cradleboard on her back. Her daughter had grown so much in recent months that in another few weeks Winona would have to wean her of the habit. As comfortable as the cradleboard was, at the end of each day her shoulders ached terribly.

Spying her husband approaching, Winona smiled and slowed so he could pull alongside her mare. She winked at Zach, who scrunched up his nose at his sister. "Three days and all is well," Winona remarked.

"Maybe not for long," Nate said. He related the latest news, adding, "Spread the word among the women. They're not to wander off alone after we make camp. Have them go everywhere in pairs, even into the bushes. And make sure they carry rifles. There are plenty to go around, thanks to Ashworth."

"Did you hear what he did last night?" Winona asked.

Nate shook his head.

"Clay Basket took him his supper. She had made stew from a deer her man had killed. Ashworth turned up his nose when she put it in front of him."

"Typical greenhorn."

"I am not finished, husband." Winona chuckled. "He ate three helpings and six of her biscuits."

"You don't say?" Nate said. "Maybe he's not hopeless, after all." Twisting, he surveyed the ridge and the towering mountains beyond, bothered by the sensation of unseen eyes watching their every move.

"Is something wrong?" Winona probed. After a dozen years of being by her man's side day in and day out, she was sensitive to his every innermost feeling.

"A case of bad nerves maybe," Nate said.

Winona doubted it. He wasn't the type to jump at shadows, at anything else.

The hour passed quickly. Between two hills

that served as the gateway to a wide canyon, Nate called a halt. The horse herd was ushered into the canyon for safekeeping until dawn. Little forage was available, but Nate would rather have the animals hungry than missing. He directed that extra sentries be posted, and that at least four fires be kept lit all night.

Richard Ashworth observed all this while seated on a log in front of his tent. Munching on a piece of pemmican given him by one of the squaws, he reflected that he was glad King had come along. The man had proven invaluable in so many respects, among them a knack for getting the trappers to do work long and hard without complaining.

Ashworth went to take another bite, then saw his watchdog giving King what could only be described as the evil eye. "Don't you dare, Emilio," Ashworth said. "You're not to lay a finger on him. Ever."

The giant didn't answer. Emilio had promised himself that before the expedition was over, he would show the big mountain man why he was the most feared member of La Cosa Nostra in all of Little Italy. No one put a hand on him and lived to tell of it. No one at all.

Nate came toward them. Ordinarily he would have ignored the swarthy giant, but after three days of being glared at, he wasn't in the mood. Walking right up to Emilio, he said, "I don't like how you stare at me all the time, mister. If you have something on your mind, speak your piece."

Ashworth was on his feet and between them before Barzini could reply. "Now, now, Nate," he said casually. "I realize there has been some bad blood between the two of you, but let's put it behind us, shall we? We're all on the same side."

"Tell that to him," Nate said.

"Emilio means you no harm," Ashworth declared, and he nudged the hulking brute, trying to prompt him into confirming it. The giant stayed silent.

"I have enough to keep me busy without having to worry about him slipping up on me when I least expect it," Nate said. He was inclined to goad the man into a fight then and there to settle matters.

"I give you my word that he won't," Ashworth said, even though he suspected that given the opportunity, Emilio just might. The man broke bones and killed people for a living; he was not about to adhere to any rules of proper conduct.

"Maybe it would help if you were to give him some work to do so he doesn't stand around staring at folks all damn day," Nate mentioned.

"He already has a job."

"You could have fooled me. All he ever does is follow you around."

"Believe it or not, that's what he is supposed to do," Ashworth said. "Emilio is here to guarantee that the money invested in our expedition isn't wasted."

Nate's curiosity was piqued, but before he could learn more, a strident sound brought the entire camp to a standstill. It was the piercing scream of a woman.

Chapter Twelve

Nate King was in motion before the last wavering note of mortal terror died on the wind. It had come from the northwest, where dense forest bordered the encampment. His Hawken clutched in his left hand, he sprinted in that direction. Hardly had he gone 20 yards when he was joined by Henry Allen and a knot of somber trappers.

Every person in camp had stopped whatever they were doing to stare into the dark woods. Mothers were gathering children. Men gathered weapons.

Nate saw his son racing toward him and stopped the boy cold with a shake of his head. "Find your ma and sister," he hollered. "Stay with them until I get back."

Zach was too disappointed for words. If there were hostile Indians about, he wanted to be in the thick of things. It was the dream of all Shoshone boys his age to one day be great warriors, and the only way to do that was by counting coup in battle. But he obeyed his pa without hesitation. He knew his father was counting on him to safeguard his mother and sister, and he wouldn't let his pa down.

Nate spied a grizzled mountaineer who was on sentry duty crouched at the edge of the woods. At the same moment, the man spotted him and beckoned urgently. Jogging over, Nate sank to one knee. "See anything, Weiss?"

"Two women with baskets left a short while ago," the man revealed in his heavy German accent. He jabbed his rifle at a ravine barely visible through the trees. "They went that way to get roots, I think." Weiss shuddered. "That scream! May I never hear its like again!"

More mountaineers were converging at a brisk clip. Nate picked Henry Allen and four other dependable men to accompany him. To Clive Jenks, he said, "Double the guard on the camp and the stock. Have everyone stand by their guns until you hear from us."

"What if you don't make it back?" Jenks wanted to know.

"Then you get promoted," Nate said. He didn't mean the remark to be humorous, which was just as well, since no one cracked a smile. Nate rose to hasten off.

"Hold on, King. I'm coming with you."

None of the mountain men had noticed when Richard Ashworth and his gigantic shadow arrived on the scene. Threading through the group, Ashworth proudly clasped the heavy Hawken he had purchased in St. Louis and announced, "As leader of this expedition, I am responsible for all your lives. If there are dangers to be confronted, then I must confront them. Lead on, my good fellow. I'll be right behind you."

Nate hesitated. The New Yorker had no business tagging along; it might get him killed. But there was no time to waste debating the point, so Nate merely nodded once and sped into the brush. A carpet of pine needles enabled him to move as silently as a specter. The other mountaineers did the same. To his mild surprise, Emilio Barzini was equally skilled at moving stealthily. For one so huge, the Sicilian was amazingly swift. Only one of them was making any noise.

Ashworth noticed King shoot him a sour look and wondered why. Seconds later he stepped on a dry twig and several of the other men gave him the same kind of look.

Realizing that he was not being quiet enough, Ashworth slowed. He scoured the ground closely and avoided dry twigs and leaves. For several yards he made no sound whatsoever. Pleased with himself, he glanced up to see if the rest had noticed how well he was doing and discovered that he had fallen at least 20 feet behind. He hurried to catch up.

Nate was skirting a thicket when the crack of another twig to his rear caused his temper to flare. Ashworth's intentions were honorable, but the man was a bumbling simpleton when it came to stealth. Whatever had attacked the women, whether man or beast, was bound to know they were coming.

The mouth of the ravine appeared. Nate raised a hand and instantly Allen and the rest of the mountaineers halted. Even Emilio Barzini. Only Ashworth took a few more strides before noticing and stopping.

Hunched low, Nate soon found the tracks of the two women. They had been walking side by side, probably chatting, paying scant heed to the woods around them. They should have known better.

The tracks disclosed that one had been a Flathead, the other a Nez Perce. Nate tried to recollect who among the mountaineers were hitched to women from those tribes as he padded on into the ravine. It would have been better to hug either wall in order to avoid the thick brush, but he stayed right on their trail to find them that much sooner.

Their steps meandered from bush to bush. Nate found where the Nez Perce had dug a hole to extract a few roots. Farther on, they had stopped. Both sets of toes had turned toward the right, as if they both had heard something and pivoted to see what it might be. Apparently, they had not been alarmed. Both had gone on, wending among boulders and clusters of plant growth.

A bend in the ravine hid whatever lay beyond. Nate motioned for the those behind him to exercise even greater caution. The Tennessean came forward and glued himself to Nate's elbow. Together they crept to the turn. Raising their rifles, they peeked around.

Ever since hearing the scream, Nate had feared the worst. He had witnessed so many atrocities over the years that he had come to regard them as part of the normal course of life in the Rockies. So he was inwardly prepared for whatever they might find. Or so he thought.

"Dear God!" Allen breathed.

Nate's stomach roiled. Bile rose in his throat but he swallowed it. His mouth suddenly went bone dry as he slid warily forward.

It was the Flathead. She had been quite lovely in life, with a healthy bronzed complexion and hair almost as long as Winona's. In death she was starkly pale, her tresses disheveled.

Part of her paleness could be blamed on the loss of blood. Someone had slit her throat from ear to ear and a large scarlet puddle framed her shoulders and head.

But that was not all her assailants had done. Her beaded dress had been slit from top to hem, then parted as one might part the pages of a book. Next she had been gutted, her intestines yanked out and strewn over her thighs. As if that were not enough, her breasts had been sliced off. Her throat, evidently, had been slit last.

"The vermin would have done more if they'd had the time," Allen whispered.

Nate was inclined to agree. Her attackers had known the scream would bring rescuers. So they had not dallied any longer than necessary to finish her off.

The Tennessean looped wide to scour for prints as Nate stepped to the body. Almost tenderly, he folded the dress up over the woman's exposed parts as best he was able. Her wide, blank eyes sent a tiny chill rippling down his back. He could well imagine the same horrid fate befalling Winona. More than ever, he was upset that she had seen fit to come along.

Allen signaled by chittering like a chipmunk.

Going over, Nate studied the trail left by the departing warriors. "Crows!" he growled, wishing he had killed Little Soldier when he had the chance. Scuff marks showed where they had dragged the Nez Perce off. She had fought them, to no avail.

"Want I should go after them?" Allen volunteered.

Just then a loud gasp heralded the arrival of the others. Richard Ashworth was shocked to his core. The only corpses he had ever seen had been immaculately arranged ones at formal funerals. He blinked at the spreading pool of blood, at the pink gap where her throat had been slashed, at twin moist spots on her chest. Dizziness made him stagger. He would have fallen, but he thrust an arm against a boulder for support.

Emilio Barzini was a human statue, his features inscrutable. The ghastly condition of the woman did not effect him in the least. He had seen quite a few mutilated people in his time; he had even mutilated a few himself. Compared to them, the Indian woman was in good shape.

Ashworth tried to tear his gaze from the awful spectacle, but couldn't. Taking deep breaths to clear his head, he abruptly had to bend and empty his stomach.

Nate waited for their leader to compose himself before speaking up. "Ashworth, I want you and your shadow to get back to camp. Hanson, go with them and fetch a blanket to cover the body. Find her man. He'll have the final say on what we do with her."

"That would be Lyle Cornish," another mountaineer mentioned, and frowned. "Poor fella, he was right fond of that filly. Bought her last year for two horses and a pile of blankets."

Ashworth did not understand how the trappers could stand there so calmly and coldly talk about the woman as if she had been an article of commerce. He said as much.

Nate glowered. There was only so much stupidity he would tolerate. "You're a fine one to talk," he responded. "If it weren't for you, she would still be alive."

The accusation jarred Ashworth out of his daze. "What are you blathering about?" he snapped. "I had no more to do with her death than I do with the rising and setting of the sun."

Nate did not have time to spare but he paused anyway. "That's what you think, hoss. You were the one who stopped me from making worm food of that weasel back on the Green River."

Ashworth did not see the link. "So?"

Stabbing a finger at the Flathead, Nate could

not help but raise his voice in anger. "Crows did this, greenhorn! Do you have any idea what that means?"

Bewildered, Ashworth glanced from one trapper to the next. Their collective accusation hung as thick in the air as smoke over a fire. "Oh," he said lamely, not knowing what else to say. Then, as the full magnitude of King's comment sank in, he blurted much louder, "Oh! But I only did what I thought was right! How can you fault me for that?"

Nate nodded at the corpse. "Ask her, mister. She's the one your good intentions killed." Turning, he nudged Henry Allen. "We'll go together."

Ashworth watched the two mountain men dash off. "My word!" he said, more to himself than anyone else. Looking at Hanson, he asked, "How do they know Little Soldier is involved? It might be other Crows."

Hanson offered no answer. Nor did any of the other men. Ashworth, stunned, feeling very much the pariah, headed for camp. His legs had never felt so leaden.

Nate glanced back once to insure Ashworth was doing as he had directed. Devoting himself to the tracks, he soon figured out that the Crows had made for a gap high in the right wall.

A talus slope had to be negotiated. Slick with small stones and loose earth, it was as treacherous as ice. Nate climbed carefully, sideways, placing each foot down firmly before lifting the other. He tried not to make any noise but it was hopeless. Dirt and pebbles kept sliding out from under him to rattle to the bottom.

Halfway up there was evidence of a struggle. The Nez Perce had broken free and tried to flee, but had been tackled by two of the Crows. She must have fought them tooth and nail because they had been forced to render her unconscious before they went on. The drag marks were plain as could be, even in the gathering gloom.

It would soon be night. Nate reflected that the women should have waited until morning to go root hunting. Their suppers would not have been all that less tasty without them.

Murky shadow shrouded the gap. It was barely wide enough for a broad-shouldered man like Nate. Holding the Hawken in front of him, he sidled along a serpentine crevice that slanted steadily higher. Presently, he reached the top and peered in all directions before exposing himself.

"They've lit a shuck," Allen guessed.

"Look for sign," Nate said, and located it himself seconds later. He had to get down on his hands and knees to read it. Six unshod horses had been ground hitched at that spot for quite some time. They had left in a hurry, one bearing more weight than any of the others.

"Heading west," Allen said thoughtfully. "To throw us off the scent, most likely. Their camp will be to the south, east or north. The big question is which."

"No, the big question is whether they're alone or not," Nate corrected him.

"Only one way to find out," the Tennessean said.

Nate sighed. More than anything, he wanted to go after the band and save the Nez Perce. But it wouldn't do to go stumbling around in the dark. Neither of them could track at night without torches, which would enable the Crows to spot them from a long way off. "We'll have to wait until sunrise."

"Damn," Allen said.

"You and me both," Nate confirmed. Reluctantly, he cradled his rifle and retraced their steps. They arrived at the body just as Hanson and others were bearing it away. A morose mountain man walked beside the slain woman, his callused hand resting on the bloodstained blankets, his rawhide cheeks moistened by tears.

Nate glumly brought up the rear. Since each and every day he had to live with the prospect of Winona facing a similar horrible end, he felt Cornish's pain as if it were his own.

Fully half the camp was gathered close to the woods when the party emerged. Among them was a young trapper being held by two others. "Where's my woman? What happened to Yellow Bird?" On seeing the body, he heaved and strained to be let free. Wisely, the men held on.

Virtually all eyes were on Nate as he walked toward the younger mountaineer, whose name, as Nate recalled, was Able Ferris. Terror lent his features a wild aspect.

"Don't keep me in suspense, King! I can't stand not knowing! Is she alive or not?"

There was no way around it. Nate put a hand on Ferris's arm. "The Crows have her. Allen and

I tracked them as far as we could. At first light we'll go after her."

"First light!" Ferris practically roared. "Are you mad? You know as well as I do what those bastards will do to her before morning. I'm going after her right this minute." Ferris tried to take a stride but was restrained once again by his companions.

"No!" one said. "Those devils will lift your hair for certain! We won't allow it."

Ferris ignored them and focused on Nate. "They'll listen to you. Give the word." He paused, and when Nate offered no comment, he went on, frantic. "For the love of God, you can't refuse me! What if it were your woman they stole? Would you be content to cool your heels in camp while she was being molested, or worse? No, of course you wouldn't! Damn it all. Do the right thing!"

A hush fell over the camp. Until that moment, a few people had been talking softly among themselves. But they, and everyone else, now stared at Nate, awaiting his decision. He scanned their intent faces and saw the one enshrined in his heart of hearts. She gave a barely perceptible nod.

"Release him," Nate said.

One man did but the other balked. "What in tarnation has gotten into you? Do you want both of them to be killed?"

"I want you to let him go," Nate stressed softly.

The man didn't miss a beat. "Only if I can go with him."

Able Ferris, about to run off, looked back hopefully.

This time it was Henry Allen who moved his head a fraction, giving it a curt shake. Nate understood why. The six Crows might not be alone. There could be an entire war party out there somewhere, waiting to strike when the time was ripe. Every man he allowed to go with Ferris meant one less rifleman to defend the camp. "Three men can go with you," he said. "That's all we can spare."

Ferris showed more teeth than a starved cow in a clover patch. "I'm obliged, King. I won't forget this."

"Just see that you make it back wearing your hide," Nate said as the distraught man and his two friends hurried off. Another young trapper joined them en route to the horses.

No one else moved. They awaited orders, which Nate promptly dispensed. All the women and children were to sleep in the middle of the camp, ringed by the fires. Sentries were to keep watch in pairs. Riders were to mingle with the stock in the canyon. No one was to venture outside the camp unless he was notified first.

The expedition members dispersed. Winona, carrying Evelyn, fell into step on Nate's right as he headed for the tent housing the expedition's leader. Zach imitated his mother on the left.

Winona could tell her husband was upset. "You did what you had to," she said to soothe him.

"That won't make it any easier if none of them come back," Nate replied.

"I know you. The real reason that you are upset is because you cannot go with them yourself. If you were not needed here, you would already be mounted and ready to ride."

Nate had to admit that was part of it. The other factor bothering him was being responsible for the welfare of so many people. It was one thing to be second-in-command when everything was going smoothly, quite another to have over 60 lives in the palms of his hands when those lives might be snuffed out like candles in the wind at any moment.

They were almost to the tent when an enormous shape separated from the inky mantle of night and moved to bar their path. Emilio Barzini moved slowly and held his arms out from his sides to show that he meant them no harm. His personal feud with King could wait until the hostiles were disposed off. "Mr. Ashworth asked that he not be disturbed until he says differently."

"That's too bad, because I need to see him right this second," Nate said. He brushed on past, tensed for the blow he was sure would land. But none did. The Sicilian made no attempt to stop him. Marching to the flap, he threw it open without ceremony.

Richard Ashworth had just tipped his flask to his mouth, his seventh gulp since plopping down on his cot. He couldn't shake the appalling image of the butchered Flathead from his mind. It was the single most sickening thing he had ever seen. For the very first time he seriously considered the possibility of the mountaineers dying. Not just one or two or three, but every last one, wiped out by the Blackfoot Confederacy.

Kendall and Allen and others had told him it could happen. They had warned that every soul might be lost, that all he would have to show for his hard work and perseverance would be his bleached bones lying in the middle of nowhere.

Until the instant Ashworth set eyes on the butchered Indian woman, he had dismissed their words of caution as flights of exaggeration based on unfounded fear. The frontiersmen had heard so many tall tales about the dreaded Blackfeet that they had come to believe the tribe was invincible.

Ashworth had seen through their silly pretense. The tribe didn't exist that could stand up against an organized force of 60 heavily armed men. All he had to do was drill some military precision into the oafish trappers, and they would exterminate any hostiles who stood in their way.

In his more whimsical moments, Ashworth had daydreamed of defeating the Blackfoot Confederacy and taking their chiefs back to the States in chains. He'd be hailed as a national hero for ridding the frontier of the Blackfoot scourge.

And now? Ashworth was not so sure. Anyone who could violate a young woman in so hideous a fashion qualified as a savage in the most literal sense of the word. An entire tribe of such brutes could oppose an army. What chance, then, did his 60 have if the Blackfeet waged all out war on them?

It was enough to give Ashworth nightmares. He was downing some of his precious Scotch to fortify himself for whatever lay ahead when the flap jerked open and in came the man he relied on more than any other to insure his dream came true. Startled by the unwanted intrusion when he had given specific orders that he was not to have any visitors, Ashworth sat up so sharply that he spilled some of the liquor on his chin and shirt.

"What is this?" Ashworth cried, trying to sweep the flask behind him before it was seen. "Doesn't anyone in this camp know how to respect another person's privacy? I'd rather be alone."

"Wait outside," Nate said over his shoulder to his family. "I won't be long." Hunkering, he crossed his arms on his knees and let the New Yorker fidget a few seconds. "Are you worth it?" he finally asked.

The question mystified Ashworth. "Worth it how? Financially? I'll have you know I'm one of the richest men in New York City." It was a small lie, he told himself, since he was still quite wealthy on paper. And once the expedition returned bearing more bales of beaver than anyone had ever collected at any one time before, he'd be as rich as he claimed.

"Are you a drunkard?"

Recoiling in indignation, Ashworth said, "How dare you, sir! Yes, I enjoy a few sips now and then, mainly for medicinal purposes. But I can stop drinking any time I want."

Nate had seen the signs before. He thought of all the people who were depending on the pampered greenhorn, of those whose lives would prosper or be ruined depending on the outcome of the expedition. "What you saw today was only the start of things to come. More of us will die. You have to learn to deal with it like a man, or you might as well pack up and head for St. Louis in the morning."

"Who says I'm not holding up my end?" Ashworth countered. "Just because I was ill over that poor Indian woman doesn't mean I'm not fit to lead this expedition. Trust me. I can handle whatever comes along."

As if to test that claim, gunshots rent the night.

Chapter Thirteen

Nate King paused just long enough to snap at Ashworth, who was starting to rise, "Stay put. I'll go have a look." With that, he was out of the tent in two swift bounds. Winona and Zach were facing to the southeast. "Go to our lean-to," he said. "You'll be safest there if it's an attack."

Nate very much doubted his words. As he sprinted toward the sound of the tapering shots, he listened for war whoops and heard none.

Few tribes waged war at night. Shoshones, Dakotas, Cheyennes, and Arapahoes preferred to raid enemy villages at the crack of dawn, when their enemies were still half asleep. Utes would strike at any time during the day, just so they could be back in the deep woods by nightfall. Even the Apaches, the most fierce of fighters, had never been known to launch an attack after dark.

The reasons varied from tribe to tribe. Some believed that the spirits of men slain at night were doomed to wander the earth forever. Others had more practical concerns. At night it was hard to pinpoint targets, harder still to hit a moving enemy at any great range.

So Nate had a hunch what he would find when he reached the perimeter of the camp, and he was right. As he flew past a solitary pine, he saw a half-dozen trappers on their knees, peering into the deep forest. The firing had stopped, but smoke curled from the muzzles of several rifles.

Nate, bending low, waited until he was much closer to inquire, "What was all the shooting about, boys?"

"Mr. King!" exclaimed a mountaineer fresh to the mountains. "It's Injuns, sir! They was tryin' to sneak up on us, but I cut loose and these others joined in. We drove 'em back, I reckon," he concluded proudly.

Nate scoured the woods. Other than leaves being rustled by the wind, there were no unusual noises. "Did you see these Indians?"

"Sure did," the man said. "I was makin' my rounds when I spotted a whole bunch of 'em creepin' along in a group. One of 'em stepped on a twig or I might never have noticed."

Other trappers had arrived and more were hastening to the scene every moment. One was Henry Allen, who had overheard the last remark and glanced at Nate, his lips compressed.

Nate felt the same way. There had been no Indians. The guard's imagination had fleshed out shadows; his fear had done the rest. "Any sign of them now?"

"No, sir," the sentry answered. "They hightailed it without loosing a single arrow. We must have scared them silly. They'll know better than to try a stunt like that again."

"That they will," Nate agreed, rising. He wasn't going to give the sentry a scolding over a bad case of nerves. Every man was entitled once in a while. Besides which, since the guard had gotten the nervousness out of his system, he'd settle down and do right fine from then on.

"The danger is past," Nate declared. "Everyone can go back to whatever he was doing." He moved off, a flick of a finger enough to get Allen to join him. "Pass the word to Jenks. There's a new rule," he said. "From now on, pair up a hiverman with the younger men on watch. Savvy?"

The Tennessean nodded. A hiverman was a trapper who had spent at least one winter in the mountains. Nate hoped that pairing experienced mountaineers with those less so would prevent another incident like the one that just happened.

"One more thing," Nate said. It was important that someone else know about their leader's secret habit, in case something happened to him. "Just between the two of us."

"This coon's lips are sealed."

"Our booshway has a fondness for the hard stuff. I caught him sucking on a flask as if it were his sweetheart's nipple."

"Was he whiskey-soaked?"

"Not that I could tell. But it's a cinch he can't

go two hours without a nip."

"Then he must have a stash." Allen wore the look of a bobcat about to devour a sparrow. "It'd be easy to cure him of the habit."

Nate pondered a bit. "We can't," he decided. "It's his right, so long as it doesn't put any any of our lives at risk. We'll let him go on thinking he's pulled the wool over our eyes. But keep your own on him."

Allen sighed. "He's no mountanee man, but at least he's not a flash in the pan. He's willing to face whatever we do, come what may."

Nate was grateful for the reminder. "That's another thing. See that he doesn't do as he did up in the ravine ever again. I don't want him waltzing into the middle of a racket and getting himself killed. Without him, none of us will ever add a cent to our pokes."

"Never thought of it that way," Allen said. "It makes him the only one this outfit can't do without."

"Indispensable," Nate concurred.

The man from Tennessee snickered. "Goodness gracious! You do come up with some real tongue twisters. That's what happens when a body reads too damn much."

It was common knowledge that Nate was fond of books. In his cabin he had a small but cherished collection that included the current works by James Fenimore Cooper, his favorite. "Guilty as charged," he quipped.

Allen became sober again. "About those stinking Crows. Some of the men are thinking about heading out in the morning to go help Cornish. They don't know I know."

"How many?"

"Eight or nine. Brickman is behind it."

"We can't spare them."

"Figured as much. Let me handle it. I'll have me a little talk with Brickman before I turn in. Make him see the light."

"What if he refuses?"

"I'll remind him of that disagreement I had with that fella from Georgia."

Nate remembered it well. Three years ago, at a rendezvous, Allen and another man had gotten into an argument when Allen won big at a game of cards. The gent from Georgia had accused Allen of cheating, but as anyone who knew the Tennessean would attest, there wasn't a dishonest bone in his body. One thing had led to another. The Georgian had pulled a knife.

Nate had been nearby. He had heard the ruckus and gone over to behold a knife fight the likes of which few men were privileged to see. Both men had been born and bred in the mountains of the South. Both had been extremely skilled. For long minutes they had thrust and parried and feinted and cut until, at long last, Henry Allen's blade had sunk to the hilt in the Georgian's chest.

"Let me know if he gives you any trouble," Nate said.

"He won't."

They veered apart, Nate bending his steps to the cluster of lean-tos at the center of the encampment. On either side reared the hills, partially blotting out the stars. To the west was the mouth of the canyon. The horse herd filled it from front to back. Many of the animals were milling about. They disliked being hemmed in, and Nate didn't blame them. He had never been fond of being cooped up himself.

It was early yet. Most of the women were still out and about, gathered near the four crackling fires. Winona, Zach, and Evelyn were at the one closest to their lean-to, Winona brushing the girl's hair while their son cleaned his rifle. They did not notice Nate until he was right on top of them.

"Papa!" Evelyn gurgled happily, throwing out her arms.

Nate set his Hawken down and picked her up. "How's the apple of my eye doing?"

"I miss you," Evelyn said.

"Sorry I'm away so much, but it can't be helped," Nate said. "I have a lot to do these days looking after all the folks we're traveling with."

Winona saw the corners of his mouth twitch down and came to his rescue to spare him from feeling as if he were neglecting them. "You are doing what you have to, husband. We have no complaints."

Zach stopped cleaning his gun long enough to ask, "Pa, what was that fuss about a while ago? There was some talk of Indians."

Nate related the event, and as he talked the tension slowly drained from his rock hard body. It was the first time all day he had been able to relax. He cast aside his troubles, treated himself to a steaming cup of black coffee from one of the four pots the women kept going every hour of the day, and leisurely sipped.

Winona was glad to see her man take it easy for a while. The strain of being responsible for so many was taking a toll in wrinkles around his eyes where there had been none before and in his seldom being able to sit still for more than a few minutes at a stretch.

"How about supper?" Nate said. "I know it's late and most everyone else has filled his belly, but I'm so hungry I could eat a buffalo raw."

Evelyn puckered her lips in disgust. "Could you really?"

"Only with a lot of salt and garlic," Nate joked.

Winona rose and walked to their lean-to. When she came back, she carried a small covered pot which she set on a flat rock by the fire. "It should not take long to heat up," she said.

Nate didn't ask what it was. He'd rather be surprised. As it turned out, she had made rabbit stew, one of his favorites, laced with tangy onions and herbs and a few chopped roots. He happened to scoop one of the roots out with the first dip of his big wooden spoon, and vivid images of the unfortunate Flathead almost made him lose his appetite. Shaking his head to dispel the memory, he dug into the stew with relish, chewing each morsel thoroughly to savor the meal to its fullest.

Zachary laughed. "Pa, I never saw anyone who likes to eat as much as you do."

"Wait until you're older, son," Nate said with his mouth full. "There's nothing like a good meal to perk a man up when he's had a rough day."

Winona arched an eyebrow. "Nothing?"

"Well, almost nothing," Nate backtracked to redeem himself.

Zach was bent over his rifle barrel, rubbing hard. "I know what you mean, Pa," he commented without looking up.

"You do?"

"Sure. Hunting and fishing and riding a horse do the same." Zach stopped rubbing a moment. "That is what you meant, isn't it?"

"Of course," Nate said, glad to have been spared an embarrassing explanation. He finished his meal, his ears registering every sound made in camp and every noise in the woods beyond.

Owls hooted. A few birds screeched. In the distance coyotes yipped. Not to be outdone, wolves gave throaty voice to plaintive howls. Once a panther screamed just like a woman in labor. Another time a guttural grunt warned of a roving grizzly bear.

Most newcomers to the West would have trembled at the nightly chorus, convinced that at any minute a ravenous beast was going to spring out of the gloom and pounce on them. But to Nate, the sounds he heard were the same as a lullaby. They told him that all was well, that no two-legged fiends were abroad.

If the forest had been totally silent, then there would have been cause for worry.

The pot empty, Nate stretched out on his back, cupped his hands under his head, and admired the myriad of stars ablaze in the heavens. A minty scent tingled his nostrils as a warm shape molded itself to his side.

"You should get some sleep, husband. I will wake you if you are needed."

"Later," Nate said. "I have to check on the horse herd before I turn in."

"A short while would not do any harm."

To humor her, Nate closed his eyes. He thought that he would lie there a few minutes and get up, but when he opened his eyes again, the fire had burned low and almost all the women were gone.

Winona, gently rocking Blue Flower in her arms, smiled to herself. Her man had needed the rest whether he would admit it or not. "All is well," she informed him as he sat up. "There was no trouble. The only one who came by to see you was Henry Allen."

"What did he want?" Nate asked, yawning.

"He said to tell you that Brickman has seen the light. I did not understand but he claimed that you would."

Nate stretched, then helped himself to more coffee to dispel lingering drowsiness. He was mildly peeved that his wife had let him doze so long, yet he had to admit he'd needed it badly. Evelyn and Zach were both out to the world, Zach hugging his rifle in his sleep.

The camp was quiet. Here and there a handful of people were talking in hushed tones, and to the east one of the guards was humming a ballad.

"Do you regret coming?" Winona asked.

Taken aback by the query, Nate paused with the tin cup tipped to his lower lip. "No, not really.

It's the only way I could repay Kendall."

"But you regret that we came along, don't you?"

"I haven't tried to hide the fact," Nate noted.

"Quit fretting over us, husband. What will be will be. Each of us must do as we think is right and live with the consequences."

Nate swallowed more coffee to keep from making a remark that might get him in hot water. He mused that Winona's outlook was fine so long as a person only had his or her own hide to watch out for.

"We will turn in," Winona said, and lowered her voice to say playfully, "I will keep your blankets warm for you."

"I won't be long," Nate said. He kissed her cheek. Polishing off the brew, Nate claimed his Hawken and strolled toward the canyon. The pale starlight was adequate for him to distinguish objects close at hand but not those at any distance.

Nate had to pass scattered trees and large boulders to reach the horses. A stately oak was one. Intent on spotting the men riding herd, he walked under the overspreading limbs without giving it a second thought. He was abreast of the trunk when a slight scraping sound came from above. Stopping short, he glanced up.

The act of halting saved his life. For hurtling down toward him was a powerfully built figure wielding a long knife. The knife swept at his face, but missed. Had Nate kept on walking, it would have penetrated clear to his jugular.

Nate tried to throw himself backward but the figure slammed into his left shoulder and they both crashed down, his attacker on top and raising the blade for another blow. For a frozen moment Nate saw the man plainly.

It was Tall Bear. Even in the dark, his mashed lips and charred cheek were evident, as was the hatred that contorted his face. He had stripped to his loincloth and moccasins. An amulet, or charm, hung around his neck. In addition to the knife, he had a short club wedged under his loincloth above his right hip.

All this Nate saw in a span of heartbeats. As the knife speared at his neck, he jerked to the right. The blade thudded into the ground, nicking his ear. Nate had dropped the Hawken when he fell but he still had his pistols and he aimed to get at them. Heaving upward, he dislodged the Crow, who tumbled but recovered in half the time it took Nate to push to his knees and claw at his flintlocks.

The knife stroked at Nate's hand, forcing him to snatch it away or lose fingers. Tall Bear, hissing, lunged, seeking to bowl Nate over by sheer brute force.

No outcry rose in the camp. No shots were fired. No one knew that the warrior had slipped in past the perimeter guard. No one knew that Nate was fighting for his life. Nate shifted as Tall Bear came at him and grabbed the Crow's arm. He levered it as he might a pump handle.

Tall Bear's mouth went wide but no howl of pain came out as he catapulted head over heels and hit hard.

Nate dived on top. On the spur of the moment

he had changed his mind. Rather than resort to a pistol, Nate intended to take the Crow alive. Tall Bear had to know what Little Soldier's plans were, and Nate was going to wring that information from him.

They grappled, Nate locked onto the warrior's knife arm, Tall Bear clamping a hand on Nate's throat. The Crow squeezed but he didn't have a solid grip; the worst he could do was gouge his fingernails into Nate's skin.

Rolling to the right, Nate resorted to a tactic he rarely used. He drove his forehead into the warrior's chin, butting like a bull. Sometimes that was enough to knock a foe out. In this instance, Nate was the one who saw dazzling fireflies pinwheel before his eyes and felt his limbs grow momentarily weak.

Tall Bear saw his chance. He flung his knife high, sneered in triumph, and cleaved the air, the tip of his blade pointed at a spot to the left of Nate's sternum.

The Crow was a shade too slow. Realizing that he would be mortally stricken if he did not do something, Nate King had drawn a pistol as the tiny lights burst in front of him. He cocked it as the knife elevated. He jammed it against the warrior's stomach and fired as the knife descended.

The heavy lead ball sheared through Tall Bear's innards like a cannonball through a scarecrow. He was flung onto his back, a hole at the base of his spine as big as his hand. Mouth working, he tried to form words but none came out.

Nate slowly straightened up. The shot had been

muffled by the Crow's body. It was doubtful anyone had heard. He palmed his other pistol on the off chance enough life remained in the warrior to animate his limbs.

The hatred never left Tall Bear's eyes. With his dying breath he tried to spit. Then his body convulsed, his head flopped up and down, and he expired with a loud exhale.

Where there was one Crow, there might be more. Nate reloaded the spent pistol, scooped up his rifle, and jogged toward the part of camp where most of the single mountaineers had spread out their blankets. Locating the Tennessean among 40 sprawled forms proved easier than it would seem since he knew of Allen's penchant for sleeping in the darkest spots. As Allen liked to put it, "A red devil can't slit your throat if he doesn't know where you are."

Nate threaded among prone forms, moving with the utmost care so as not to awaken anyone. He distinguished the vague outline of a sleeping form off by itself, next to a small pine, and hurried over. As he bent to shake Allen's shoulder, the lanky trapper's ripcord frame uncoiled and a pistol was flourished inches from Nate's nose.

"Oh, it's you," the Tennessean said. "Don't you know any better than to go skulking around in the middle of the night? Are you looking to have your head shot off?"

"The Crows," was all Nate had to say to bring Allen to his feet. Nate filled him in while Allen donned his ammo pouch, powder horn, and possibles bag.

"Find Jenks. We'll round up six other men and make a sweep of the whole camp," Nate said. "Quietly, though. There's no need to rouse everyone else unless Little Soldier is up to something."

"I wish to blazes I'd get that bastard in my sights for two seconds."

"That makes two of us."

But a thorough search turned up no other Crows. Nate had every tree inside the perimeter checked. Every boulder was circled. Every inky patch of ground was warily probed.

The men riding guard on the horse herd were alerted and scoured the canyon from one end to the other. Like Nate and his bunch, the riders came up empty handed.

It was past one in the morning when Nate finally sank down inside the lean-to next to Winona and tried to get to sleep. His mind had a will of its own. It raced like an appaloosa. Over and over again he reviewed the precautions he had taken to protect those who were relying on him. Over and over he tried to pinpoint mistakes he could have made. There might be flaws the Crows could exploit, flaws he'd correct if he could only figure out what they were before Little Soldier attacked.

And attack the Crow leader would. Nate knew it as surely as he lived and breathed. Instinct, premonition, intuition, whatever it was called, it blared in his brain that the Absarokas craved revenge and would stop at nothing to get it.

After the longest while, Nate slept. But he didn't enjoy his slumber. He tossed and turned and woke up at the slightest noise, even when one of his loved ones rolled over in their sleep.

Nate was actually pleased when a faint pink band framed the eastern sky. He was up before any of the women and made a fresh pot of coffee. Hunkered by the fire, he let the flames warm his limbs and the coffee warm his stomach.

One by one other trappers rose to greet the new day. Not a solitary cloud marred the azure blue of the heavens. The air was so crystal clear that the first war whoop from the depths of the canyon rang as clearly as the peal of a bell. Nate leaped to his feet, spilling his coffee and not caring. There were more whoops, then the crack of rifles. Mountaineers shouted. Some cursed. Last of all came the sound Nate prayed he wouldn't hear, the drum of over a thousand heavy hooves as the horses were panicked into motion.

The Crows had stampeded the herd—straight toward the camp.

Chapter Fourteen

"Stampede!" Nate bawled at the top of his lungs as he cast the tin cup down and dashed toward the family's lean-to. Others who were awake took up the refrain, mingled with shouts of, "Run for your lives! Run! Run!" and "Head for the trees!"

Winona had been half awake when the commotion broke out. She'd heard the rumble to the west and in her drowsy state had attributed it to thunder. Then she heard her husband, and in a flash she was up and out of the lean-to with Evelyn in her arms.

Zach King was only a few steps behind. He had been in a deep sleep, dreaming of counting coup on a score of Dakotas who had raided his uncle's village. Automatically, he grabbed his Hawken, ammo pouch, powder horn, and possibles bag as he bolted.

Nate pointed toward the hill to the north, the nearest of the two. "That way!" he shouted to be heard above the uproar. "Don't stop for anything!" Giving his wife a hasty kiss, he said in her ear, "I'm sorry. I have to help the rest."

"I understand," Winona responded. "Do what you must."

Nate ran off. Winona started to do the same. She stopped, though, causing Zach to nearly bump into her. "Our parfleches and blankets! We must save what we can!"

Zach wasn't so sure that was the right thing to do. He'd heard his pa tell them to run for their lives. Taking time to save their effects might put them in jeopardy. But he turned to help anyway. He wouldn't desert his mother and sister, even if it cost them dearly.

Winona glanced to the west. The canyon was about ten flights of an arrow distant. Other than a enormous roiling dust cloud, there was no sign yet of the horses. She had the time to save their possessions if she hurried.

Other women were doing the same. Frantically folding blankets and snatching up everything they could, they fled in panic, some toward the hill to the north, the others southward. No one went to the east since that was the direction the horses would naturally take.

It took only seconds for Winona to throw several blankets over her shoulders. She handed two full parfleches to Stalking Coyote, who looked as if he were certain they were going to be killed at any moment.

Winona was stooping to pick up a water skin when a shrill scream snapped her erect. Her first thought was to wonder how horses had gotten there so fast? The horses were in sight, their lead ranks formed in a wide line that stretched from hill to hill. Nostrils flaring, manes flying, they were not about to stop for anyone or anything.

She saw a mountaineer try to turn them. A man she didn't recognized, mounted on a sorrel, rode directly into the their path. Firing his pistols and hollering, he bore down on them as they bore down on him. The outcome was inevitable. At the last instant the man attempted to rein the sorrel around and flee. The sorrel was broadside when the front row of horses smashed into it, plowing sorrel and rider under a driving wedge of hammering hooves. Faintly on the breeze fluttered an all too brief screech.

"Ma?" Zach said. Those horses were much too close for comfort. He didn't see how his mother and he could possibly reach the trees before the herd overtook them.

Winona gave him a push and barked, "Run!" She suited action to words, weaving among the lean-tos until she hit open ground, at which point she raced like the wind.

Little Evelyn, in her childish innocence, cackled with glee, liking the new game they were played.

The thunder grew louder and louder. The encampment was a whirlwind of men and women fleeing. Some didn't make it. Screams punctuated the thunder, making Winona regret that she had dallied. Their possessions were not worth their lives.

The tree line seemed so impossibly far away. Winona focused on a lightning-charred stump at the edge to the exclusion of all else. Make it there, she told herself. Then they would be safe!

Zach stayed at his mother's side even though he could have outdistanced her if he had applied himself. He was on her left, between her and the onrushing herd so that whatever fate befell them befell him first.

Scattered shots rang out. A chorus of whinnies rose skyward with the column of dust. The ground itself seemed to shake, and several of the lean-tos collapsed without being touched.

One of the blankets slipped off Winona's shoulder. She didn't bother to stop to get it. The herd was so close that she could see their wide eyes, their flattened ears. The horses were less than the flight of a single arrow away. Not much closer was the north hill, their only hope of survival. She girded herself and ran a fraction faster.

Zach was debating whether to try to drop a few of the lead horses in the slim hope that those behind would part to either side and go around them. It was a long shot, but it was the only one they had.

Winona's legs ached but she forced them to keep going. The trees reared larger and larger before her. Just when it seemed a sure thing that they would gain safety, the unexpected happened. Evelyn picked that moment to wriggle and push against her. To Winona's utter dismay, her daughter slipped from her fingers.

Zach was horrified. "Ma!" he cried, slowing to cover them as she whirled.

Evelyn had landed on her side, apparently unhurt. She grinned merrily as Winona seized her. Spinning, Winona flung herself at the vegetation. In her ears pounded imminent death. Her legs stretched to their limit. Another blanket fell. Evelyn wriggled again but this time Winona held on.

Then the trees closed around them. Winona's foot stubbed on an exposed root and she pitched forward, bracing herself on her elbows and knees to spare her daughter. Gasping for breath, afraid that the horses might still trample them underfoot, she swiveled to see the herd streak past, row after row of terrified animals, raising so much dust that it seeped down her throat and brought tears to her eyes.

Belatedly, Winona thought of her son. "Stalking Coyote!" she cried, pivoting. "Where are you?" Her heart leapt to her throat. There was no sign of him! She peered under the ranks of horses, fearing what she would discover.

"Up here, Ma."

Winona glanced up. Zach had been a step behind her when they reached the hill. The horses had been almost upon him. In desperation, he had jumped as far and as high as he could. A low limb had offered sanctuary. He had let the parfleches drop and caught hold with one hand. From there it had been simple to swing up and over and brace his back against the trunk to watch the herd pound on by.

"We did it," Winona breathed, amazed at their deliverance. None of the horses entered the trees, although a few came awfully close to doing so. She covered Blue Flower's mouth and nose to spare her child from the dust. "We're safe here."

"We are," Zach said, "but what about Pa?"

To answer that crucial question, Zach would have had to join his father minutes ago as Nate King sped through the camp urging people to leave their effects and flee. Most obeyed. Others insisted on gathering their belongings.

A young white woman was on her knees, carefully folding clothes that she slid into a large leather bag. Nate paused in front of her lean-to. "Are you loco, woman? Light a shuck before it's too late!"

"But these are the only clothes we have," she protested without looking around.

"You can't wear them if you're dead," Nate pointed out, and dashed on to help an older woman swing a cradleboard onto her back.

The camp was in utter turmoil. Most of the women had kept their heads, but a few were near hysterical, shrieking as they dashed every which way. A few children bawled their lungs out. Some of the men were running back and forth with no evident purpose, so rattled that they couldn't think straight.

Nate had drifted nearer to the south hill than the north one. He was about to turn and rejoin his wife when it dawned on him that he was the only one who could save those too foolhardy or terrified to save themselves. Jumping onto a log, he bellowed, "Listen to me, all of you! Head for that hill now or you'll answer to me!" He pointed and repeated his order.

A few of those who heard him hesitated. But within moments every last soul in sight was involved in a mass exodus, abandoning the camp and their possessions.

The herd was dreadfully near. Nate held back, goading others on, giving those who stumbled a boost, shoving those who were not going fast enough. A few other mountaineers took their cue from him and helped out.

Nate glanced repeatedly at the horses. They were only 50 yards away, narrowing the gap rapidly. He spotted a woman lugging several parfleches much too heavy for her and went to lend a hand, then drew up short on spying an infant seated all by itself a dozen yards back.

The baby took priority. "Drop those bags!" Nate yelled at the woman as he darted toward the child. The woman heard him but shook her head.

With the thunder of hooves drumming loudly in his skull, Nate sprinted to the infant and grabbed her up. She was no more than a year old, dressed in a small buckskin garment adorned with fringe and red beads. Her large, trusting eyes fixed on his as he rotated toward the south hill.

There might not be time to reach it. Nate bounded like an antelope, passing the woman burdened by parfleches. "Leave them!" he shouted, and again was ignored. He could do no more for her, not while he had the child. Speeding on, he glanced to his right and realized the woman would never reach safety. The panicked herd was that close.

Ahead, a woman screamed as she tripped. Scrambling upright, she flung the articles she carried down and ran, limping from a hurt ankle.

Nate came alongside her and hooked his free hand under her elbow to propel her forward. They were the last, except for the stubborn soul bearing the parfleches. He didn't bother looking at the horses again because they were so near that he could see them clearly out of the corner of his eyes.

Nate took three more strides and then he pushed the woman with all his might and hurled himself at the trees just as something slammed into his shoulder. For a moment he thought that he would be bashed to the earth and reduced to so much shattered bones and pulp, but the impact actually helped, adding momentum to his own leap. Brush rushed up to meet him. Tucking his arms around the child, he crashed into a thicket that cushioned their fall and rolled.

Thorns tore at him. Branches gouged him. A rock scraped his cheek. Over and over he tumbled, to come to rest against a low mound of grass covered earth. The infant giggled as he held her up to see if she had been harmed. She was fine.

Meanwhile, the herd drummed on past, scores upon scores of wild-eyed horses passing over the exact spot Nate had occupied seconds ago.

Twenty feet in, there was a commotion. Some of the horses plunged and snorted, as if to avoid an obstacle. Others ran right over it.

Nate swore that he heard a sickening crunch. To the west, shooting broke out, rifles and pistols blasting without cease. He had no idea what it meant, but he soon noticed that the number of horses had tapered, that small groups of them went galloping by where before it had been a riotous mass. The swirling dust eliminated any chance he had of learning the reason.

On both sides and behind him people coughed and sputtered and cried. Nate heard a woman calling a name again and again.

"Melissa! Melissa! Oh, God! Where are you?"

On a hunch, Nate let himself be guided by the female's voice and came on a blubbering woman on her knees, her hands in her hair, her face streaked with tears. "I believe I have something of yours," he said.

The woman snatched the baby and pressed the child to her bosom. "She's alive! Oh, thank heaven!" The mother gripped Nate's wrist. "And thank you! I can never repay you for what you've done!"

"No need," Nate said. He had to pry her fingers loose before he could make his way back to the tree line. The dust had begun to thin but it was still too thick for him to see more than a dozen feet. Most of the horses going by were farther out. In twos and threes the animals made for the open plain.

Nate wondered about his wife and children. He was impatient for the stampede to end so he could go look for them. As the horses became even fewer, he cautiously advanced.

A gust of wind fanned his face, then another. The breeze picked the perfect time to gain strength. In under two minutes the dust had dissipated to swirling tendrils.

It was worse than Nate had anticipated. Broken personal belongings of every kind were scattered everywhere. Dotted among the debris were human forms, most crushed beyond recognition.

All that remained of the stubborn woman who had insisted on keeping her parfleches was a flattened smear of flesh and ruptured bones. Her skull had been broken in three segments. One, relatively intact, included her right eye and part of her nose. The eye was wide with astonishment, as if at the instant of dying she had not believed that it was happening to her.

To the north, remnants of the herd were galloping off across the flatland. Once in the open, dozens had slowed. A handful had taken to grazing.

To the west, Nate saw 15 to 20 riders rounding up other horses. Among them was Henry Allen, who caught sight of him and hurried over.

"This coon is mighty glad to see you breathing, hoss," the Tennessean said, adding grimly as he surveyed the camp, "We've lost too many fine people this day."

"Do you know where Jenks is?"

"Over yonder," Allen said, indicating the hill to the south. "Ran into him a few minutes ago. He's in one piece but as riled as a wet hen. Says he wants to wipe out the whole Crow nation."

Nate was scanning the devastated encampment also. North of where the lean-tos had been was the tattered remains of Richard Ashworth's tent. Hardly enough was left to construct a kite. A small kite. "What about the booshway?"

"Haven't laid eyes on him yet." Allen took a shorter grip on his reins as his mount nervously pranced, then gazed out over the prairie. "It could have been a hell of a lot worse. Me and a bunch of the boys were able to stop most of the herd from getting out of the canyon. Only about a hundred and fifty broke through, and of those, only about a hundred reached the prairie."

"Round up the closest ones. Then we'll go after the rest," Nate said as he jogged off to find his family. "And give a holler if you see the greenhorn."

"Will do."

The majority of the lean-tos had become so much kindling. One, defying all odds, still stood, the items in it untouched. Littering the ground were torn clothes and blankets, ruptured parfleches, and battered cooking utensils. A single fire flickered feebly.

Nate came to the approximate spot where his lean-to had been and scoured the vicinity. Ten feet away lay the body of an Indian woman, her body twisted and crumpled like a child's busted doll. His gut balled in a knot, he walked over. A floodtide of relief washed over him when he discovered it wasn't Winona.

"Pa, we're over here!"

No words had ever sounded so sweet to Nate as the hail of his oldest. Zach, Winona, and Evelyn were just emerging from the woods that lined the lower slope of the north hill. He ran to meet them, smiling the entire way, stopping at arm's length to regard the three of them with heartfelt affection. "I thought—" he began slowly, barely able to speak thanks to a constriction in his throat.

"We know," Winona said. "We thought the same." She set Blue Flower down.

The mountain man and his Shoshone maiden stepped into each other's arms and stood silently holding one another. Evelyn tugged at her mother's dress but Winona paid no heed.

Zach politely looked away. One thing he had learned during his short life was that his ma and pa were as fond of hugging each other as a bear was of eating honey. A few years ago their displays of affection had embarrassed him; he could never say why. But of late, he had begun to notice girls in a whole new light, and with his new interest had grown a whole new appreciation for the love his folks shared. He hoped that one day he would meet a girl who cared for him as deeply as his ma did for his pa.

The crack of a twig brought Nate down to earth. Stepping back, he saw the expedition's leader and a hulking figure walk from the pines.

Richard Ashworth was in near shock. He had been on his cot when the alarm sounded, and he had shuffled to the flap to ascertain why everyone was in an uproar. In his befuddled state, he had not made much sense of the shouts and the rumbling in the distance.

Usually Ashworth had to indulge in several long

sips from his flask before he was fit to greet a new day. On this morning, the sudden appearance of Emilio had done the trick.

"Dress quickly," the Sicilian had said, brushing past him without so much as asking permission to enter.

"How dare you!" Ashworth had protested.

"If you're not ready when I am, I'll carry you," Emilio had said, going to a pair of expensive leather carrying cases Ashworth had purchased in New York City. Linked by a wide strip, they sported silver clasps and studs. "I'd suggest you hurry."

Suitably motivated, Ashworth had hastily donned attire while his shadow gathered up an armload of his clothes and other effects. As he draped his cape over his shoulders, the ground under them had trembled as if from an earthquake. He had moved to the flap and nearly fainted. Thankfully, Emilio had hauled him out by the wrist and sprinted toward the forest with a speed belying his huge bulk.

They had barely reached safety. Crouched behind a tree, Ashworth had seen the camp destroyed, had seen lives snuffed out in the blink of an eye, had seen valuable supplies rendered worthless. Worst of all, he had watched his tent topple, seen it fall and be tromped under a legion of hooves.

Ashworth had yet to recover. Now, blankly halting in front of Nate King, he said, "What caused this disaster? Why did our animals stampede?"

"I should think you would have guessed," Nate

said. "Blame your old friend Little Soldier."

"The Crows again?" Ashworth bleated, his horror growing. Now, in addition to the life of the Indian woman, he had to shoulder a large measure of blame for the destruction of their camp. It numbed him to realize that if he hadn't stopped King the other day, Little Soldier would be dead and the Crows would not be harassing them.

"What do we do? Have half the men go hunt the bastard down?"

It was Emilio who asked. Nate was inclined to make a sarcastic reply, but he held his peace. "It's up to your boss. We could do it that way, but we'd lose a lot of time—days, maybe weeks if he reaches Crow country before we catch him."

Ashworth gestured at the devastation. "Surely you're not suggesting that we let this atrocity go unpunished?"

Under different circumstances, Nate would have laughed. This was the same man who had begged him not to harm a hair on Little Soldier's head! "Not at all," he answered. "I think two or three men can do what has to be done. Myself, Allen, and one other should be ample."

"I'll go," Emilio offered. He was amused when the frontiersman and the silver spoon both betrayed surprise. He ventured no explanation. Why should he? They had no business knowing that it was his job to keep Ashworth alive until the pelts were sold. Nor need they learn that since he couldn't take it for granted Little Soldier wouldn't attack again, he had to dispose of the Crow before the Crow disposed of Ashworth.

"We can manage without you," Nate said, suspicious of the Sicilian's strange change in attitude.

"Afraid I'll stick cold steel into you when your back is turned?" Emilio said, insulted. "I don't need to sneak up on someone to kill them. When your time comes, we'll be face-to-face."

The lack of propriety jarred Richard Ashworth back to normal. "See here, Emilio! I won't have talk like that, do you understand? What if the Brothers were to learn that you have a habit of threatening anyone who so much as looks at you crosswise?"

Nate saw a flicker of—something—cross the giant's features. "Who are the Brothers?" he inquired, and he was puzzled when the two men shared a look that implied it was a mutual secret.

"Business associates of mine," Ashworth said. "Now, if you'll excuse me." He trudged off to forestall additional question, Emilio at his heels. When they had gone a suitable distance, he remarked, "That was careless of me. I doubt any of these bumpkins have heard of your employers, but it wouldn't do to let the cat out of the bag, as it were. I'll be more careful in the future."

Emilio merely grunted. The silver spoon's blunder had given him yet another excuse to eliminate Nate King just as soon as King outlived his usefulness. Emilio couldn't wait.

Chapter Fifteen

The final tally of the expedition's losses was lower than Richard Ashworth had feared it would be but still much too high in one crucial respect: the number of lives lost. Three mountain men, four women, and one child died in the stampede. Eight more suffered mild injuries. Allen thought that was bad enough. But then, two days later, Nate King came to him and mentioned it was unlikely they would ever again set eyes on Cornish and the three trappers who had gone with the young mountaineer to save Cornish's Nez Perce wife. "They should have been back by now," Nate said sadly. "Something must have gone wrong."

The two days were spent rounding up the stock that had stampeded onto the prairie. Eighty-one horses were recovered. Combined with the 297 that Henry Allen's quick thinking prevented from running off, Ashworth was pleased to have 378 animals at his disposal. Only 22 were gone for good.

As for the expedition's supplies, the toll was not as severe as Ashworth had feared. True, many of his prized personal possessions were lost, as were those of the married mountain men and their families. But most of the supplies carried by the packhorses had been piled to the south of the mouth of the canyon and had been spared when the horses broke out.

On the morning of the third day, as the first flush of color tinged the eastern sky, Nate King and Henry Allen rode up to the lean-to that served as Ashworth's quarters.

Ashworth was expecting them. Wrapped tightly in his cape against the morning chill, he tried to hide his anxiety. He had grown to rely heavily on King and did not want to lose the man. "I don't like this," he said bluntly. "Why can't we just move on?"

Nate arched an eyebrow. "You were the one all fired up to get revenge the other night as I recollect," he reminded their leader.

Ashworth fidgeted, shifting his weight from foot to foot. "The stress of the moment," he grumbled. "Little Soldier is probably long gone by now. You'll be wasting your time."

"We can't let him get away with what he did," Nate responded. "Don't worry. One way or the other, we'll catch up with Jenks and you well before the expedition reaches Blackfoot country."

"I still don't like it." Ashworth refused to be

mollified. "Your rightful place is here with us."

Nate was spared further argument by the arrival of the giant Sicilian. Emilio Barzini straddled a big sorrel that would have dwarfed any other man. His immense bulk lent it the aspect of a child's pony. "I'm ready when you are," he rumbled.

Nate nodded at Ashworth, wheeled the black stallion, and headed west. Over a shoulder he said to the giant, "We'll ride Indian fashion in single file. Allen will bring up the rear. You stay between us. Try not to make much noise if you can help it."

Emilio grunted in acknowledgment. He didn't resent being treated as if he were incompetent. He would freely admit the other two men had more experience in the wilderness. But where it counted the most—being able to kill another human being without batting an eye—he was their equal, if not their superior. Let them lead him to the Crows. Then they could sit back if they wanted and watch a professional at work.

Nate swiveled in his saddle just before the foliage enveloped him. Winona, Zach, and Evelyn were near their new lean-to, staring sorrowfully. Zach waved; so Nate returned the favor and all three smiled.

Putting them from his mind in order to concentrate on the job at hand, Nate made a sweep of the rugged terrain bordering the canyon. He found the Crow trail easily enough. Only four warriors had taken part in stampeding the herd. Their tracks led southward.

Fortunately it hadn't rained since that fateful morning. The sign was clear enough for Nate to urge his mount to a trot more often than not, stopping only now and again to verify that they had not strayed off the trail.

No one spoke. Nate and Henry Allen were quiet out of habit, using expressions and gestures to communicate. Emilio was content to follow their example. He had never been much of a talker anyway. He liked to let his actions speak for him.

It was the middle of the morning when they located where the Crow camp had been, in a steep gully rimmed by tall trees. The ashes of the fire were cold to Nate's touch. He walked in ever-widening circles, his nose bent to the spoor. There had been nine warriors, all told, and they had headed south in a body the day after the stampede. The four Crows hadn't been alone.

Nate was examining the prints when Henry Allen called his name. The Tennessean stood on a low mound that partially hid whatever lay beyond on the gully floor. Rising, Nate strode over. He nearly gagged when a revolting stench made his stomach churn. It was an odor he knew all too well.

Cornish and one of the men who had gone with him had been stripped naked and staked out. Their mouths had been sewn shut, no doubt so they couldn't scream when the torture started. Both had been skinned in parts, narrow strips peeled from their bodies as a man might peel an orange. Their ears had been hacked off, their noses removed. The rest was unspeakably vile, vicious even by the savage standards of the frontier.

Nate saw that their eyes hadn't been gouged out, but that was only so they could see what the warriors had been doing to them. He imagined that Little Soldier had forced the Nez Perce woman to watch the whole thing.

Emilio regarded the Crow handiwork with interest. Having tortured more than his share of fools who incurred the wrath of his employers, he recognized the work of a master when he saw it. Whoever mutilated the frontiersmen knew exactly what he had been doing. Every cut and blow had been calculated to inflict supreme pain. The mountain men had suffered the torment of the damned.

Two of the men with Cornish had been spared. Nate guessed that Little Soldier would take the pair back to the Crow village to parade them in triumph, then give them the same treatment accorded their friends. Cornish's wife would be compelled to take a Crow warrior as her mate, perhaps even Little Soldier himself.

Buzzards and other scavengers had been at the bodies. Nate spent five minutes covering the grisly remains with stones and dirt. It was the best that could be done under the circumstances. Mounting, they rode out.

More than ever, Nate was determined to give Little Soldier his due. If the atrocity went unpunished and word spread among the various tribes, the mountaineers would be seen as weak, as fair game for any hotheaded young warrior who wanted to make a name for himself among his people.

Nate pushed hard. Where possible, they galloped. They took brief rests only when their horses flagged. Sunset came and went and still they forged on. Nate had a fair notion of roughly where the Crows were heading; so he no longer needed to rely exclusively on their tracks to guide him.

Riding at night was always a risky proposition. Obstacles were harder to avoid. Ruts and animal burrows could cripple a horse. Low branches might poke out the eye of an unwary rider. A man could not afford to let down his guard for an instant.

Nate had an added problem in that he didn't like having the Sicilian at his back the whole time. It gave him an uncomfortable feeling. Several times the skin between his shoulder blades prickled, and when he look around, he would catch the giant staring at him.

Despite everything Emilio had said, Nate didn't trust the man. He wouldn't put it past Barzini to kill him if given the chance. It wasn't bad enough that Nate had to be on the lookout for the Crows and wild beasts; he also had to be wary of one of his own party.

Henry Allen seemed to be aware of Nate's feelings. Nate noticed that the man from Tennessee always stayed close to him when they stopped and never drifted far behind when they were on the go. It helped that Allen was watching over him, but not enough to dispel the uneasy feeling that nagged Nate from the moment they left Ashworth.

Close to two in the morning, Nate finally called a halt. A cold camp had to suffice. The horses were tethered where they could graze. The three men turned in.

Nate did not judge it necessary to take turns standing guard. Few Indians were abroad at night, and if any predators came close, the horses were bound to act up, awakening him. As for Barzini, Nate just had to trust in Providence.

Before sunrise the three avengers were back on the trail. Nate munched jerked venison Winona had packed, savoring the tangy taste. Her jerky was always softer than his and twice as delicious.

Noon passed. The hoofprints revealed that the Crows had been taking their sweet time. Evidently Little Soldier believed his band had gotten clean away.

Toward late afternoon Nate glimpsed dark shapes pinwheeling in the sky far ahead. He hoped against hope that they weren't what he thought, but they were. Half-a-dozen buzzards circled a high country meadow. The object of their interest was sheathed by tall grass.

Nate motioned. Allen fanned out to the right. Emilio, seeing this, went left.

The corpse lay on its side, a pool of dry blood framing the head like a dark scarlet halo. The mountain man still wore his buckskins and moccasins. He had taken three arrows low in the back, three more higher up.

Flattened grass told the story. The man had

slipped his bounds and tried to escape on foot. Six of the Crows had ridden him down. Out of spite or anger or perhaps because he had struck one of them in getting away, they had turned him into a pincushion, then lifted his scalp.

Allen dismounted to examine the blood. Rubbing some of it between his fingers, he said, "Couldn't have been more than eight hours ago. We're gaining."

"Not fast enough," Nate commented.

A shallow grave, hastily dug, served their purpose. Nate galloped southward yet again. He had been through the particular stretch of mountains before them and believed that he could guess where the Crows would make camp that night.

"Hidden Lake?" Allen called out, as if he could read Nate's thoughts.

"That would be my hunch."

Situated on a tableland bordered by snow-capped peaks, the small lake was regularly visited by the Crows. Warriors ventured to the heights above to snare eagles for the feathers so prized in headdresses. Since the lake contained no beaver, it was of little interest to the whites. Only a few mountaineers had ever been there.

Nate was one. He recalled that on the other side of the tableland lay a lush valley where Little Soldier's village was bound to be. Unless the wily Crow could be stopped before he reached it, dispensing justice would be impossible.

Another sunset painted the sky in vivid hues that no artist could ever rival. Twilight gathered and deepened. Nate had to rely on his heels to spur the stallion on at a brisk clip. The forest came alive with typical night sounds.

A series of switchbacks brought them to the tableland shortly after midnight. A break in the trees rewarded them with a glimpse of the lake, its tranquil surface reflecting both the stars on high and the glow of two small fires at the water's edge.

"We did it!" Henry Allen whispered.

Nate studied the fires, which were spaced dozens of yards apart. Given the size of Little Soldier's war party, it was odd that the Crows had more than one. He held the stallion to a slow walk and wound through the trees to a cluster of huge boulders. Sliding down, he ground hitched his horse, then waited for his companions to join him.

Emilio kept his face impassive but inwardly he was more excited than he had been since he killed his first man years ago. The prospect of clashing with fierce savages on their own terms was a rare treat.

Emilio had always liked a challenge. When he first started working for the Brothers, he had relished the chance for heady combat, the thrill of pitting his sinews against those of his victims.

All too often, though, the men Emilio had been sent to dispatch had proven to be weaklings or craven cowards who put up little or no resistance. Killing them had been like swatting gnats. They were insignificant, pitiful creatures, hardly meriting any effort. He had derived no enjoyment from slaying them.

Enemies worthy of the name were few and far between, but the Crows promised to be a rare test of Emilio's skill. He hoped their prowess had not been overrated. Should they prove as easy to slay as their white counterparts, he would be tremendously disappointed.

Nate would rather have left the Sicilian there, but he could think of no excuse to justify it. "Stay behind us," he told the giant. "Move as silently as you can."

"You won't even know I'm here," Emilio said.

Doubting that very much, Nate moved into the pines. He counted on hearing the clomp of heavy footsteps, on the crackle and snap of twigs, but the only sound he heard was the sigh of the wind and the distant howl of a wolf. Thinking that the Sicilian had lost sight of them in the dark and fallen behind, he glanced back and was surprised to discover Barzini practically breathing down Allen's neck.

Only someone with exceptional skill could move like that, Nate mused. There was more to the giant than he had suspected.

Waist-high cattails lined the lake. Once Nate reached them, he bore to the left and followed the shoreline to a vantage point 60 yards from the fires. One was almost out; the other would not last more than half an hour unless wood were added. The glow bathed the sleeping forms of four warriors and hinted at the presence of more.

A single Crow was awake, but barely. Seated near the dancing flames, he had his forearms resting on his knees and his cheek on his arms. He yawned frequently. Twice he raised his head and shook it vigorously in order to keep from drifting off.

Nate couldn't see Little Soldier. The Nez Perce woman, Yellow Bird, was slumped over by the fire that had nearly gone out, her posture one of total despair.

Bound and left lying within inches of the lake was the last of the four men who had intended to rescue her. Sam Guthrie was his name, Nate remembered. Guthrie hailed from Indiana; he had only been in the mountains a couple of years. Shadow wreathed Guthrie's face, so Nate couldn't tell if the man was awake or not.

A hint of movement signified that Henry Allen was leaning toward him. Nate tilted so the Tennessean could whisper in his ear.

"Something ain't quite right, hoss."

The same disturbing feeling gnawed at Nate. All appeared to be as it should, yet he couldn't shake the nagging thought that he was overlooking an element he shouldn't.

Emilio couldn't understand what the mountain men were waiting for. They had found the Crows. It was time to kill or be killed. Sliding a hand up his right sleeve, he palmed one of his stilettos. Handcrafted by a master knifemaker in Sicily just for him, it was twice the size of an ordinary stiletto, but still perfectly balanced and sharper than the keenest razor.

The trappers were studying the camp. Emilio saw no need to waste more time; so he slipped on around them and stalked the warrior keeping watch. The man's head bobbed. It wouldn't be long before he joined his fellows in slumber—or if Emilio had his way, his ancestors in the grave.

Nate was being cautious. He refused to commit himself until he was certain no nasty surprises awaited them. Then he saw a massive shape outlined against the backdrop of trees, a shape moving through the very center of the Crow camp much as might a stalking grizzly, and he realized that his wishes no longer mattered. They were committed, whether they wanted to be or not.

"That blamed jackass!" Allen whispered.

Nate begged to differ, but he never uttered a word. *They* were the jackasses, for not having noticed sooner that the Sicilian had given them the slip.

Emilio had his rifle in his left hand, the stiletto in his right. He was within two paces of the guard when he set the rifle down. The Crow rose up and looked around, but not to his rear. Emilio smirked and closed in. Hooking his left wrist under the Indian's chin, he clamped down on the man's windpipe even as he effortlessly jerked the Crow erect and plunged the stiletto into the warrior's back. A single thrust was all that Emilio needed.

The Crow went limp. Not a sound had been made except for the soft hiss of steel slicing apart flesh. Emilio carefully eased the body to the ground, arranged it to give the illusion the man was asleep, and stepped to a Crow who actually was. Clamping his free hand over the warrior's mouth, Emilio plunged the stiletto between two of the lower ribs. The warrior gave a convulsive twitch, then went limp. Just like that, Emilio had extinguished a second life.

Nate was flabbergasted at the ease with which the Sicilian slew the Crows. Four of them were dead before Nate and Allen collected their wits and moved in to lend a hand. Allen slanted toward the Nez Perce while Nate hastened to Guthrie.

All went well until Nate put a hand on the captive. The moment he did, Guthrie shot up off the ground and bawled like a stricken calf for its mother. It was an automatic reaction on Guthrie's part, born of fear and desperation. And it had a predictable outcome.

The shriek brought every last Crow to his feet. For a few fleeting seconds the tableau froze, Allen still yards from the woman, Emilio with his stiletto jutting from the ribs of a fifth warrior.

In that frozen interval, the missing element revealed itself. Off to the southwest, Nate spotted the tethered horses. In the dark it was difficult to be exact, but he could clearly tell that there were far more than nine. In a flash of insight he realized why there had been two fires: Little Soldier's band wasn't the only one camped at Hidden Lake. Another group had already been there when Little Soldier arrived. There were far more than nine warriors. Thirty, perhaps. More than enough to slay Nate, the Tennessean, and the Sicilian combined.

A warrior in front of Nate galvanized into life, reaching for a knife on his left hip. Nate leveled his Hawken and fired, the shot smashing the man to the earth. He clubbed another warrior who tried to stop him from reaching Yellow Bird as Henry Allen's Kentucky boomed and fully half the Crows vented strident war whoops.

Bedlam ensued. Nate glimpsed the Tennessean backpedaling toward the reeds as a knot of enraged Crows closed in. A pistol barked and one dropped.

Over by the fire, Emilio was hemmed in on three sides, his back to the water. His rifle was yards away, and it might as well have been on the moon. Several warriors leapt forward, weapons upraised. In a twinkling he produced another stiletto, and with one in each hand, he met his attackers head on.

Nate reached Yellow Bird. Her face aglow with hope, she twisted and extended her wrists for him to cut her free. But as he squatted, something streaked under his right arm from behind, brushing the fringe on his buckskin shirt.

An arrow materialized in the Nez Perce woman's side. She recoiled at the impact, glanced forlornly at Nate, and pitched forward without an outcry. Nate started to lift her, to drag her off so he could extract the shaft, but there was no need. Yellow Bird had breathed her last.

Whirling, Nate drew a pistol and put a ball into the forehead of the warrior who had shot the arrow.

Since to stay and fight courted certain death, Nate's intent was to grab Sam Guthrie and head for the hills before all of them resembled porcupines. But no sooner did he turn toward the bound mountaineer than Guthrie pushed to his knees and drew attention to himself by shouting, "King, for God's sake, get me out of here!"

It was a fatal mistake. A pair of Crows were closer. At Guthrie's yell, they were on him like two furious panthers, ripping at his chest and neck with long blades of steel. Guthrie was dead before the echo of his shout died on the wind. Everything had gone terribly, utterly wrong.

Nate retreated toward the lake, expending his second flintlock on a warrior armed with a club. Henry Allen had disappeared in the cattails, along with seven or eight Absarokas. The Sicilian was half buried under a berserk mass of Crows striving their utmost to count coup on him. At least six corpses testified to their failure.

All of Nate's guns were empty. He shoved the spent pistol under his belt beside its mate and took one more step backward. Water soaked his foot up to the ankle. He could go no farther.

A ragged line of Crows advanced; among them was Little Soldier. The bloodthirsty leader was urging his fellow warriors on while bouncing up and down like a man half demented. Then Little Soldier looked at Nate. "You die, white dog! We take your hair, Grizzly Killer, and hang on post for whole village to see!"

Nate scanned the semicircle of feral bronzed faces that confronted him. Barring a miracle, Little Soldier's boast might just turn out to be prophetic.

Chapter Sixteen

Nate King dropped a hand to the hilt of his Bowie knife. He pictured Winona, Zach, and Evelyn, and he wished that he could have lived long enough to see his children grow up and have children of their own. But he had always known the odds were against him. Few who called the wilderness home ever lived to a ripe old age. Those who did were the exceptions, not the rule.

As the 11 Crows slowly converged, Nate prepared to sell his life dearly. He saw some of the warriors tense for the fatal lunge, saw knives and lances and arrows glint dully.

At that exact instant, a thunderous bestial bellow drowned out all other sounds. It was so loud, so like thunder, so startling in its ferocity that the Crows paused and glanced around to isolate the source.

Nate already knew who was responsible. He had seen Emilio Barzini throw off the warriors trying to smother the Sicilian by sheer weight of numbers. He had witnessed Emilio straighten up and utter the roar of savage glee. So when all eyes swiveled toward the giant, Nate seized the moment, spun, and flung himself into Hidden Lake.

The water was ice cold. It was hard to swim while holding a rifle and wearing buckskins, but it was either that or go down under the blood-drenched weapons of the Absarokas. And Nate wanted more than anything to live. He pumped his arms in powerful strokes while kicking for all he was worth. A sharp cry made him look back. The Crows had discovered that he was escaping. All 11 rushed to the water's edge but only two dived in after him.

There was no sign of Allen. The Sicilian fought on, a slender blade in either hand, leaving a trail of littered bodies as he retreated toward dense brush.

Nate could only afford a short glance. He had to outdistance the pair of warriors eager to slit his throat. One floundered, a poor swimmer. But the other was a human fish and cleaved the surface as smoothly as a sturgeon. Water splashed off a tomahawk the man held.

Nate's plight was compounded by his clothes. Buckskins were heavy enough dry; wet, they seemed to weigh a ton. They impeded his every movement. Yet he could hardly take the time to strip off his shirt and leggings. He had to swim as fast as he could and pray it was good enough.

It wasn't. A wolfish yip alerted Nate to the proximity of the Crow, who had overtaken him not 30 feet from the shore. Stopping, Nate rotated to face his adversary. The warrior raised the tomahawk, his teeth flashing white in the night.

Even though the Hawken was an extra burden, it was just as well that Nate had not discarded it. The rifle came in handy. He jabbed, the stock connecting with the Crow's forehead.

The warrior shrugged off the pain and swatted at the Hawken, his tomahawk glancing off the polished wood, then backed up a few feet to get out of range.

It was a stalemate. Nate couldn't turn to flee or the Crow would be on him in the bat of an eye, nor could the Crow close in so long as Nate held him at bay with the Hawken.

Then an arrow cleaved the water less than a foot from Nate's right elbow. Several warriors on the rocky beach were taking careful aim with their bows. Even in the dark, they were uncannily accurate, and sooner or later one would score.

Nate had to get out of there. The nearest cover was a belt of cattails to the east. He began to paddle toward them, never taking his gaze off the warrior with the tomahawk. The man pounced, swinging overhand. Nate swept the Hawken up to block the swing, shifted, and drove the stock at the Crow's temple. If he had been on land, the blow would have dropped the warrior in his tracks. But, lacking firm footing, the best Nate could do was clip his enemy. The man backed up, shaking his head, dazed but unhurt.

Another arrow sought Nate's life. Then a third. The archers came closer with each try. Nate continued toward the reeds, deflecting a flurry of strikes as the Crow with the tomahawk attempted to stop him.

Nate realized he could never get away unless he disposed of the warrior first. He resorted to a ruse. Suddenly throwing himself at the cattails as if frantic to flee, he watched the Crow out of the corner of his eye. When the man hurtled forward to stop him, Nate reversed direction, giving the warrior no warning, no time to react. He speared the barrel at the Crow's throat.

The man jerked to the left to avoid it, but was a shade too slow. A gurgling gasp burst from his lips. Pressing a hand over his neck, he swayed, wheezing loudly for air.

Nate didn't waste another second. Barreling into the cattails, he shouldered his way to the north, staying low so the Crows couldn't see him. Whizzing shafts rained down, most wide of the mark but a few much too near to suit him. One even nipped his shoulder but only tore the buckskin.

Moving rapidly, Nate veered toward the shore. A line of trees reared out of the inky veil. He lifted a leg to dash from cover and into the forest when a cluster of indigo forms appeared between the reeds and the pines.

Nate ducked and froze. The Crows were so close that he could have flicked a pebble and hit one. They halted abreast of his position. Words were whispered. Some commenced poking into the reeds while others scoured the tree line and the undergrowth.

No shouting or sounds of battle arose from the Crow camp. Nate wondered if the Sicilian had gone down. And what about Allen? Had the Tennessean made good his escape? Or had the Crows added one more victim to their long string?

Another warrior showed up. Commands were snapped. Nate couldn't see the man's face, but the voice he identified. It was Little Soldier.

The Absarokas spread out in twos and threes. Little Soldier and one other stayed put, the Crow leader with his back to the lake and his hands on his hips.

Nate could have gone on. It would have been infinitely safer for him to have slipped quietly off than it was for him to do what he did, namely, to noiselessly part the stems in front of him and stealthily glide toward the man who had caused the expedition so much grief. His guns were empty but he still had his Bowie and his tomahawk. Either would do, but this time he relied on the weapon favored by his adopted people.

Little Soldier and the last warrior were talking softly, Little Soldier gesturing at the trees, the other man at the reeds. Apparently they were arguing over where Nate had gone.

As Nate stepped onto dry land, he glanced to the right and the left to verify no other Crows were close by. Placing the Hawken down, he stalked his quarry. He was only a few feet from them when his soggy buckskins squished loud enough to be heard in St. Louis.

The two Crows whirled. Little Soldier took one look, pivoted on a heel, and sprinted into the forest while bawling at the top of his lungs. The other man brought up a club.

Nate struck before the warrior could. As the Crow toppled, Nate wheeled and plucked the Hawken up on the fly. He was in among the reeds again before help could arrive. Wading to the outer fringe, he hurried eastward.

Nate presently reached the easternmost point and swung around to the north. When he was due south of where the horses were hidden, he inched to the shore again. No Crows appeared this time. Dripping wet, he emerged from the cattails and dashed into the trees. Once under cover, he made his way to the boulders.

More than anything, Nate wanted to reload his guns. But that had to wait until he could thoroughly dry each one and inspect the black powder in his powder horn to insure it had not been rendered useless during his swim.

Nate was relieved to spot the black stallion and the other two horses right where they had been left. He wasn't about to run on out there, though, when Crows might be lurking in the brush, waiting for someone to do just that. Instead, he circled the boulders.

A stealthy tread brought Nate to a halt. Through the trees flitted a black specter that would pass within an arm's reach of the trunk behind which Nate hunkered. Nate reversed his grip on the Hawken, holding it like a club. The figure paused, as if sensing his presence. In a few seconds it took another stride. Nate had every sinew balled into a knot and was rising to swing when the outline of a beaver hat awakened him to the mistake he had nearly made.

"Henry?"

The Tennessean smiled broadly and clapped Nate on the shoulders. "This coon is mighty tickled that you gave those red varmints the slip!"

"Have you seen Barzini?" Nate whispered.

"Neither hide nor hair," Allen responded. "I had my hands so full dodging the devils that were after my own skin that I couldn't help out either of you."

Nate stepped to a boulder and knelt at its base. "We can't leave until we know for sure," he said.

"Know what?" a deep voice replied, so near to Nate that he jumped.

An immense living block of manhood rose up out of the shadows. Emilio was delighted by the startled looks the mountain men bestowed on him. For all their vaunted prowess, they would be no match for him in a life or death clash.

"How long have you been hiding here?" Allen inquired.

Emilio did not like the inference. "I've been waiting for the two of you, not cowering in fear. It's taken you so long I was sure the Indians had wiped you out."

Nate was amazed that the giant had eluded the Crows and even more astounded that he had beaten them to the boulders. There was much more to Emilio Barzini then met the eye. "I thought the same about you."

"They tried," Emilio said with a hint of contempt. The Crows had fought well, but no better than some whites he had gone up against. In that respect, they had been a distinct disappointment, although the score or more of cuts and nicks on his arms and chest were ample proof that he should not regard them too lightly.

"I think I made worm food of three of them." Henry Allen mentioned.

"I killed four, maybe five," Nate said.

Emilio smirked. "Is that all? Twelve of them fell before me, and two others I crippled for life." His broad chest swelled. "They will not soon forget this night."

"You made worm food of a baker's dozen?" Allen said skeptically. "Who do you reckon you are? Samson? Or did you rip trees up by the roots and bash the Absarokas over the head with them?"

"I do not like being mocked," Emilio warned, his voice rising.

Nate defused the dispute by interjecting, "I saw you kill at least seven of them. That's more than any one man has ever done at one time before."

"It was nothing," Emilio said, and meant it. "I have done better." He alluded to an incident years ago. At a waterfront tavern in southern Italy he had become embroiled in a dispute with a group of sailors, and when the final chair had been broken and the last bottle smashed, 15 broken, dying, or dead men had been left lying on the floor.

Nate rose. "So between the three of us, Little Soldier lost upwards of twenty warriors. That won't sit well with his people. Whenever a man is lost on a raid, it's considered a bad omen."

Henry Allen nodded. "You're right there, hoss. Losing that many will make him awful unpopular for a long spell. He won't have any influence among the Crows. Hell, it wouldn't surprise me if they refuse to let him lead them from now on."

"Then we've done it," Nate said. "We can head on back."

"Done what?" Emilio wanted to know. In the Old Country, a debt wasn't settled until the offending party had been eliminated. An eye for an eye was the day-to-day creed by which his people lived. By his reckoning, honor would only be satisfied when Little Soldier was killed.

"We had to avenge the raid or risk being branded as fair game for any war party that comes along," Nate refreshed the Sicilian's memory. "And that's exactly what we've done."

"Little Soldier still lives."

"But he does so in shame," Nate said. "To the Crows and the Dakotas and some other tribes, that's a fate worse than death. No one will listen to him. No one will want to go on raids with him."

Emilio began to understand. "We have made an outcast of him?"

"Not exactly, but the next best thing," Nate answered. He did not know how else to explain Indian customs to someone completely ignorant of Indian ways. Especially among the Crows, where valiant exploits were the basis by which warriors advanced in rank, losing a battle was a stigma of the highest magnitude. No man was even rated a warrior until he had counted coup, and any man who had not done so by the time he reached 20 years of age became a slave of the women.

"So let's light a shuck," Allen advised, stepping to his mount. "That greenhorn booshway of ours is going to need our advice when he gets to Blackfoot country."

Nate did not need any prompting, as eager as he was to be reunited with his loved ones. Forking leather, he rode northward.

Emilio brought up the rear. Despite their explanations, he thought it strange that the mountain men had let their enemy live. In the Old Country, no one would have been so stupid. A live enemy could always make trouble later on. What was to stop Little Soldier from causing more trouble at some point farther along the trail? No, if it had been up to him, he would not have rejoined the brigade until the vicious Crow had given up the ghost.

Nate wanted to ride all night and into the next day but their horses weren't up to it. He called a halt about three and let everyone sleep until the middle of the morning.

Refreshed, they rode until nine that night. Nate was so confident the Crows wouldn't bother them again he built a fire himself and made coffee. During the afternoon Allen had dropped a grouse at 75 yards, and Nate roasted it on a makeshift spit. They turned in early, their bellies full for the first time in days.

When they reached the site of the stampede, the sight of the row of graves dispelled Nate's lighthearted mood. Scavengers had been at them. Two graves had been dug open, the remains partially consumed. Tracks revealed the culprits.

"Damned coyotes!" Allen complained. "Remind me to shoot the next six or seven I see."

It didn't take long to slide the putrid body parts back into their holes and cover the defiled corpses with more dirt. Nate also took the precaution of layering every mound with large rocks and broken limbs to deter any more digging.

Emilio helped, but he thought the effort a waste of energy. When a man died, that was the end of it. Whether his body was formally interred in an expensive coffin in a mausoleum or left to rot in the open was of no consequence. As an Old Country saying had it, "The dead tell no tales, the dead feel no pain. What matters to them the sun or the rain?"

Emilio would have left the graves as they were. He wouldn't have seen fit to deprive the coyotes of their feast. So what if the bodies were eaten? The dead men didn't care. Why should the living?

A six-year-old could have tracked the expedition from that point on. The trail left by the horse herd alone was over a hundred yards wide and dotted with enough droppings to fertilize each and every tilled acre in New York for an entire year.

Nate rode hard but still couldn't overhaul the brigade before nightfall. Camp was made in a ravine where their fire was safe from the wind and prying eyes. Since they hadn't bothered to drop fresh game during the day, their supper consisted of jerky and the last of their pemmican.

To say that Nate was surprised when the Sicilian unexpectedly addressed him would be an understatement. The man had hardly said two words to either Allen or him except when they spoke first.

"How soon before we reach Blackfoot country?" the giant inquired.

"Most of their villages are a week's ride north of here," Nate disclosed, "but we could run into them at any time. They like to think of themselves as the lords of the mountains, and they roam pretty much wherever they please."

"How do they compare to the Indians we just fought?" Emilio wanted to learn. In light of how poorly the Crows had fared, he was beginning to think that all the stories he had heard about Indians were exaggerations, at best, or outright lies, at worst.

"If you're asking me how tough the Blackfeet are," Nate said, "I'd have to say they're the best fighters north of the Missouri River. They're afraid of no one."

"And they hate whites with a passion," Allen threw in.

"Why?" Emilio asked.

Nate responded. "Blame Lewis and Clark."

"Who?"

Henry Allen snorted. "You're an American and you've never heard of them? Where the blazes were you back then? Why, they were wrote up in every blamed newspaper from Maine to the Gulf of Mexico. I daresay they're just about two of the most famous gents who ever lived."

"I am new to America," Emilio revealed. "You

must excuse me if my knowledge of her history is flawed."

Nate leaned back against a boulder and bit off a piece of pemmican. "Meriwether Lewis and William Clark were picked by President Jefferson to explore the country between the Mississippi and the Pacific Ocean. On their way back, Lewis tangled with a bunch of Blackfeet who tried to steal the guns of his party. Two of the warriors were shot, and the Blackfeet have never forgiven us for that. Ever since, they've done all in their power to make life miserable for any whites they catch."

Admiration flowered as Emilio listened. These Blackfeet, he mused, were a lot like his own people. They apparently valued their honor above all else, and never let a wrong go unavenged. "How many trappers have they killed?"

"No one knows for sure," Nate said, "because most of the time there are no witnesses. But a lot of men have gone into their country to trap and never come out again."

"I'd swear an oath on the Bible that they've rubbed out thirty or forty," Allen remarked. "Some were good friends of mine."

Nate stared soberly skyward. He had lost friends, too, one a preacher who had rashly believed it was possible to convert the Blackfeet despite Nate's assurances to the contrary. Some men, he had learned the hard way, believed what they wanted to believe, whether it conflicted with reality or not.

Emilio was still not satisfied. "Do these Blackfeet only attack small groups of whites or will they go up against large parties as well?"

"They'll go on the warpath against anyone anytime," Nate made clear. "About six years ago a war party of sixty-nine Blackfeet went up against more than two thousand Crows. The Crows won, but it cost them dearly."

The more Emilio heard, the more his admiration grew. He hoped that he would have the chance to test his mettle against the Blackfeet, just as he had against the Crows.

Since the Sicilian was being so talkative, Nate casually asked, "What can you tell me about those business associates Ashworth talked about?"

"Who?" Emilio feigned.

"The Brothers, I think he called them." The subject had bothered Nate ever since Ashworth mentioned them. By rights it was none of Nate's business, but Ashworth's secretive behavior had convinced him that something was amiss.

"Mr. Ashworth is the one you should ask," Emilio hedged. He didn't like the mountain man prying. Were it not for Ashworth's insistence that they needed King to get them safely in and out of the mountains, Emilio would have liked to snap the trapper's neck later that night while King slept. The Southerner's, too, just for the hell of it.

Nate didn't press. If Ashworth and the Sicilian wanted to keep the matter secret, that was their affair. Stretching, he said, "I reckon I'm going to turn in. If we get an early start, we should catch up to the brigade by noon."

By ten, as events came to pass. The Ashworth

Expedition had stopped on the south bank of the Snake River. It was much too early to make camp for the night, so Nate figured Jenks had done so to water the stock, until he noticed that the horse herd had been drawn up under heavy guard and that the women and children were behind a protective barrier of supplies.

"There's been a racket," Allen guessed.

Nate saw no evidence of a battle as he descended a steep ridge and applied his heels to the stallion. But there was no denying the nervousness of the horse guard, one of whom threw a Kentucky to his shoulder as Nate and the others burst from a stand of cottonwoods and willows. The man was set to fire when an older mountaineer trapper shouted something that made him lower his weapon.

"Nate! Are you a sight for this coon's tired eyes!" the old-timer declared as the three men rode up.

"What's the trouble, Ferris?" Nate got right to the point.

"What else?" the grizzled trapper responded. "Blackfeet."

Chapter Seventeen

Richard Ashworth was a nervous wreck. Nothing was going as it should of late. So much had gone wrong, in fact, that he was inclined to think his precious expedition had become jinxed.

It had been one thing after another. The death of that poor Flathead woman. The abduction of the Nez Perce. The stampede, with the attendant loss of lives and provisions. And now, when the man he most relied on to guide his judgment was gone and might have fallen victim to the Crows, a new problem had reared its unwanted head in the form of the notorious Blackfeet.

As if all that were not bad enough, two days had gone by since Ashworth had enjoyed a sip of Scotch, and he wanted some badly. There was an ache in the pit of his stomach, an ache that would only go away if he indulged. But he only had a little Scotch left in his flask, and he was saving it for a special occasion.

Hands entwined behind his back, Ashworth paced in front of the piled supplies and wondered if perhaps his great brainstorm was truly as flawless as he had imagined back in New York City.

A commotion brought an end to Ashworth's pacing. He looked up. Never had he been so glad to see anyone as he was to behold his second-in-command returning, along with the Tennessean and the gigantic Sicilian.

"King!" Ashworth exclaimed happily, rushing forward to meet the mountain man halfway. But someone else got there first. Ashworth had to stand and wait while the trapper's Shoshone wife embraced King for a full minute. Impatient to confer, he hastened forward as soon as they separated. "King!" he repeated. "It's about time you've shown up. Jenks claims were in big trouble."

Nate let his eyes linger on his lovely wife a few seconds before he turned to the greenhorn. Zach and Evelyn were nearby, dutifully waiting for him to notice them. He gave each a smile, and he would have gone to them had his arm not been gripped and had Richard Ashworth not spun him around.

"Haven't you heard a word I said, mister? The men riding scout saw a party of Blackfeet who took off into the deep woods. Jenks is afraid the heathens went to get reinforcements so they can attack us in force."

Nate yanked his arm loose. It galled him to be

manhandled, and it incensed him even more to be treated as if he were at the New Yorker's beck and call, as if he could be bossed around like some sort of lackey. "So I've heard. Where is Jenks now?"

Ashworth gestured to the northwest. "He rode off with fifteen men about an hour ago to track the Indians. I'm worried that the Blackfeet got them."

"Clive Jenks has spent more years in the Rockies than most. He knows what he's doing," Nate said. "He'll be back when it suits them."

"And what are we supposed to do in the meantime?" Ashworth demanded irritably.

"We wait."

Ashworth was about to reply that he was tired of waiting, that he wanted to get the brigade moving again, that he didn't think King was taking his responsibility seriously enough, but he never uttered a word. Something in King's eyes, a flinty gleam that hinted at latent violence, held him in check. Swallowing his pride, he stepped back, soothing his ruffled feathers by telling himself that it was best to use tact and diplomacy when dealing with men who were little better than the savages they lived among and took to wife.

Winona could tell that her man was upset. Taking his hand, she steered him to the children and was rewarded by a huge smile as Nate gave each a big hug in turn.

"What happened with the Crows, Pa?" Zach asked.

"I'll tell you all about it tonight before we tuck you in," Nate promised, scooping his daughter up. Blue Flower giggled and pecked him on the cheek.

"Missed you, Papa."

"Missed you, precious."

A low cough intruded. Nate twisted. Henry Allen was still mounted and standing in the stirrups, a hand over his eyes to shield them from the glare of the sun.

"Riders coming," the Tennessean reported. He squinted. "It's Clive, sure enough."

Ashworth overheard and clasped his hands. "Hallelujah! At last something is going my way. Let's hope he made wolf meat of the Blackfeet, as you mountaineers like to put it."

Jenks was grinning when he reined up, which Nate took as a good sign. Ordinarily, the man was a stickler for always believing the worst that could happen, would happen.

"Howdy, hoss," Nate greeted him. "What's this about Blackfeet skulking about?"

"The scouts figured as much," Jenks said. "But we followed the tracks of four unshod cayuses off to the northwest to a spot where one of the Injuns climbed down. Saw his moccasins prints as plain as day. They weren't Blackfoot."

"Flathead, then? Or Nez Perce?" Nate said, since both tribes occupied territory in that direction.

"Neither," Jenks said. "I never saw prints like these, Nate. Whatever tribe those Injuns belonged to, it's a new one on me."

In itself, the news was a relief. The Blackfoot Confederacy had yet to learn of their presence. Nate speculated that maybe the four warriors were from a tribe living up in Canada. He'd heard tell that there were as many tribes in the north country as there were in the southern Rockies and the plains, many of whom had never had contact with white men and would naturally run off at the sight of a party the size of the fur brigade.

"We can move on then," Nate announced. "Spread the word. From here on out, we push twice as hard."

The words were music to Richard Ashworth's ears. He had half a mind to celebrate by finishing off his Scotch, but he refrained. Noticing the Sicilian, he walked over as Barzini led his mount off. "How did you fare in your foray against the Crows?" Ashworth inquired.

"It was educational," Emilio said. His all-too-brief time away from Ashworth had brought into sharp focus exactly how much he despised the man. Emilio couldn't wait to be done with his job and get back to New York. The knowledge that it might be another two years was enough to shake even his iron-willed resolve.

One thing alone kept Emilio there. The Brothers had hinted that if he performed well, they would bring his sweetheart over from the Old Country. Maria was the only person in the world Emilio cared for. He had courted her before he went to work for the Brothers; they had looked forward to the day they would be man and wife.

His departure for America had spoiled their

plans. Once a month she wrote him, begging that he send for her so they could be together again. And at long last, after Ashworth sold the furs and he disposed of the man, her wish would be granted.

Suddenly Emilio realized that the silver spoon had gone on talking.

"Why anyone in his right mind would live in these mountains is beyond me. Just between the two of us, my good fellow, giving up all the comforts civilization has to offer to live like an animal is insane. Wouldn't you agree?"

Emilio almost laughed. This from a man who had concocted so mad a scheme to recoup his family's fortune? He changed the subject. "From now on, you are not to wander out of my sight. Is that understood?"

Ashworth halted in midstride. "What?"

"You heard me. My employers can't afford for anything to happen to you. It wouldn't do to have the Blackfeet take you captive."

"I'm perfectly capable of taking care of myself," Ashworth said, indignant at being treated as if he were an infant. "I've done just fine these past few days while you were gone."

Emilio moved closer, towering over the other man, intimidating him on purpose. "It's not open to debate. You will do as I say of your own free will or I will force you to do it. Either way, I must do as the Brothers expect of me."

Before Ashworth could stop himself, he complained, "Sending you along was a mistake. They shouldn't have done it."

"For once we agree on something," Emilio responded.

Ashworth tried to think of a witty retort but couldn't. He resigned himself to once again having a hulking shadow at his elbow every waking hour of the day. Feeling glum, he sat on a log and looked on as the mountain men loaded supplies onto packhorses. In short order Nate King had the brigade ready to move out. Ashworth took his position at the head of the column, waved an arm overhead, and their trek resumed.

Nate had a definite destination in mind. In order to make the expedition a success, the brigade had to bring in more plews than anyone ever had before. To do that, they had to trap virgin streams and rivers, waterways white men had never touched, where the beaver were thicker than the blades of grass on the prairie. One region in particular offered that prospect.

Deep in the heart of the Bitterroot Range, below the divide in remote wilderness through which the Salmon River and countless smaller streams meandered, existed perhaps the last area where beaver could be found in abundance, where they were as numerous as they had been in the central Rockies before the coming of the white man.

Or so Nate had heard from the few hardy souls who had ventured into the region and lived to tell of what they had seen. To a man, they had lost their horses and their fixings and almost their lives to roving bands of Blackfeet, Bloods, or Piegans, for the Bitterroot Range lay in the very heart of Blackfoot country.

Years back a smaller brigade had gone in there with the intention of cleaning out the beaver. Less than half made it back again, without a single pelt.

Nate had discussed it at length with Ashworth. They had a plan, and if all went well, they would succeed where everyone else had failed.

As the brigade journeyed ever deeper into the foreboding fortress of mountains, Nate doubled the scouts during the day and the guards at night. No sign was seen of Indians, but there was plenty of evidence of beaver: their lodges, their dams, their runs, trees gnawed through, and the beaver themselves in more numbers than he had seen at any one time since he first came to the Rockies.

"Lord, this is paradise," Henry Allen commented one fine morning as they wound along a wide stream in which several beaver frolicked, unconcerned. "Tell me I've died, hoss, and gone to heaven."

The other mountaineers felt the same way. Nate had seen it mirrored in their joyful eyes, in their happy expressions, in the general air of contentment that had come over every last trapper. They were in their element, about to do that which they did best. After several seasons of hardship and want, they were on the verge of realizing a dream come true. But only if they took steps to insure the Blackfeet wouldn't drive them off.

Nate found a suitable spot in a verdant valley rife with elk, deer, and mountain buffalo. As soon as he called a halt, he set the men to work. One detail was assigned to chop down cottonwood trees, another assigned to trim them. A third dug holes in the shape of an 80-foot square. A fourth sunk the cottonwoods into the ground to a depth of two and a half feet.

Working in unison, the mountaineers erected their stockade within ten days. It included two bastions ten feet square at opposite angles and railed parapets on all four walls. Shelters were added inside, solid buildings that would keep out the wind and the cold during the winter months. Suitable quarters for the married trappers were set up. The single men had to make do with a long, low barracks that was more than adequate for their simple needs.

Ashworth insisted on holding a formal ceremony. He was so proud of Fort Ashworth, as he dubbed it, that he had one of the trappers unfurl an old Stars and Stripes the man owned atop a 20-foot pole.

The expedition leader also gave a speech, mercifully short, in which he urged the men to exert themselves to their utmost, and to show the crude red man that the white man was not to be denied once he set his mind to a task. To prove to the vile Blackfeet that they were superior to them in every way, and that if they harassed them, they would pay dearly.

Nate could not help but notice that the speech did not go over very well. Most of the mountaineers didn't think of Indians as inferior, only different.

That evening Nate called all the trappers together and laid down the rules they must follow. Most stemmed from sheer common sense.

No one was to go into the forest alone. Trapping parties were to consist of ten men, minimum. Half would lay and raise their Newhouses while the rest stood guard. All peltries were to be turned over to Jenks, who would keep the official tally.

Horses were always to be hobbled when left unattended, even when close to the stockade.

Never were more than three trapping parties to be gone from the fort at any one time. The corral attached to the rear of the stockade was to be guarded day and night, and the ground around both to be cleared of all plant growth for over a hundred yards so no hostiles could sneak up on them.

The women were never to go to the river without an armed escort. Children were prohibited from playing in the woods. Dogs were to be kept on leashes. The stock was to be watered in small bunches throughout each day.

Nate tried to think of everything. Their lives depended on it. He personally made sure that trappers manned the bastions 24 hours a day. And he set a policy that no Indians other than direct kin of the mountaineers were permitted in the stockade after sunset.

Richard Ashworth had little to do. He was tremendously impressed by his lieutenant, so much so that he seriously considered offering King a small percentage of the profits should the undertaking prove successful. He decided against it, however, since it might set a bad precedent. Once word got around, Allen and Jenks and some of the others might take it into their heads to demand more money, too. And he couldn't have that.

Emilio was largely bored. He hovered over the silver spoon like a hawk over one of its brood. Also of special interest were the two expensive leather carrying cases he had saved that day of the stampede. No one other than Ashworth and he knew what was in them, and he made certain that Ashworth kept them locked at all times so no one else would find out.

With so many mouths to feed, all the boys and quite a few of the men spent most of each day in quest of game for the cooking pots. Young Zachary King was rated one of the better hunters. Thanks to the tutelage of his father, he could track and shoot better than most boys his age.

As a result, Zach spent most of his time hunting in the company of another boy named Zeb Gilcrest. Zeb's pa was from New England, his ma a Flathead. The pair had hit it off the first time they met back on the trail, and when not with their families, they could be found roving the nearby woods in search of deer or squirrels or rabbits.

Five days after the dedication of Fort Ashworth, and one day before the mountaineers were to branch out into the adjacent waterways and commence trapping, Zach and his friend happened to be hunting south of the stockade. They had gone farther than ever, over a mile, and young Gilcrest kept glancing back and frowning.

"Don't you think we've gone far enough, Zach?" Zeb asked. "Remember what your pa told us."

"He'll understand," Zach said, riveted to a set of fresh elk tracks they had been following. A big old bull was heading south toward the Salmon River. It could provide hundreds of pounds of meat, enough to feed whole families for weeks. He wasn't about to let it get away if he could help it. "Another mile won't make a difference."

"I don't know," Zeb said anxiously. "Your pa was clear as could be. He told us never to go past that knoll we crossed five minutes ago or he'd see that we regretted it."

"He'll forgive us if we get this elk," Zach predicted.

"I hope you're right."

The tracks wound toward a gap in a pair of hills that flanked the valley. It gave Zach an idea. "Let's climb the first hill," he proposed. "We might get a clear shot at the bull from up there."

"Fair enough," Zeb said, "but I'm not going a step farther than the top. My pa will tan my backside good if he hears I disobeyed your pa."

Small pines dotted the steep slopes. Zach gripped the ends of low branches to keep from losing his footing as he ascended. Well shy of the crest the trees thinned, and he had to scramble like an oversize salamander to reach the level summit. There he paused to catch his breath and survey the surrounding countryside.

Miles to the south glistened the Salmon. To the east and west majestic mountains reared. The Bitterroot Range boasted a breathtaking natural beauty that awed even a boy like Zach, who had lived among mountains all his life.

"Whew!" Zeb Gilcrest declared, joining him. "That was some climb! I'm plumb tuckered out!"

"You need to get more exercise," Zach said, poking his rifle at his friend's ample midsection.

"Don't you start in on me," Zeb scolded. "I get enough of that from my folks." He patted his stomach and chuckled. "Can I help it if I like to eat? I was born with a bottomless pit." Zeb paused, his eyes drifting past Zach. "Say, who's that?"

Zachary turned. Silhouetted against the flowing waters of the Salmon was a lone rider. The distance was too great to note any details other than the shadowy shape of the horse and the man astride it. He watched intently as the rider came northward toward them.

"Must be a mountanee man out hunting," Zeb said.

"Alone?" Zach was doubtful. "All the hunters are supposed to go out in pairs." Scooting toward a thicket on the south slope, he said, "Come on. Let's hunker down and spy on this coon a spell."

"What if it's an Indian?"

"All the more reason," Zach said. "Our folks will need to know if there are any hostiles about." Reaching the growth, he squatted behind some weeds higher than his head. His friend was quick to join him.

"I don't know," Zeb used his favorite expression. "What if he spots us?"

Zach wagged his Hawken. "We're armed, aren't

we? And we can shoot as well as the next man. What do we have to worry about?"

The rider was in no great hurry. For minutes on end he would be in the open, then disappear behind a hill or knoll and not be seen for some time. Not until he was under a mile off did Zach catch on to the fact that the mystery man was paralleling the exact route the brigade had taken from the Salmon. "I'll be! That cuss is tracking us."

"Huh?"

"Use your noggin," Zach said. "He's following the sign we left weeks ago." He pursed his lips. "Too bad it hasn't rained since."

Firs hid the rider for more than a quarter of an hour. When next he appeared, he was only 200 yards off, across a meadow that separated their hill from another.

"Tarnation!" Zeb Gilcrest said. "It's an Injun!"

"Maybe a Blackfoot!" Zach said, fingering the Hawken's trigger. Should that prove to be the case, he couldn't let the warrior ride off to tell the rest of the tribe where to find the expedition. It would be up to Zeb and him to stop the man or scores of lives might be lost.

"What's he doing now?" Zeb wondered.

The warrior had knelt to pick something up. Straightening up, he broke it apart in his hands.

"Horse droppings," Zach guessed. "He can tell how old the sign is by how dry the droppings are." It was an old trick that took a lot of practice to get down pat. Zach should know. His father had been trying to teach it to him for years, and he still misjudged more often than he got it right.

"He's coming right for us!"

The warrior had swung onto his pinto and started across the meadow. Just then, to the north of the fort, a rifle cracked faintly. Instantly the rider drew rein. He sat there a while, head cocked.

Zeb fidgeted. "Reckon he knows we're here?"

"No, but he will if you won't be still," Zach whispered. He had never realized his friend would be so excitable in a crisis, and he was glad he had learned it before they encountered a real threat, like an entire war party.

"Look!"

The rider had angled to the east, toward dense trees. He was almost close enough for them to see his features but he was staring back toward the Salmon River.

"Turn this way. Darn it!" Zach said. A clear glimpse of the man's hair and buckskins would help him determine which tribe the warrior belonged to.

Then the warrior shifted to study their hill. Zeb Gilcrest gasped. Zach's pulse raced, and he tried to tell himself that he was imagining the whole thing, that it couldn't possibly be who he thought it must be. Yet there could be no mistake. The rider was none other than Little Soldier.

Chapter Eighteen

Richard Ashworth was taken back when Nate King, Henry Allen, and Clive Jenks glanced at him as if he should have his mouth washed out with soap. All he'd asked King's son was, "Are you sure it was the Crow, boy? Or could your imagination have been playing tricks on you?" He'd given the youngster a pat on the head. "After all, boys your age are prone to flights of fancy."

Zach bristled at the suggestion he was a mere child who couldn't be trusted. "I know who I saw, mister," he stated coldly. "It was that murdering Absaroka, big as life."

"We both saw him," Zeb Gilcrest threw in. "And the two of us couldn't be wrong."

Ashworth spread the fingers of both hands and touched the tips together. "All right. Let's assume that you actually did. What in the world is Little

Soldier doing so far from his own country alone?"

The Tennessean had an answer. "The polecat wants to get back at us—that's what. He's by himself because the other Crows wanted no part of it."

Ashworth indulged in a laugh. "I don't see why he even bothered. What can one man hope to do against all of us? It's ridiculous."

"Is it?" Nate said soberly. On the face of things, the greenhorn had a point. But Nate wouldn't put anything past their nemesis. The Crow wouldn't have come all that distance unless he was fairly confident he could get his revenge. Little Soldier must have a plan of some sort, but what?

Jenks cleared his throat. "The varmint can't have gone far. I say we round up about forty men and go after him."

"He'd hear that many riders coming from a long way off," Nate said. "Two men should be enough. Allen and I will go—and Zach so he can show us where he saw Little Soldier last."

Zachary swelled with pride. To be allowed to ride with the men was an honor. He was the first to the horses, the first to mount. There was a short delay while his father and the man from Tennessee saddled up. Then they trotted on out the gate and raced southward.

Nate was so preoccupied with pondering Little Soldier's presence that he almost overlooked the fact that they had passed a certain knoll he had set as one of his son's boundary markers. Twisting, he said, "I thought I told you not to go beyond that point."

"We were after a big elk, Pa," Zach said, hoping that would be enough to justify his breach of conduct. Another excuse occurred to him. "And if we hadn't, we never would have spotted the Crow."

"I'll let it go—this time."

From the top of the hill Zach pointed out where he had initially seen Little Soldier and the route the warrior had taken. "He disappeared into those trees yonder and we lit a shuck for the fort."

"You did the right thing." Nate held his Hawken cocked as he descended to the meadow and crossed to the spot his son had indicated. Unshod hoofprints led into the pines. They advanced slowly, making as little noise as was humanly possible. Nate preferred to catch sight of Little Soldier before the Crow caught sight of them.

The trail looped to the north. Once past the hill, the Absaroka had ventured to the tree line and from there stared out over the valley dominated by Fort Ashworth. Apparently he had sat a while studying everything, then backed into the pines and continued on a northerly bearing.

Five hundred yards farther on, directly abreast of the stockade, the Crow had again moved to the edge of the trees for a better look. It must have pleased him immensely, Nate suspected, to have found them. But would Little Soldier try to burn the stockade to the ground? Run off their stock all by himself? Pick off trappers one by one?

The warrior had gone north again, then westward, making a partial circuit of the valley. Abruptly, for no evident reason, the Crow had reined to the northeast and ridden off at a trot.

"Where could he be off to in such a hurry?" Allen whispered.

Nate shrugged. It did seem as if Little Soldier had a definite destination in mind, but there was nothing in that direction except limitless miles of untamed wilderness. Plus the Blackfeet, of course, inveterate enemies of the Crows. Little Soldier was taking his life into his hands by going into the heart of their territory.

For over an hour the two Kings and the Tennessean dogged the warrior's trail, and at the end of that time they were no closer to their quarry than they had been when they started. Nate checked the sun, which hung low in the western sky. He hadn't thought to bring extra provisions along. All he had was enough jerky for about four meals, in a parfleche saddlebag.

"The big question is whether we see this through to the end or head on back," Nate commented when they paused on a switchback to give their animals a breather.

"I'd rather go on," Zach said, thrilled by the likelihood of a fight with the Absaroka.

Henry Allen nodded. "Something tells me that, if we let him slip away, a lot of lives will be lost."

"Then it's unanimous," Nate said. "We may go a little hungry, but we don't give up until we've put a permanent end to it."

Sunset caught them in thick timber where the shadows lengthened so quickly they were in near total darkness within minutes. Nate had to accept that they wouldn't catch Little Soldier that day, and he called a halt at the next clearing they came to.

A cold camp was in order. Nate limited himself to a single piece of jerky, but gave a handful to his son. Allen had pemmican, which he offered to share. Nate declined, saying, "It might have to last us a while. We'd better go easy."

Their saddle blankets served as bedding. Nate tossed and turned all night, and he was grateful when dawn's light spurred them on their way.

Not quite an hour after the sun rose, Nate found where Little Soldier had bedded down. "We're not that far behind him," he remarked.

"By nightfall he'll be buzzard bait," Allen predicted.

They tried. They really tried. By prodding their horses on even when the animals flagged, by taking fewer rests than they should, by refusing to stop to eat, they covered as much ground as they normally would in two days of riding. Yet it wasn't good enough. When darkness fell, Little Soldier was still ahead of them.

"Damn it all!" Allen groused. "What's his hurry? Where is he so all fired eager to get to?"

"I wish I knew," Nate said.

Zach had not said much all day. It had taxed him to keep up with the men, and he couldn't wait to close his eyes and drift off. Half asleep, he mumbled, "Who can tell with a mad wolf like him? Little Soldier is crazy enough to do anything."

That was what worried Nate. The Crow would stop at nothing to savor his vengeance. And whatever Little Soldier had in mind, it was bound to be the last thing they would ever expect.

Another day dawned crisp and clear. Nate had to stomp his feet and flap his arms to get his circulation going. He missed having a cup of coffee so much that his mouth watered at the notion.

"Today is the day," Allen declared.

Nate didn't share his friend's confidence. It was obvious that Little Soldier's horse was more than a match for any of theirs. They would be lucky if they caught sight of him.

As if to confirm Nate's hunch, tracking the Crow became more difficult. Early on, the warrior changed direction. His tracks wound eastward a while, then to the southeast, then to the northeast again. Over and over the pattern was repeated.

"What in the hell?" Allen said at one point. "If I didn't know better, I'd swear he was lost."

By early afternoon their horses were in need of rest. They had climbed to the crest of a sawtooth ridge and Nate was about to suggest that they stop for a while when his son blurted out and jabbed a finger eastward.

"There he is, Pa! See him?"

Below the ridge lay open prairie. Scattered across it, grazing contentedly, were hundreds upon hundreds of buffalo. Maybe half a mile out was a solitary rider, weaving among them.

"He's slowed down some," Zach observed.

Nate scanned the herd of shaggy brutes. "He had to because of the buffalo. He's being careful not to spook them into stampeding."

Zach eyed the beasts with trepidation. He had yet to go on a buffalo hunt. His father joined the Shoshones once or twice a year on a surround, as they were called, and although he had begged to go along the last few times, his pa had refused, claiming he wasn't quite old enough. "Are we going on down there?" he asked.

"We have to," Nate said, taking the lead. "It's our best chance yet to catch him."

Buffalo were quirky critters. At times they would panic at the mere sight of a man on horseback. At other times they would totally ignore him. Nate tried to gauge the mood of the herd by the number of great hairy heads that raised up to warily regard them as they reached level ground. A few of the older bulls fringing the main body looked up and snorted, but none pawed the earth or lowered their horns in preparation for a charge.

Nate deemed it safe to do as Little Soldier had done. "Keep in single file," he whispered over a shoulder. "And whatever you do, don't make any loud noise."

Buffalo had the distinction of being the largest creatures on the continent. Adult males stood six feet high at the shoulder and weighed close to 2,000 pounds. Females were only a foot or so shorter and weighed a little over half as much.

Their bulk, combined with their unpredictable temperament and their wicked spread of curved horns, made them supremely dangerous.

At birth, a buffalo usually had a yellow coat with a light red stripe down the spine. Gradually the coat darkened with age, so that by the time a buffalo attained full stature, it boasted a rich, dark brown hide thick enough to keep a person warm in the coldest of winters. Small wonder the Indians prized buffalo robes above all else for their bedding.

Zach gulped as he approached the first group. The bulls were so big that he could have sworn they dwarfed him and his horse. When one looked up at him, he immediately froze in the saddle. The bull was chomping grass, its huge jaws moving up and down, the crunch of its iron teeth enough to bring goosebumps to Zach's skin.

Nate checked to see how his son was doing. It took more gumption than most possessed to ride through the center of a buffalo herd, and he was proud at the courage Zach displayed.

A few of the buffalo moved out of their way, but most stood firm and had to be skirted. Nate swung past several young bulls and angled to the right to bypass a cow and a calf. Suddenly the calf snorted and came toward him. So young that its legs wobbled, it acted more curious than upset.

The same wasn't true of its mother. Grunting, the cow spun and regarded them with her dark beady eyes. She took a few steps to head off her offspring, but the calf skipped past her, coming straight toward the black stallion.

Nate had to rein up or risk bowling the calf over. The stallion flared its nostrils and pricked its ears, but didn't give in to the overpowering fear that many horses experienced when in close proximity to buffalo. The calf stopped and sniffed at the stallion's front legs, then moved toward the back ones, its muzzle rubbing the stallion's belly as if in search of teats.

To keep the horse from bolting, Nate patted and stroked its neck. The calf reached the black's tail, realized there was no milk to be had, and bawled its displeasure. That was the signal for the cow to stalk forward, grunting louder than before, its ponderous head swinging from side to side.

Zach was positive the mother was about to charge his pa. He remembered what his father had mentioned about always aiming behind the foreshoulder and did so. A buffalo's skull was too thick for any ball to penetrate, even the larger calibers.

The cow stomped the ground once. It uttered a rumbling snort from deep within its barrel chest. Catastrophe was averted when the calf pranced back to its mother's side and the pair moseyed off among the others.

Nate rose in the stirrups to catch sight of Little Soldier, but the warrior was nowhere to be seen. Moving on, he fought shy of any brute that acted the least bit belligerent. Twice he had to swing wide of wallows where bulls were rolling over and over in an effort to get some relief from the insects that plagued them.

Buffalo gnats were the bane of the buffalo's existence. Resembling animated black beads, the gnats would swarm over the great beasts, burrowing into their hides and causing large sores to form.

The wallows reeked of bull urine. Nate made it a point to hold his breath when going past.

Threading through the herd made for slow going. Nate developed a crick in his neck from constantly twisting it right and left. He smiled when the last of the beasts appeared.

Little Soldier had headed to the northeast once more. Nate brought the stallion to a gallop. A sea of high grass stretched before them as far as the eye could see. To the north, a pack of gray wolves shadowed the herd, waiting to pick off the sick and the aged.

Once, that would have bothered him. When Nate first had come to the mountains, he had been horrified by the constant violence, by the daily battle for survival every animal endured, by the unending struggle to keep from being killed for food.

Big insects and fish ate little insects. Birds ate the big insects. Eagles and ospreys ate the fish. Bobcats ate the birds. Larger predators, such as panthers and wolves, preyed on deer, antelope, and buffalo. Grizzlies ate anything and everything.

It had bothered Nate that the whole purpose of existence seemed to be for creatures to slay one another. Even humans got into the act, with Indians and whites killing one another at the drop of a feather.

Back in New York City, where Nate's every want had been provided by markets and stores and tailors and barbers, he had somehow come to the conclusion that the natural state of man was one of comfort and ease. Having his every need provided on a silver platter, as it were, had blinded him to the truth that in the natural scheme of things it was dog eat dog.

City life did that to a person. It warped his thinking, made him believe that the world owed him a living when the frank truth was that the world didn't owe him a damn thing.

A dot on the horizon brought an end to Nate's musing. "Little Soldier," he said for the benefit of the others.

"Reckon he's seen us, Pa?" Zach asked.

"I doubt it," Nate said, but slowed anyway. It was best if they take the crafty Crow by surprise. "We'll hang back until dark and jump him after he's made camp."

The sun arced steadily higher. The temperature climbed.

"Are they what I think they are?" Allen inquired, pointing.

Rising up over the rim of the world materialized three buttes. They were harbingers of of an area where the prairie gave way to arid ravines and gorges. And wafting skyward from one of those gorges were tendrils of smoke.

"A campfire," Nate said unnecessarily. The others could see for themselves. He scoured the terrain for the Crow, but the only things moving were a pair of antelope heading in the opposite direction.

Taking cover behind boulders the size of a Shoshone lodge, Nate rummaged in one of his parfleches and came up with his spyglass. Many trappers relied on them, a practice started by Lewis and Clark, who had packed a few on their famed expedition.

Nate swept the wasteland from north to south. The gorge was bordered by brush and boulders, enough to conceal them but not their mounts. "We'll get as close as we can with the horses, then investigate on foot," he directed.

In a gully 70 yards from the gorge, Nate tied the stallion to mesquite. Climbing to the rim, he pretended to be part of the landscape for almost ten minutes until he was convinced no one had spotted them. Then he zigzagged to a weed-choked slope that brought them to the top of the gorge.

Flattening in the shadow of a rock monolith, Nate peered over the edge. He expected to find the Crow settling down early. Instead, he saw a half-dozen warriors, armed to the teeth. At his elbow there was a soft intake of breath.

"Bloods!" Zach whispered. By some accounts, they were more fierce than their allies, the Blackfeet and Piegans. When he'd been much younger, his father and Shakespeare McNair had nearly been rubbed out by a Blood band, and Zach had never forgotten how scared he had been listening to his Uncle Shakespeare relate their narrow escape.

Nate saw a small spring. It explained why the band had stopped there. Six painted horses were tethered nearby, as well as five others. Several warriors had coup sticks, from the ends of which dangled scalps. Dry blood on a few marked them as recently acquired.

The Tennessean leaned toward Nate. "It's a war party on their way home after a raid on the Sioux."

"I wonder if Little Soldier knows they're here," Nate whispered.

The very next second Zach stiffened. "Pa, look across the gorge!"

A head and shoulders had risen above a row of weeds. The Absaroka was intent on the six Bloods. He watched them for the longest while before vanishing in the growth.

Henry Allen sighed. "Too bad. I was hoping they'd add his hair to their collection. Come to think of it, the Bloods probably aren't partial to fleas."

Nate grinned. "We still have a job to do. So let's get to it. We'll fetch our horses and circle around to pick up his trail on the other side."

"Not so fast, hoss," Allen said, nodding.

Little Soldier had reappeared, only lower. Exercising skill worthy of an Apache, he was working his way down the gorge toward the Bloods.

"What in the name of all that's holy is that idiot Injun up to?" Allen said. "Even he can't be fool enough to think he can defeat six Bloods by his lonesome."

Nate was mesmerized. It was insane for the Crow to tempt fate, yet Little Soldier didn't stop until he had reached a clump of scrub trees a stone's throw from the war party. Nate had a clear shot but he didn't take it. The Bloods were bound to come on the run, and he had no hankering to trade lead with them.

Little Soldier observed the warriors go about various tasks. One man, an unstrung bow resting in a quiver slung across his back, began to gather wood for the fire. His hunt brought him ever closer to the Crow's hiding place. Little Soldier inched toward him.

"I do believe that mangy Absaroka is sunstruck," Allen whispered. "It's too bad the Bloods will have the honor of gutting him. I was looking forward to stuffing his innards down his mouth and making him eat them."

Zachary glanced at the Southerner, trying to tell if he was serious or not. He went to ask, then was glued to the tableau below as Little Soldier unexpectedly jumped up and trained the rifle on the Blood carrying the wood.

"Dumber than a buffalo chip," Allen quipped.

The other Bloods had seen and started to dash to the aid of their companion, but they stopped short at a yell from the Crow. Little Soldier strode into the open, motioning for the Blood in front of him to drop the dead branches. Then he marched the warrior at gunpoint back to where the others stood.

To Nate, it was total madness. The moment Little Soldier dropped his guard, the Bloods would be on him like a pack of ravenous wolves on a buffalo calf. The Crow wouldn't stand a prayer.

"Well, look there!" Allen whispered. "Up the gorge a way! This is fixing to get mighty interesting."

A seventh Blood was on his way back to camp, a pair of dead rabbits in his left hand, a lance in his right. He reached a bend in the wall and saw his fellow warriors. Stopping, he set the rabbits down, then slunk along with his back to the wall. Taking two or three steps at a time, he closed in on the unsuspecting Crow.

Nate was stupefied when Little Soldier lowered the rifle and held it in the crook of an elbow to free his hands for sign language. The angle was all wrong for him to see what the Crow said, but the expressions of the Bloods left little doubt that it had not gone over well with them. Little Soldier addressed them again, his hands flying, unaware of the seventh warrior who had slanted toward him and was almost within hurling range.

"I wish Jenks were here to see this," Allen said. "He always claimed that ornery Crow has eyes in the back of his noggin."

The seventh warrior proved Clive Jenks wrong. Rather than throw his lance, he sneaked up behind Little Soldier, planted himself, and rammed the butt of his lance against the Crow's head three times in as many seconds. Little Soldier crumpled.

Henry Alley chuckled. "So who says there isn't any justice in this world of ours?"

"Let's get out of here," Nate proposed. "They're bound to check to see if Little Crow was alone."

The three of them sped to their horses, walked the animals until they were far enough from the gorge to mount without being spotted, and trotted westward. No outcries rang out.

"We can breathe easy now," the Tennessean commented.

Nate hoped so. But a tiny voice deep inside warned him not to take anything for granted. Where there were seven Bloods, there might be more.

Chapter Nineteen

Nate's misgivings seemed to be unfounded. They reached Fort Ashworth without incident. When the news spread among the mountaineers that their hated enemy had fallen into the merciless hands of the Bloods, there were whoops and cheers, and a number of trappers discharged their guns into the air.

Richard Ashworth was in his quarters, relishing a sip of his precious Scotch, when the first shots sounded. Sitting upright so abruptly that he nearly tipped his chair over, he hastily capped his flask, slid it into a pocket, and bolted outside, fearful that the fort was under attack. He was stunned to see his men beaming and hollering and jumping up and down like young children.

Ashworth, spying King and Henry Allen, hailed them. "Good heavens! What is this all about?"

Nate was tired and hungry and anxious to see his wife, but he took the time to relate what had happened. He had gotten so used to Emilio Barzini being at Ashworth's shoulder all the time that he didn't give the Sicilian's presence a second thought.

Henry Allen laughed when Nate mentioned Little Soldier being taken by surprise by the returning Blood. "Ain't it grand?" he declared, his Southern drawl more pronounced than usual. "That coon won't be plaguing us anymore. No, sir!" He slapped his thigh in glee. "Maybe we should hold us a frolic!"

"A what?" Ashworth said.

"A regular rip-snorting jollification," Allen clarified.

Ashworth still didn't understand. But Nate lit up like a shelf full of candles. The idea was so wonderful that Nate was almost sorry he hadn't thought of it himself. "Hoss, you are a shrewd one! A frolic is just what we need. It'll give the boys a chance to let off some steam before they settle down for the long trapping season ahead. And the women will be tickled silly."

"See here," Ashworth interjected. "What exactly are we talking about?"

"Celebrating," Nate said. "Holding a party."

Ashworth blinked. "Is that wise? I mean, what if the Blackfeet should hear us?"

"We won't be making any more noise than we did constructing the fort," Nate noted. "And our hunters have been shooting off guns for weeks now without being discovered." He gazed out the gate at the vista of valley and mountains. "We're so far into the Bitterroots that it's doubtful the Blackfeet will find out we're here for a long time. I reckon a frolic might be just what the sawbones ordered."

Ashworth could see that the frontiersmen were thrilled, but he didn't share their enthusiasm. "We'd be taking a great risk," he pointed out.

Nate was already thinking of the tasty eats the women would whip up. "Haven't you ever heard that all work and no play is bad for the soul? A body needs to his let down his hair now and then or his innards can get twisted into knots."

Ashworth had heard some feeble arguments in his time, but King's homespun wisdom was atrocious. "Listen. I really regret having to do this, but I'm afraid I must put my foot down. There will be no celebration. And that's final."

Nate glanced at the Tennessean, whose disgust was transparent. "Don't you trust my judgment any longer?" he asked the greenhorn.

"Of course," Ashworth said. "It's just that I have too much at stake to endanger our enterprise with a few hours of needless carousing."

"Needless?" Nate countered. "When was the last time these people had a chance to relax and enjoy themselves?"

"I'm sure I don't know," Ashworth said, annoyed that the mountain man was making an issue of it. "I hired them to work, not to indulge themselves."

Emilio Barzini had listened to the exchange with interest. He didn't give a damn about the grungy trappers and their heathen women. The dispute, though, gave him an opportunity to put Nate King in his proper place. Stepping up beside Ashworth, he said brusquely, "You'll do as Mr. Ashworth wants, whether you like it or not."

Nate stiffened. "No one asked for your opinion."

"It's not mine that counts," Emilio said smugly. "It's Mr. Ashworth's. And if he says no, the only celebrating that will be done will be over my dead body."

Henry Allen's right hand, unnoticed by anyone else, had fallen onto a flintlock. "That can be arranged, you walking slab of meat! Lift a finger to try to stop us and you'll be the only man in camp with a nose in the middle of his forehead."

Ashworth saw the Sicilian start to lift his right arm and remembered the stilettos Barzini carried up each sleeve. He quickly stepped between them. "Enough of such talk!" He couldn't believe that two grown men were ready to kill each other over such a trifle.

Emilio almost disobeyed. He'd meant to antagonize Nate King into doing something rash. It had never occurred to him that the Southerner might challenge him. "I don't like being threatened," he said.

Nate resented the giant's attitude. "Then maybe you should learn to keep your mouth shut until someone asks your opinion," he stated.

An insult was on the tip of Emilio's tongue, his right hand inches from the hilt of the blade up his shirt.

"Enough!" Ashworth practically screamed. Without thinking, he turned and gave Barzini a push to get the Sicilian to back down. It was like trying to push a building. The giant didn't budge. "Must I keep reminding you that the Brothers would not take kindly to your rank disobedience? You will desist this instant!"

Emilio stared at Ashworth's bobbing Adam's apple. He couldn't wait to squeeze it between two fingers until it popped like an overripe fruit. "As always," he said, making no attempt to conceal his sarcasm, "your every wish is my command."

Nodding, Ashworth faced the trappers. "It's obvious you're determined. Very well. Against my better judgment, and to preserve harmony in our camp, I will accede to your request." He paused, positive he was making the biggest mistake of his life, but at a loss to know how else to deal with the situation. Widespread unrest might result otherwise. "You may hold your frolic."

Word spread like wildfire. A mountaineer by the name of Fester, who never went anywhere without his cherished fiddle strapped to his back, was picked to organize the music for the affair. Winona volunteered to see to it that the womenfolk made enough sweetmeats and cakes.

Shortly after sunset, the festivities commenced. Richard Ashworth perched on a crude bench in front of his quarters to watch. Accustomed as he was to formal parties where elegance was the byword, he was dumbfounded by what followed.

First, the band practiced awhile. It consisted of two fiddles, a flute, a bearded rowdy who pounded away on a pair of small Indian drums, and a set of bagpipes furnished by a mountaineer of Scottish extraction.

Ashworth almost cackled when they started playing. He compared the sound to a legion of cats with their tails caught in meat grinders. But as the mountain men warmed to the task, their music took on a pounding beat that somehow struck a resounding chord in his breast. He caught himself tapping his toe to the rhythm and immediately stopped.

As the expedition members gathered in a large circle, Ashworth saw several men passing out jugs. When one came near him, he called out, "Say, my good fellow! What is that you have?"

The man, acting as sheepish as a thief caught in the act, slowly came over. "The handle is Bowen, sir. Rufus Bowen." He held out the jug. "You're welcome to keep it if you want. We had to make do with berries and roots, but it goes down real smooth after six or seven swallows."

With that, the trapper was gone, melting into the crowd before Ashworth could think to stop him. Puzzled, Ashworth pulled the cork and put his nose to the hole. A scent reminiscent of red wine made his mouth water. "They couldn't have," he said to himself, and tipped the jug to his lips.

Ashworth had never tasted liquid fire, yet that was exactly the sensation he had as the contents burned a scorching path down his throat. His stomach flipflopped. His eyes watered. His nose felt as if it were being pricked by a thousand pins.

He tried to take a breath and swore that his lungs had collapsed. A massive hand, smacking him squarely on the back, jarred him back into possession of his faculties.

"Are you all right?" Emilio asked. The man looked as if he just swallowed a goose egg.

"Fine," Ashworth sputtered, his voice suddenly like sand paper. Shaking his head, he gawked at the jug. "How could they?" He had given specific orders that no alcohol of any kind was to be consumed so long as the mountain men were in his employ. Scott Kendall, and later Nate King, had told him that he might as well try to stop the mountaineers from breathing as get them to give up liquor, but he had insisted. Sobriety bred efficiency, in his estimation.

Emilio overheard the question and answered. "It explains all those baskets of berries the women brought back from the woods. I wondered why there were so many."

Ashworth didn't bother to mention that the Sicilian had misunderstood. He, too, had seen women bearing large baskets crammed to the brim with small reddish berries of a type he was unfamiliar with, and other baskets containing long roots, equally as unknown back in the States. It had never occurred to him that they would be put to use in the way they had. The ingenuity involved staggered his perception of the mountain men as unschooled louts.

A squeal of delight raised Ashworth's gaze to the open space, where couples were lining up to dance. When he saw Nate King's wife take King's arm as daintily as any true lady, he didn't snicker. It was beginning to dawn on him that there was much more to these people than he had ever imagined.

The music screeched in earnest and the couples swirled into motion. For a few moments Ashworth had the illusion of being at a grand ball in one of the swankest clubs in New York City. In his mind's eye, he saw wealthy men attired in the finest of fashion whirling powdered, coiffured, pale-skinned beauties. Then he blinked, and before him were lusty men in greasy buckskins swinging raven-haired, bronzed savages in buckskins.

By rights, Ashworth told himself, he should find the scene highly amusing. Even contemptible. Yet it held an odd attraction he couldn't explain—a certain quaint charm that stirred his soul in a manner it had never been stirred before.

For all their earthy habits, for all their gruff flaws the mountaineers and their women were really no different from the cream of society back east. Should he hold it against them that they were rough around the edges? No, he thought not. Rather, he admired them for their natural earthiness, for their total lack of pretense. They never pretended to be other than what they were. In that respect, they were more inherently honest than the high-society crowd Ashworth associated with back home.

A fiery tingling in Ashworth's throat made him realize that he had taken another swallow from the jug without being aware of doing so. This one went down easier than the first, but it still moistened his eyes and made his insides feel as if they were about to explode. The taste was tart but pleasant.

Ashworth treated himself to a third gulp and a fourth. Before long, half the jug was gone, and he was stomping his feet to the music, as well as humming along. His head felt strangely light and airy, his thinking was clear.

Raising the jug, Ashworth kissed it. He had found a marvelous substitute for his prized Scotch. Perhaps, he mused, he could get one of the squaws to provide him with a steady supply. He'd pay handsomely.

Suddenly Ashworth sensed another person was close to him. He started on seeing Nate King, Henry Allen, and a mountaineer he didn't know, as well as two Indian women. "My word!" he said, grinning. "You shouldn't sneak up on someone like that!"

Nate King picked up the jug and shook it. He wasn't surprised that their leader had indulged, just at the amount that Ashworth had downed. Half a jug was enough to put the average mountaineer flat on his back. "I'm sorry to bother you," King said, "but Harvey has a proposition."

"A what?" Ashworth said. It was a bit of a shock for him to discover that the music had stopped and everyone was helping himself to refreshments. Maybe he wasn't as clearheaded as he liked to think.

The scarecrow of a trapper who had accompanied King cleared his throat. "An offer for you,

Booshway—or actually, it's my daughter who wants to do it, not me. I told her a refined man like yourself probably wouldn't be interested, but she wouldn't pay me no heed. You know how women are. When they take a notion into their heads, there isn't a man alive who can change their minds. I never have figured out why our Maker made them that way, but there must be a purpose. If—"

Ashworth held up a hand to silence the man before Harvey talked him to death. "Pardon me, my good fellow. But could you get to the point?"

Harvey nodded. "Fair enough. Red Blanket wants to tickle your hump ribs in a way that won't make you laugh."

Ashworth felt certain that he was befuddled by their concoction. He had no idea at all what the man was talking about. "She wants to what?"

Henry Allen nodded at the entrance to Ashworth's private quarters. "She wants to live in your lodge."

"My what?" Ashworth said, beginning to comprehend, but convinced that they couldn't possibly be saying what he thought they were saying.

Nate took it on himself to set the greenhorn straight. "Red Blanket wants to live with you, if you'll have her." He saw the New Yorker's eyes widen in amazement, and he went on before the man made a comment that would bring the wrath of her people down on all their heads. "Hear us out," he added quickly.

Too befuddled to collect his wits, Ashworth nodded. "Be my guest."

"Red Blanket's mother is a Flathead, and her people are a bit more"—Nate had to rack his brain for a delicate term—"forthright about these kinds of matters. If a woman takes a shine to a man, she isn't always shy about letting him know. And Red Blanket has taken a fancy to you."

Richard Ashworth looked at the jug. Was it possible, he asked himself, that he had passed out and was dreaming? He studied the young woman, who had a complexion as smooth as the most expensive china and black hair that would be the envy of any socially prominent woman he had ever met. She met his gaze with a frankness that was shocking, on one hand, and oddly stimulating, on the other.

"Don't ask me why she likes you," Nate went on. "She's taken it in her head that you're the man for her, and she'd be honored if you'd take her for your woman."

"My word!" Ashworth exclaimed, at a loss to know the proper form of etiquette in such a situation.

Nate hunkered to look their leader in the eye. It was important that Ashworth understand what was at stake. "You can say no if you want to, just so long as you do it politely." He stressed the last word and was relieved to see understanding blossom in the other man's eyes. "Say the wrong thing and you'll wind up insulting not only her and her mother, but the Flatheads as well. And since they go out of their way to be friendly to all whites, we like to return the favor. Savvy?"

"Yes," Ashworth said, winking. He assumed

that King was going into detail to spare his feelings, to let him know there was an easy way out.

Harvey stepped forward. "Then what will it be, Booshway? You could do a heap worse. We've raised Red Blanket proper, and she's as decent a girl as you're going to find anywhere. I've never let her sell herself to the men as some of the girls her age do just to get themselves a lot of foofooraw."

Ashworth squared his shoulders and elevated his chin to convey an impression of dignity. He planned to decline, to tell the upright father and the doting mother that, while he was as flattered as could be, he had his duty as leader to think of. He fully intended to say no. It was the word in his mind, the word his mouth was supposed to utter. Yet incredibly, he heard himself say, "I've be delighted to have the young woman move in with me."

Nate King figured that their leader was too drunk for his own good. "Are you sure it isn't the firewater talking?" he asked, at the risk of offending Harvey.

Ashworth had a second chance. He opened his mouth to say that was exactly the case, that their peculiar liquor had rendered his mind virtually numb, that he wasn't thinking straight. Instead he replied, "Nonsense. Have her move her things in whenever she wants."

Red Blanket showed her fine white teeth. Her mother clasped her hands and smiled. Harvey stood straighter, saying, "However much you want to give will be fine by me. Like I told you, we're not interested in gewgaws."

Constantly being unable to make sense of what was being said vexed Ashworth. Just once, he wished, they would speak plain English. "I'm sorry—"

Nate again intervened. "It's customary to give her folks something. The more you give, the more you honor them."

A kernel of suspicion formed in Ashworth's mind. Despite Harvey's claims to the contrary, it was entirely possible that the trapper had offered his daughter just to increase his own worldly goods.

"A horse, a knife, some blankets—anything will do," Nate elaborated.

Ashworth took a sip to stall so he could ponder. Placing the jug on the bench, he rose, fully expecting to keel over. But his legs worked well enough for him to shuffle to the doorway and beckon King. When Emilio Barzini made as if to follow them, he waved the Sicilian off. "No, no, just Mr. King and myself, if you don't mind."

Nate had no idea what the man was up to. Telling Harvey to wait, he followed their leader in. The flickering glow from the fire outside enabled him to see the greenhorn stumble to a table and bend to fumble with a lantern.

"Close the door, would you?"

The Sicilian was framed in the entrance, and he did not appear happy. Nate, at a loss to know why, gripped the latch. "You heard the man," he said, shutting the door almost in the giant's face.

Ashworth stepped to his cot, leaned down, and

pulled his matched set of costly leather carrying cases out from under it. Patting them, he asked, "Do you know what's in here?"

It was a mystery to Nate. He'd seen how Ashworth fawned over them and concluded they must contain Ashworth's stock of Scotch. "No," he responded.

Placing a finger to his lips, Ashworth said, "Shhh!" Then he snickered. "It's a secret. Promise me that you won't tell anyone."

"You have my word," Nate said, hoping the New Yorker wasn't about to down a lot of Scotch on top of the rotgut he'd already consumed. The man would be sick for a month.

Ashworth fiddled with the clasp. Either his finger had changed to lead or the button was a lot harder to work than it ever had been. As last he got it open and flipped the flap back to expose his secret. "See this?"

Nate had to move closer. Where he thought there would be bottles of Scotch, he saw hundreds of dollars in coin and scrip. "Planning to start your own bank?" he joked.

"It's all I have left in the world, all that remains of my initial capital," Ashworth confided. "Six hundred eighty-seven dollars out of fifteen thousand. But if all goes well, in two years I'll return to the States with over one hundred fifty thousand dollars worth of beaver pelts. Even allowing for the money I must repay the Brothers, plus interest, I'll have more than enough to continue living in the style to which I have grown accustomed."

Finally, Nate had a clue to as to who the Brothers were. They had backed Ashworth's venture. But right away he saw a major flaw in their enterprise, and he was about to reveal it when Ashworth nudged him.

"I brought you in here, King, because I value your advice. How much should I pay for the woman? A hundred dollars? Two hundred?"

"Ten should be enough."

Ashworth arched a brow. "That's all? But I thought the more I pay, the better."

"She wants you, hoss, not your money. And you heard Harvey. He's not looking to fleece you. Ten dollars will make him as happy as a lark."

Ashworth counted out the right amount, then closed the case. "Now remember. This is our little secret." Draping an arm over the mountain man's broad shoulders, he steered Nate to the door. "I can't thank you enough for having my best interests at heart, and I want you to know that I'll never forget it."

Not quite sure what the man meant, Nate smiled and said, "Any time." In his experience, it was better to humor those who were liquor-soaked. As they stepped from the small room, the greenhorn clapped him on the back.

"Just think, my friend! We stand on the threshold of prosperity! Nothing can obstruct us now! Absolutely nothing."

Nate could envision a few thousand obstructions, every one of them painted for war and thirsting for white blood. So far, their luck had held. But for how much longer? Time would tell.

Chapter Twenty

Trapping season commenced a week later. The mountaineers could hardly wait to lay their first traps. They reminded Nate King of racehorses straining at the bit to be off.

Three parties of ten men each were sent out to work the adjacent waterways. The men were advised to set up base camps, then work in pairs. Once a section had been trapped out, they were to proceed to the next. When they had as many plews as their pack animals could tote, they were to bring the bales to the fort.

Richard Ashworth was a nervous wreck until the first group came back. The success of his scheme to recoup the family fortune depended on the skill of the rough-and-tumble men he had reluctantly grown to admire. If they failed to live up to his expectations, he would be ruined financially. Not to mention having to answer to the Brothers for the loss of their investment.

Then a party of ten returned. When Ashworth set his eyes on the eight glorious bales of prime beaver hides they brought with them, he nearly cast off his usual reserve and whooped for joy. As it was, he crouched and ran a hand over the wonderfully smooth, soft fur, in a state of giddy rapture. When a shadow fell across him, he spoke without looking around.

"Look at them, Emilio! Your lords and masters would be immensely pleased if they were here right now."

"Are you talking about the Brothers?" Nate King asked.

Surprised, Ashworth rose. He was so used to Emilio hovering over him like a mother hen that he'd taken it for granted the shadow was the Sicilian's. "As a matter of fact, I am," he admitted. "They sent Mr. Barzini along to look after their interests."

The statement reminded Nate of the night of the frolic. "I've been meaning to talk to you about that."

"In what regard?" Ashworth asked, on the defensive. His arrangement with the Brothers was supposed to be a secret. And he was sensitive about being criticized. Yes, he had put his life and all his property at risk by going to the notorious pair for the capital he'd needed, but he'd done so only as a last resort. The banks had all refused to lend him a cent. And his so-called friends had turned their backs on him when he'd needed them the most.

"You mentioned something about wanting to earn one hundred fifty thousand dollars," Nate brought up.

"That's my goal, yes. Why?"

Nate put a hand on the bale and fingered the top hide. It was of excellent quality. "I just don't want you to hold it against me if you don't make that much. Some brigades haven't made more than fifteen thousand a year."

Momentary panic welled up in Ashworth but he suppressed it and said, "I'm not a complete incompetent, I'll have you know. I did my homework, as it were, before I left New York. The brigades you mention were poorly organized and badly managed. Our brigade, on the other hand, is a model of precision. And thanks to your leadership, it is fifty times more efficient than any of those others."

"Yes, but—"

"I'm not done," Ashworth said. "Those other brigades worked streams and creeks that had been trapped many times before. We, however, are in virgin territory, trapping where no white men have ever been. You know as well as I do that it will increase our haul tenfold, if not more."

"True, but—"

"I'm still not done. I happen to know for a fact that the brigade headed by Smith, Jackson, and Sublette earned over eighty-four thousand dollars some time back for a year's worth of trapping."

Nate waited for the greenhorn to go on. When

Ashworth stood there swelled up like a rooster spoiling for a fight, he chose what he had to say carefully. "I'm not trying to rile you, Booshway. But that was when the beaver market was at its peak. Prices have dropped since—"

"Not all that much," Ashworth said defensively.

Nate knew a lost cause when he saw one. The New Yorker had his mind made up and nothing was going to change it. "True. All I'm saying is you shouldn't hold it against us if you don't earn the full sum you want. To be honest, I think you'll do right fine. One hundred thousand, at the very least."

"You really think so?" Ashworth said, overjoyed. It was less than his goal, but still far more than he needed to repay the Brothers and have enough left over to last him for years. He walked off humming to himself.

Nate watched the man go, shaking his head. To think that he had once been a lot like Ashworth, so caught up in the quest for wealth that he'd never realized there was more to life than money and the things it could buy!

The mountains had set Nate straight. Or rather, the true nature of things had. Whereas in the city a person could get by with barely doing a lick of work and never having to lift a finger to prepare his own food or make his own clothes, in the wild it was the opposite. If a person didn't hunt, he starved. If he didn't stitch clothing together, he went around buck naked. Every man and woman had to make do for himself or pay the ultimate price. Whenever a person got too big for his britches in the wilderness, reality up and slapped him across the face to jolt him back to a right frame of mind.

That point was brought home to Nate again several days later when he left with nine men to trap a stream northwest of the fort. Ashworth protested, saying that Nate's rightful place was at the stockade. But Nate wasn't about to be a coffee cooler while his men were out doing all the hard work. He had to do his fair share. So bright and early one morning he left at the head of a new group, his trusty Hawken in the crook of his left elbow, a parfleche filled with food, courtesy of Winona, slung over his back.

Nate was glad to get away from the fort and Ashworth for a spell. There were times when the greenhorn pestered him half to death with silly questions and worries.

Of late, though, a subtle change had come over their leader. Ever since taking up with Red Blanket, Ashworth had been much less prone to get agitated over trifles.

Nate put the Booshway out of his mind as he entered the thick forest and rode toward a craggy peak miles off that reared above the stream they sought. By the next day they had set up camp in a spacious clearing.

Game was everywhere. Deer that had never been hunted fearlessly watched them go about their business. Elk roamed the slopes above, coming down to the stream twice each day to drink. Temperamental mountain buffalo gave them a wide berth, and they did likewise. Birds sang constantly while flitting about in nearby trees. Chipmunks scampered every which way. Squirrels cursed them in squirrel talk from high branches.

Nate paired off with a man by the name of Portis. Bright and early the next morning they headed out to lay traps. From then on, it was pretty much the same routine day after day.

First, each trap had to be set in about six inches of water near the entrance to a beaver lodge or near a run the beaver used when going onto shore and back into the water again.

To entice the beaver to step onto the trap, a secretion from their glands was rubbed onto a stick or leaf above it. This scent, known as castorium, was taken from glands of previously caught beaver.

At dawn the entire line was checked. Dead animals were skinned. Their hides were stretched over a wooden frames, then scraped and dried. To form a bale, each hide was folded with the fur side in and piled one on top of another.

The hides were not the only part of the animal the trappers used. The castor glands were removed and stored in small boxes the trappers carried at all times.

Last of all, the mountaineers saved the tail for their supper. Beaver tail was rated just about the most delicious fare around. Only the meat of painters, known back in the States as mountain lions, was considered better.

It was a routine Nate knew so well that he could practically do it in his sleep. Yet he never tired of the work, never grew bored with the chores involved. After two weeks in the field, his group was ready to return to Fort Ashworth but they stayed over one last night for the hell of it.

Under a breathtaking starry sky the likes of which no citified mortal had ever beheld, Nate and his companions puffed on their pipes, indulged in coffee, and shared tall tales. It was just this sort of relaxed camaraderie that had attracted so many young men to the trapping profession over the years, and it saddened Nate to think that the reports of a drastic downturn in the beaver trade had proven true. In a few years, some predicted, beaver would be replaced by a new material on the market, an improved type of silk.

Nate sighed, cast off his gloomy thoughts by downing more coffee, and heeded Portis, the accepted master at weaving stories.

"Must of been back during the winter of twenty-one or twenty-two, I reckon," the old man said. "I had me a dugout up in the Tetons and figured on stayin' put until the thaw so I could get an early start layin' my line. Well, let me tell you, brothers, that was the worst winter any coon ever saw that ever lived. It snowed day and night from October until June, and when it was done, the snow was piled clear to the tops of the Pilot Knobs, as some call 'em nowadays."

"It's a wonder you weren't buried alive," a mountaineer commented dryly.

"There's a tale in itself," Portis said, and took a puff. "I would have been if not for some mangy wolves. They dug me out and saved my bacon."

"Wolves?" someone else said with skepticism as thick as curdled milk.

Portis nodded. "It was like this, you see. I woke up one mornin' and went to step outside, but I couldn't open my door for all the snow piled against it. There was snow over every window, even at the top of the chimney. I figured I'd freeze to death and no one would ever be the wiser. Then I go me a notion."

"Uh-oh," another man said, smirking.

"I had me a side of elk hanging in the back; so I cut off a piece. Then I gathered up all the straight limbs I had for my firewood and other long pieces of wood and lashed 'em together with my whangs. By the time I was done, I had me a pole pretty near a hundred feet long."

They were hooked. Even Nate listened attentively as a younger man asked, "What did you do next?"

"You ain't figured it out? Why, I tied that elk meat to the end of my pole, poked the pole out the window, and kept on pushin' and shovin' until I could tell I'd poked clean up through that mountain of white fluff." Portis leaned forward, his eyes agleam. "You see, I had me the idea that there was so much snow, not many critters could find something to eat. The scent of the elk would draw 'em from miles around."

"And that's where the wolves come in," guessed the skeptic.

"Yep. Wasn't long before I felt somethin' tuggin' at my pole. I pulled it back down, and sure enough, the meat was gone. So I tied on another piece and shoved it up; only this time I was real careful. When I could tell I was at the top, I yanked it a bit lower."

"Right clever of you."

"Hush, hoss," Portis scolded. "Anyway, I could hear a lot of howlin' and growlin' up above. When there was a nip on the pole, I pulled it lower again. And I kept doin' that until, lo and behold, a pack of wolves had dug clear down to my dug-out just to get their jaws on my meat."

"How many were there?"

Portis shrugged. "Oh, twenty or thirty. I bashed each one on the head with my tomahawk as it came through the window. By the time I was done, I had me a heap of wolf peltries and a big ol' tunnel to reach the outside world." Inhaling on his pipe, Portis concluded, "Yes, sir. We don't have winters like that anymore. But if we ever do, you boys recollect my trick and you'll make out right fine."

The skeptic got in the last word. "Hellfire, Portis. If bullshit was water, we'd all be drowned to death."

At first light the next morning Nate led his merry band to the southeast. They had been alert for Indian sign the entire time, but had not seen so much as an old campfire. As near as Nate could tell, that region had rarely, if ever, been visited by the Blackfoot Confederacy.

It was early afternoon when the trapping party came to a meadow and started across. Nate suddenly noticed that the grass ahead had been trampled. The logical conclusion was that deer or buffalo were to blame, but when he reached the flattened area, he saw a heel print in a small patch of bare earth.

Raising an arm to halt his men, Nate showed the partial track to Portis and the two of them made a sweep.

"It was Injuns," the older man declared. "Twenty or thirty, in a hurry, headin' due south."

Nate gnawed on his lower lip. Had the moment he feared arrived? "Maybe they were just passing through. It could be a war party on its way to raid the Crows or Shoshones."

"Could be," Portis allowed, his tone implying differently.

A decision had to be made. Nate swung onto his stallion and reined it around. "I'll follow them and make sure they've left our neck of the woods. You take the boys on in and tell the greenhorn not to let anyone else leave the stockade until I get back."

"What about the other parties out trappin'?" Portis asked. "Should I send somebody to warn 'em?"

"Jenks and Thomas can take care of themselves," Nate answered. "We'll need every man we can spare at the fort if the Confederacy makes a move against us."

"Whatever you say, Cap'n."

With a nod, Nate was off, trotting on the trail of the Indians. The war party, if such it was, had gone by earlier that day and couldn't be very far ahead. In a couple of hours he found where they had crossed a creek at a gravel bar. In the mud were plenty of distinct prints, enough for him to suspect that they were made by Bloods.

Nate had about assured himself that the band had no intention of lingering in the vicinity when the trail abruptly veered to the east. It troubled him. If the Bloods kept on as they were doing, they'd pass south of Fort Ashworth by no more than a mile or two. Much too close for his liking.

The mountain man rode faster, rising in the stirrups every so often to survey the landscape he was about to cover. An ambush was always a possibility.

Nate grew puzzled when the Bloods again changed course, bearing to the southeast this time. It was almost as if they were searching for something, and he prayed it wasn't the fort.

Twilight aroused the birds to full chorus. With so many sparrows and robins and jays whistling and shrieking all at once, picking out background noises was difficult. But Nate still heard a faint yell somewhere in front of him.

Taking no chances, Nate dismounted and clutched the reins in his left hand. He advanced quietly, creeping cautiously through high firs until a low spine of land offered a vantage point. Hitching the stallion to a pine, he took his spyglass and climbed to a notch between enormous boulders.

There was no need for the telescope. In plain view below lay the Blood camp. Nate counted 21 warriors, most gathered in a council, others tending to a fire and butchering a black-tail buck.

South of the camp stood a lone warrior. As Nate

looked on, the man cupped his hands to his mouth and yipped shrilly, just as a coyote might do. The cry was answered from deep in the woods.

Nate knew what that meant and his blood ran cold. He did not have long to wait before another band of Bloods arrived—or so he believed until he got a good look at their hair and their buckskins.

The newcomers were Piegans, allies of the Bloods and the Blackfeet in the Blackfoot Confederacy. There were 18, their faces painted, armed for war.

Nate's mouth went dry. It couldn't be a coincidence that the two bands had linked up so close to Fort Ashworth. They must be searching for it. Even worse, the presence of the Bloods and the Piegans hinted that the dreaded Blackfeet themselves might also be converging on the brigade.

The mountaineers had to be warned. Sliding down the slope, Nate replaced the spyglass, mounted, and lit a shuck for the stockade. He had to cross two ridges before he would reach their remote valley, and as he crested the first, he was shocked to see more Indians below, working their way toward him.

Quickly reining the black into thick cover before he was spotted, Nate bent and covered its muzzle with one hand to keep it from nickering and giving him away when the warriors went past.

It wasn't long before a fierce figure materialized on the rim. The warrior looked both ways, then motioned to those behind him and jogged into the trees, heading in the same direction as the camp of Piegans and Bloods.

Nate's anxiety mounted as one man after another rose into view and dogged his fellows. Their attire, their war paint, their hair, marked them as Blackfeet. Almost 30 went by. Thankfully, the stallion stayed still the entire time.

Delaying long enough for the warriors to get out of earshot, Nate flicked his reins and resumed riding. His alarm for the safety of his family and the mountaineers spurred him to a reckless speed.

Sixty-six warriors! Nate kept thinking. Sixty-six warriors in that one area alone! How many more might be scouring the mountains for the expedition? He didn't like to dwell on it. If the Confederacy wanted, the combined tribes could put over two thousand warriors into the field, enough to repel an army. Certainly more than enough to wipe out the brigade.

All of Nate's long-suppressed fears congealed into near panic. He would never forgive himself if the expedition were to be wiped out. It didn't soothe his conscience any that he had done all that he could to safeguard every last life. Nor did it help much knowing that Ashworth would have come to the Bitterroot Range without him, had he declined.

The last ridge reared before him. Nate flew up it, his legs flailing the stallion's flanks. Having learned his lesson, he slowed near the summit and walked to the top, his rifle leveled.

The gathering darkness lent the valley a serene aspect. The fort was a brown island in a sea of emerald green. Dimly visible smoke from a dozen unseen cook fires curled above the ramparts. The gate still hung open, and a pair of hunters, bearing a deer on a long pole between them, were approaching it.

All appeared quiet, but Nate had learned long ago not to judge by appearances. Sticking to thick woodland, he wound down to the valley floor. Rather than expose himself, he turned right and paralleled the tree line.

The birds had long since quieted. Those animals abroad during the day had retired, relinquishing the wilderness to those that prowled at night, the majority of which were big predators.

Nate reined up every 50 feet or so to listen. His only warning of enemies afoot might be the muted snap of a twig or the rustle of vegetation, so he had to be constantly vigilant.

No unusual noises disturbed the tranquility. A soft breeze stirred the leaves and grass but not enough to smother other sounds. It was so peaceful that Nate was almost lulled into believing he had fretted for nothing. Not a single hostile Indian appeared to be anywhere in the valley.

Nate saw the front gate close. He went to hail the post so they would keep it open for him, but he stopped himself. As the old adage went, better safe than sorry. He continued along the edge of the trees, sheathed in the blackness of a moonless night.

Suddenly a bush on Nate's left crackled. He had

swung the Hawken and was thumbing back the hammer before he spied a small bounding form with large upright ears. The rabbit melted into the gloom, and Nate eased the hammer back down.

He moved on. Presently he was close enough to the east wall of the fort to hear the murmur of voices and the lilting tones of a woman singing. A dog barked. He couldn't see the sentry in the southeast bastion but there had to be one. It was a standing order that both bastions were to be manned at all times. No exceptions.

The temptation to slant to the gate was almost too strong to resist, but resist it Nate did. He aimed to make a circuit of the stockade, so he pushed on northward until he was about even with the northwest corner.

Not so much as an insect stirred. A few dusky clouds sailed slowly across the sky. In the distance, a wolf vented the lonesome cry of its breed.

Nate stopped. It distressed him to realize that all their hard work might be for nothing, that they might be forced to abandon Ashworth's enterprise and get out of Blackfoot country while they could still breathe. The greenhorn was bound to raise a fuss, and Nate couldn't blame him, not after all the man had at stake.

That was another thing about life. There were no guarantees from one day to the next that a person's efforts would be crowned with success. A man had to take what came in stride and make the best of it.

Annoyed that he had let his thoughts drift, Nate raised the reins to go on. As he did, a shadow separated from the trunk of a tree not 30 feet from where he sat. Even in the dark, Nate recognized the outline of an Indian. It was too late for him to try to hide. The warrior would see him. He had to sit there and hope the man went away. Then six more appeared.

Chapter Twenty-one

Nate was caught flat-footed. If he so much as jerked the reins to dash off, the Indians would spot him immediately. The only reason they hadn't noticed him yet was because they were intent on the stockade and he was slightly behind them, to their left.

Ever so slowly, Nate drifted a hand to a pistol. At that range, he'd rather use the flintlocks. As his palm closed on the smooth polished butt, one of the warriors moved, but not toward him. The man retreated into the vegetation and was joined moments later by his companions.

Nate stayed right where he was. The Indians made no noise, so he had no way of knowing if they had gone elsewhere or were crouched close at hand. He let a few minutes go by. When nothing happened, he eased from the saddle, gripped the bridle, and led the black stallion toward the north wall of the fort. He was tensed for an outcry, for the zing of arrows. The only sounds came from within the stockade.

Halfway to the northwest corner, Nate stopped to scan the forest. He was sure as he could be that he was being watched by unfriendly eyes. Yet if so, why didn't they fire on him? What were they waiting for?

Nate went on, completely forgetting about the northwest bastion until a harsh command rang out.

"If'n you're white like it looks you are, you'd best pipe up or I'm gonna blow your brains out!"

"It's Nate King," the mountain man said, stepping out from the wall so the sentry could see him clearly. "Is that you, Blake?"

"Sure enough," the other mountaineer responded. "What the devil are you doin' out there by your lonesome? Where's the rest of your party?"

Nate went rigid. "Portis and the rest aren't back yet?"

"Haven't seen hide nor hair of 'em," Blake said. "Were they supposed to be?"

"They should have been here before sunset." Nate vaulted onto the black. "Keep your eyes skinned. The Confederacy knows we're here."

"The hell, you say!"

At a gallop Nate made for the gate. Blake gave a yell and two men were opening it for him. Nate dashed inside, ordering them to close it promptly. As his moccasins slapped dirt, expedition members converged, among them the booshway and Henry Allen.

Ashworth had been treating himself to a few sips from the jug Red Blanket kept filled at all times when he'd overheard the guard's challenge. As he'd stepped to his door, men had been shouting that there were enemies afoot. "What is this business about Indians?" he demanded.

Briefly, Nate related what had happened, closing with, "Portis should have been here along ago. Either he's lying low because he knows the Confederacy are watching the fort, or he ran into trouble."

Henry Allen frowned. "Either way, boss, there's nothing we can do about it until daylight."

Unfortunately, the Tennessean was right. Nate wasn't about to lead another party out into the woods and waltz into an ambush.

Ashworth regarded the high sturdy walls of the fort and commented, "I don't see why you're so upset. We have more than enough men to hold off a horde of savages."

"You're forgetting a few things," Nate said. "Jenks and Thomas are both miles from here with their own trapping parties. Add them to the men with Portis, and we're shy twenty-nine."

Allen took up the accounting. "Since we lost seven when we tangled with the Crows, that leaves us with two dozen on hand to defend the fort. Plus the women, and sprouts old enough to hold a rifle. That gives us about thirty-eight guns."

Not enough, Nate reflected. Not if there were as many Indians out there as he feared there might be. "Put two men in each bastion. Have four men man the gate. Change them every three hours. If they see or hear anything out of the ordinary, anything at all, they're to notify us right away. Savvy?"

Nodding, Allen hustled toward the long barracks.

Ashworth was more amused than alarmed. It seemed to him that the mountain men had a knack for always expecting the worst. They were as safe behind the thick walls of the fort as if they were camped out in New York City. The Indians couldn't possibly get at them. Stifling a yawn, he said, "Well, if the excitement is over for the nonce, I'll retire. Wake me if the heathens presume to attack us."

"I won't need to," Nate said. "You'll hear their war whoops." Irritated by the greenhorn's failure to appreciate the gravity of their situation, he turned to go and nearly bumped into his wife, son, and daughter.

"Come, husband," Winona said, sensitive to the anger simmering within him. "I will make you some coffee and you can relax." Switching Blue Flower to her left arm, she clasped Nate's callused hand.

Young Zachary dogged their heels. Boiling with excitement, he couldn't make up his mind whether he wanted the Confederacy to attack so he could count coup and rise in standing as a Shoshone warrior or whether he was simply being selfish and it would be best for all concerned if the Indians left them alone. Ashworth seemed to think they were safe enough, and Zach was inclined to agree. But he could see that his pa was worried. And his pa never fretted without cause.

Winona felt the tension in her man's fingers. She gently massaged them, saying, "Come what may, we are together." One of her most deep-seated fears was that her man would be slain while off trapping or hunting, that he would die alone and in agony with none of his loved ones around him to make his passing easier. She'd even had occasional nightmares about never knowing his fate and living the rest of her days in misery.

Their small quarters consisted of a framework of saplings covered with heavy robes. Winona got a fire going under the vent hole at the top, then filled the coffeepot with water. She was disturbed by her mate's silence, by his uncharacteristic brooding. "Are you all right?" she made bold to ask.

"Never ignore your instincts," Nate said so softly that she could barely hear.

"Everyone knows that. So?"

"So I know it, too, and ever since Scott Kendall showed up at our place, my instincts have been telling me to fight shy of Ashworth and his brigade, that bad times were just over the horizon. And what did I do?" Nate snorted. "I ignored my instincts. I told myself that everything would be fine, that if I took enough precautions we'd outwit the Blackfeet and their allies and get out of this in one piece."

"We will."

Nate looked her in the eyes. It pained him that his neglect might cost those he cared for to pay dearly. "There's no use in trying to fool ourselves. We're in for a racket the likes of which we haven't seen since we went up against the Kelawatsets on the Columbia."

Winona almost shuddered. They had been part of an expedition traveling to the Pacific Ocean. It had been ambushed by the Kelawatsets and nearly wiped out.

Zach also remembered, and suddenly he wanted no part of the Blackfeet. He could always count coup another time. It was more important that his family and friends be spared.

Nate had nothing more to say until the coffee was done. Moving to the opening to get the benefit of the crisp night air, he sipped and pondered. Everyone depended on him to see them through the hard times ahead, and he didn't want to disappoint them. If worse came to worst, he had to have some sort of plan.

Winona joined him. Sitting so that their shoulders touched, she studied his profile. She never tired of watching him when he wasn't aware of it. They had been together for more winters than she cared to dwell on, yet she still thought of him as the most handsome man she had ever met. Perhaps it was due to their bond, to the love they had nurtured year after year, to the entwining of their paths for all eternity.

Nate glanced at her, his heart swelling with affection. Not once during their marriage had she ever given him cause to complain, or to regret taking her as his wife. Truth to tell, it secretly astounded him that she had stayed with him as long as she had. He never had understood what she saw in him, but he was profoundly grateful for her love.

"Care to share your thoughts?" Winona prompted.

"I was thinking of that time the Apaches took you captive. For a while there, I was afraid I'd never see you again." Nate swallowed some coffee. "Losing you or our holy terrors is the one thing that scares me silly. I couldn't go on without you."

"And you will not have to." Winona tried to bolster his spirits. "We are going to be fine."

As if to prove her wrong, from outside the stockade wavered a horrendous scream. Rising to an earsplitting pitch, the cry lingered on and on, strangling off to a pathetic whine. It pricked the short hairs at the nape of Nate's neck and made his heart thump louder in his chest. He was in motion before the scream died, passing his cup to Winona and grabbing his rifle. "I'd rather you stay here," he said as he dashed out.

Other mountaineers were heading for the parapets on the run. Among them was Henry Allen. Nate fell into step beside the Tennessean, who spoke without breaking stride.

"It's begun, hoss. I reckon our booshway is about to learn a powerful lesson, if he lives through it all."

A ladder brought Nate to the narrow walkway above the gate. A half-dozen mountaineers had beaten him there and were scouring the wide-open space that bordered the post. Nate was glad that he had seen fit to insist they clear the brush and trees. The Blackfeet and their allies would have a hard time launching a sneak attack, even in the dead of night.

"I saw movement yonder," one of the trappers manning the southeast bastion shouted. "By that big oak to the southwest."

Nate had seen the tree many times. Leaning over the top of the stockade, he tried to distinguish activity near it. Just then a new sound fell on their ears, a sound equally as chilling as the scream even though it was far less sinister.

They all heard a robust laugh, a savage, gleeful taunt. It was the laugh of a warrior who couldn't wait to daub his hands in the blood of his enemies. It reeked of confidence, and a latent hint of raw bloodlust.

"I'd like to have that coon in my sights," Allen said ruefully.

By this time everyone in the fort was at the walls. Nate's name was shouted, and he looked down to find Ashworth clambering up the nearest ladder. He gave the greenhorn a hand. Ashworth tottered as he straightened and would have fallen if not for Nate.

"What's all the uproar?"

"I suspect the Blackfeet are making sport with us," Nate said. "They want us to know that they're out there, that we're at their mercy."

Ashworth had been cuddled on his cot with Red Blanket, on the verge of dozing off, when the scream made his breath catch in his throat. He'd never heard anything like it. Not even that awful wail made by the pretty Flathead slain by the Crows could match the terror it instilled. "They have another think coming," he blustered. "Let them try to storm our gates! Just let them!"

"Be careful what you ask for," Henry Allen said. "It has a way of coming to pass."

The ladder creaked to a heavy weight. Emilio Barzini wore a sour visage. As lithely as a cat, he jumped onto the walk and rooted himself next to Ashworth. "You should have let me know you were coming over here," he complained. For once, he had been caught napping.

Ashworth had a mind to let the Sicilian know in no uncertain terms that he could do as he damn well pleased without having to answer to him, when a new sound silenced all of them.

Nate cocked an ear. From the south came the thunk-thunk-thunk of an ax or tomahawk biting into wood. More chopping broke out until it seemed that the forest was alive with a legion of woodcutters.

"What are those red devils up to?" Ashworth wondered.

"Maybe making poles to scale our walls," Allen said. "Or maybe working on a big log to batter our gates down."

"A battering ram?" Ashworth said. "Oh, come now. It's not as if we're dealing with Greeks or Romans. You credit them with more intelligence than they possess."

Nate was going to set the greenhorn straight

but the Southerner beat him to it.

Allen pivoted toward their leader. "How long?"

"I beg your pardon?"

"How long before you take your head out of your hind end and see the world the way it really is and not as you fancy it to be? You have a habit of looking down your nose at anyone you think is dumber than you. But Injuns aren't stupid, mister. In their own way, they're as bright as any whites who ever lived."

"Oh, really?" Ashworth said. While he was willing to concede that the red race had a certain innate charm, he drew the line at ranking them with the likes of Napoleon and Julius Caesar. "Do Indians know how to make steel? Where are their great cities? Their magnificent works of art?"

"You're mixing apples and oranges."

"Am I?" Ashworth countered. "Well, then, let's put this in terms you can relate to. If Indians are so brilliant, why do they spend all their time fighting among themselves when they should unite against us? We both know that one day our population will spill across the Mississippi and claim this country for our own just as we did all the land in the East. If your precious Indians are so smart, why haven't they joined forces to stop us?"

Henry Allen didn't respond. Even Nate had no adequate answer to that one. He had tried to warn his Shoshone kinsmen that there would come a time when the whites would swoop across the prairie and the mountains like a plague of locusts, devouring everything in their path. But the Shoshones couldn't comprehend the idea of there being more whites than there were blades of grass on the plains. Nor did they understand the white concept of owning land. To them, and to most other tribes, the land had been bestowed on them by the Great Mystery for all to use. A tribe might lay claim to a particular territory in which to hunt and live, but within that territory each member of the tribe was free to wander as he saw fit and live wherever he wanted.

Richard Ashworth took the silence of the two trappers as proof that he was right. Placing a hand on the top of a cottonwood post, he reveled in his moment of triumph. Belatedly, he realized the chopping in the forest had ceased, and everyone else had noticed except him. "What can those heathens be up to?"

"We'll find out soon enough," Nate answered. "For now, let's try to get some sleep. Indians rarely attack at night. We should be safe until daylight."

It was hopeless, though. Nate tossed and worried and couldn't get his mind to stay still for the life of him. He managed perhaps an hour of sleep before first light brought him out from under the buffalo robe that covered Winona and him. She had fallen asleep with her forehead resting on his shoulder, and he exercised great care in rising without waking her. Little Evelyn slept soundly beside them, while over against the opposite wall Zach snored lightly.

The morning chill penetrated Nate to the bone. He would have liked a cup of coffee, but it could wait. Stomping his feet to get his blood flowing, he ambled to the front gate. Allen was already up there, along with a number of other mountaineers. To a man, they were gazing intently out over the valley. Not one so much as twitched a muscle.

"Henry?" Nate said on reaching the ladder. The Tennessean made no reply, standing there as one transfixed. Mystified, Nate hastily climbed. As he straightened up, he learned why everyone else had been glued in place. The same happened to him. Total horror had that effect on a person.

Twenty yards out from the fort stood a high thin pole. Sometime during the night the hostiles had carried it in close and erected it without any of the sentries being the wiser. That in itself was remarkable. More so, in a ghastly sense, was the trophy displayed on top.

It was Portis's head. The old trapper's neck had been hacked clean through and his spine snapped in half. Torn holes were all that remained of his eyes, and his tongue had been removed. The bloody stub could be seen through his parted, puffy lips.

"You know what this means, don't you?" Henry Allen whispered timidly, as if reluctant to speak loudly for fear of agitating the departed.

Nate nodded. Portis might not be the only one the Indians had gotten their hands on. "Any sign of the Blackfeet or their friends?"

"Not yet."

Footsteps pounded below. One of the youngest trappers halted, half out of breath, and pointed to the north. "The other side," he husked. "You have to see."

Two heads were perched on poles about the same distance as their counterpart to the south. Both were men Nate recognized as belonging to his trapping party. One was in the same condition as Portis. The other man apparently had incensed his captors, because they not only had ripped out his eyes and tongue, they had sliced off his nose and ears, cut off his lips, and partially scalped him.

"That was Dexter," Allen said. "He came from North Carolina. Good man, but he never did know when to keep his mouth shut."

At that moment the sentries in the northwest bastion shouted. Nate hastened over guessing what he would see and scared to death his hunch was correct.

The Blackfoot Confederacy had been as busy as bees overnight. Two more poles, two more heads. These were farther back, close to the trees; they had been in shadow until the sun had risen high enough to reveal them.

"Damn their hides all to hell!" Henry Allen declared, and Nate did not need to ask who he meant.

Other trappers were on the parapet, just as shocked as Nate and the Tennessean. Swallowing hard, Nate glanced eastward. Allen nodded.

Together they hurried to the southeast bastion. The trappers occupying it were staring at the pole to the south. "Here, what's all the fuss about at the other walls?" a beanpole demanded.

"More trophies," Nate said, and let it go at that. Stepping to the east corner, he surveyed the cleared tract between the post and the pines. Nothing. Nor did he see any poles along the edge of the forest.

"You were thinkin' there'd be some on this side?" a sentry said. "Not likely. This wall is closer to the woods than any of the others. Those buzzards couldn't do like they done to ol' Portis without one of us seein'."

"So they made do," Allen said, extending a finger.

It took a few seconds for Nate to discover what the Southerner had already spied. Deep shadow lingered on this side, only now being dispelled as the sun cleared the tops of the tall trees.

This time the Blackfeet had relied on rawhide ropes instead of poles. From low limbs in two trees dangled heads of men they all had known, men they had ate with, joked with, lived through sheer hell with.

The beanpole turned crimson. "I'll make every last one of those murderin' scum pay!" he raged, and whipped off a shot into the undergrowth before anyone could prevent him.

Nate grabbed the muzzle and pushed it down. "Enough," he said curtly. "No need to waste ammunition."

Eyes slick with moisture, the mountaineer had to try twice before he could speak. "What's one ball, more or less? We have enough to rub out a few thousand worthless Blackfeet and the like."

"And we'll need every one," Henry Allen said.

The compound was crammed with trappers, women, and kids. Word had spread, and every last soul had turned out to witness the atrocity. There was no more space on the parapets. Those deprived of the opportunity were urging the stunned dozens who were on the walls to climb down so they could have a turn. But they would have to wait. For those on top had a new sight to contend with: that of scores of painted figures emerging from the vegetation to the west and east, where the trees were closest.

"Dear God!" one of the men with Nate exclaimed.

Nate descended the ladder on the fly and raced to the one beside the front gate. Shoving through the crowd, he gained the walkway and had to shoulder several people aside to make room. Allen stayed by his side the entire time.

"Look at 'em all!" someone said. "We're doomed! Do you hear me? Doomed!"

More warriors had stepped into view to the south, two solid rows, 50 or 60 prime fighting men in each. At a sharp yip, they raised their weapons and voiced a collective bloodcurdling howl, the din loud enough to spook the horses in the corral and set many of the dogs to barking.

"There must be two hundred or better," the Tennessean said. "Some Bloods, some Piegans, but mostly Blackfeet."

Nate hadn't bothered to count them. He was focused on a particular warrior, a short, cocky fiend who strutted out in front of the rest, elevated a rifle, and roared his hatred. It was Little Soldier.

Chapter Twenty-two

Henry Allen gripped a post so hard that his knuckles turned white. "Tell me my eyes are playing tricks on me, hoss! That bastard should have been wolf meat weeks ago!"

Others recognized the brigade's sworn enemy, and word was rapidly being spread along the ramparts.

Nate toyed with the notion of trying to drop the Crow, but at that range hitting Little Soldier would have been more a matter of luck than skill. He'd wait. Sooner or later he was bound to get a better chance.

Seconds later the war whoops died. Three warriors conferred with the Crow, resorting to sign language to communicate. One of the three was a Blackfoot, another a Blood, another a Piegan.

"Why haven't they butchered him?" Allen said,

more to himself than anyone else. "That's what I'd like to know."

The parley was short. At a gesture from the tall Blackfoot, a dozen warriors darted into the woods and shortly returned forcefully hauling the three missing members of Nate's trapping party along.

"Oh, hell," Allen said. "Better for those coons if they'd been killed with their friends."

At another command from the Blackfoot, the three mountaineers were tied to trees. Then the Blackfoot walked over to a beefy trapper named Wagner, who slumped as if half dead. The Blackfoot entwined his fingers in Wagner's long brown hair, jerked the mountaineer's head up, and gazing at Fort Ashworth, lit his features with a sinister smirk. The message was plain.

"We've got to do something!" a man to Nate's right bawled. "We can't just let those sons of bitches torture our boys!"

Nate leaned on the wall and surveyed the grim faces turned toward him. "If any of us go rushing on out there, we won't last two minutes. We'd be playing right into their hands."

"Look!" someone cried. "What's the Absaroka up to?"

Little Soldier had moved to Wagner's side and was rummaging through the trapper's possibles bag. Evidently not finding what he wanted, he stuck a hand into Wagner's ammo pouch and drew out a strip of tan cloth Wagner used either to clean his guns or for making wads. Little Soldier flapped it a few times, said something to the

Blackfoot, and handed over his rifle. Next, the Crow waved the cloth overhead while slowly advancing 20 feet toward the post. "I want truce!" he hollered. "I want talk Grizzly Killer!"

Allen scowled. "Curse his bones! That polecat knows our ways too damn well." He glanced at Nate. "You're not going to go, are you?"

In response, Nate gave the Tennessean his Hawken.

"You could be making a mistake," Allen advised. "He might want to get you out there so the Blackfoot can pick you up."

"More likely he wants to gloat." Nate bent to the ladder.

"Keep me covered as best you can."

At the bottom waited Winona, Evelyn at her side. Nate steeled himself as he descended. "Before you say a word," he said, "I have it to do."

Winona had heard the Absaroka's shout. Searing claws of pure fear slashed at her heart, and she brazenly pressed up against her man and kissed him full on the lips before replying, "I know, husband. Come back to me."

Four mountaineers were ready to open the gate. Nate nodded and slipped out when they had it open just enough for him to do so. "No wider," he cautioned. "Be ready to shut it if I get cut off."

"Will do, Captain," a trapper said.

Little Soldier was still waving his flag of truce. On spying Nate, he lowered it and grinned broadly. "I knew you come, white man!" Pointing at his waist, he rotated to show that the only weapons he had were a knife and a tomahawk.

"No guns, Grizzly Killer! Savvy?"

Reluctantly, Nate pulled his twin flintlocks and turned to pass them to one of the men. Instead, Winona was there, hands outstretched. Their fingers brushed, and she conveyed more by the look in her eyes than most folks could have expressed in an entire book.

"Come on, Grizzly Killer!" Little Soldier taunted. "Are you afraid face me?"

Nate threw his shoulders back, lingered a moment to brand his wife's face into the depths of his soul, then headed across the valley. Twenty feet from the fort, he stopped. "Halfway, you coyote!" he shouted. "Prove you're not the coward everyone thinks you are and meet me halfway!"

It was a calculated gamble on Nate's part. He was hoping that the Crow wouldn't want to appear yellow in front of the Confederacy. Should Little Soldier insist that he go all the way, he had no choice but to comply; he wouldn't put it past Little Soldier to carve on the captives if he refused.

The wily Absaroka hesitated. He glanced at the rows of warriors behind him, at those to the east and west of the fort, and seemed to take courage from their numbers as well as the bows and fusees they had trained in Nate's general direction. "I come, white dog!" he cried, striding forward.

A tingle shot down Nate's spine. In light of what he had in mind, it was hard to maintain a show of calm as he also advanced. To give the impression that he posed no threat, he held his arms out from his sides.

Nate tried not to think of all the weapons fixed on him. One false move, and the warriors would unleash a hailstorm of lead and shafts. He adopted a smirk that matched the Crow's and came to a stop when they were only ten feet apart.

"Surprised, white dog?" Little Soldier asked.

"That I am," Nate confessed. "I've never talked to a dead man before."

Little Soldier's brow knit and he warily started to back off.

"I saw you taken by the Bloods," Nate hastily explained, "in a gorge east of the Bitterroots."

The Crow opened his mouth wide and covered it with a hand, a typical Indian expression of amazement. "You were there!" he bleated at length.

"When you were knocked out, I figured that was the end of you," Nate said, taking a casual step with his arms still hiked.

A gleeful cackle burst from Little Soldier. "Any other man die. Not me! I too smart for Bloods. I make deal for life."

"What sort of deal could you possibly make?" Nate started to quiz the warrior when in a rush of insight he perceived the Crow's strategy. It had been a bold gambit that confirmed the Absaroka's intense hatred. "You came all this way to enlist the Blackfoot Confederacy's help in doing what your own people refused to do? You offered to lead the Bloods and their allies to our fort in exchange for your life?"

Little Soldier was tickled. "I know maybe I die. But I never rest, never stop, until Grizzly Killer and all his people be dead."

Nate took another pace. "I'm impressed," he said to distract his enemy while sliding his leg forward yet again. "It was a stroke of genius on your part."

"Genius?" Little Soldier repeated.

"It was very smart of you," Nate clarified. He was now only six feet from the warrior. "Few men would have the grit to do what you did."

The flattery had an effect. The Crow puffed up and put his hands on his hips. "Look around you, white man! Plenty warriors! Soon you and all in wooden lodge be dead."

One last step brought Nate close enough to suit him. "Maybe so," he said, "but I'll have the satisfaction of seeing you die before we do." He lowered a hand to his tomahawk.

Little Soldier's eyelids fluttered. "You crazy, white dog? You be killed before you reach friends." He laughed a forced, nervous cackle that revealed how deeply afraid he had suddenly become.

"If I put an end to you, it will be worth it," Nate said, continuing to smile and hold one arm out so the onlooking Blackfeet, Piegans, and Bloods wouldn't suspect that anything was amiss.

The Crow's throat bobbed. "Hold on, Grizzly killer!" he said, shoving both hands toward Nate as if to ward off a blow. "Touch me, friends die!" He jabbed at the captive trio to accent his point.

"You aim to kill them anyway," Nate said harshly. "There is nothing I can do to save them. I might as well make sure that you never make life as miserable for anyone else as you have for us." He inched the tomahawk upward.

The Crow was stupefied. He began to back up, placing each foot carefully. The cloth fluttered at his feet. "Know this!" he hissed. "Many more Blackfeet soon be here. Your family die for sure! Kill me, you not be here to help them!"

"So be it," Nate declared, and sprang, the tomahawk glittering in the bright sunlight as he took a single bound and drove the keen edge at the crown of Little Soldier's head with all the might in his sinews.

The blow should have split the Absaroka's head like a pumpkin. But at the exact instant that the mountain man leapt, Little Soldier whirled to flee and tripped over his own two feet. Sprawling onto his side, he scrambled to get out of reach.

Nate closed in. It was then that the hostile warriors surged to life. Fusees boomed. Bow strings twanged. Nate paid them no heed. Lunging, he swung at the Crow's midsection. This time his tomahawk was deflected by Little Crow's. The warrior pushed up into a crouch and tried to take Nate off at the knees. Backpedaling, Nate blocked, countered, and was foiled once more.

Little Soldier was gaining confidence. Rising, he feinted to the right, pretended to go left, and went right. His tomahawk came within a hair's width of opening Nate's gut from hip to hip.

Nate drew back his arm as an arrow thudded into the soil close to his foot. Another missed the Crow by less. Startled, Little Soldier glanced at the warriors and shouted in his own tongue. The distraction permitted Nate to glide in and aim a vicious swing at the Absaroka's neck.

Little Soldier, sneering in contempt, threw himself rearward. He was still sneering when the blade bit into his flesh, still sneering when it sheared through to his backbone, still sneering when his head flopped back onto his shoulders and a scarlet geyser spewed from the nearly severed stump.

In a flash, Nate spun and sprinted toward the post. Only at that moment did he realize hundreds of savage throats were roaring in outrage and that the brigade members were urging him on with yells and shrieks. The din was almost enough to mask the pop of fusees and the zing of arrows. Balls spattered all around him as he flew toward safety. Spinning shafts came close to making the Crow's boast come true.

Nate stared at the gate, refusing to dwell on how much ground he had to cover to get there. He simply ran like a madman.

The gate was still open, and Winona appeared, beckoning, imploring. The next moment she pointed to the east and shouted, but he couldn't hear the words. Not that he needed to. A quick look revealed a cluster of warriors hurrying to intercept him. They were swift like deer, and Nate knew that he couldn't possibly reach the post before they did. Armed as he was with just his tomahawk and knife, they'd cut him down with ease.

Rifles poked over the posts above the gate, Hawkens and Kentuckys crowned by bearded faces that were fixed intently on the sights at the ends of their guns. Henry Allen was one, and at a bellow from him, seven muzzles spat lead and smoke.

Seven of the charging Indians dropped. The rest faltered, recovered, and ran on. Another volley dropped six of them, four to never rise again. The others were severely wounded and needed assistance to get out of there.

Nate could see the whites of his wife's eyes. They widened in joy as he covered the last 30 feet. Arrows whisked past him, a few imbedding themselves in the fort.

Lead smacked into the gate near Winona but she never flinched. Her own safety was of no concern when her man was in danger. She waited until he reached her, threw her arms around his heaving chest, and drew him into Fort Ashworth just as a hail of hostile fire peppered the wall on either side.

Four trappers slammed the gate shut. Nate sagged against it to catch his breath. The aroma of his wife's hair and the pulsing throb of her body against his were too exquisite for words. "For a bit there, I didn't reckon I'd make it," he commented.

"If I had known what you were going to do, I would have gone with you," Winona said, her cheek on his arm. "We have been together too many winters to be separated now. It is fitting that we pass on side by side."

Nate begged to differ. What about their children? he was going to ask. But their talk was nipped in the bud when he heard someone call his name. The Tennessean was waving for him to come up. He hustled onto the parapet.

The fallen warriors were gone. The wounded and dead had been carried into the trees, with a notable exception. Little Soldier had been left where he had dropped.

A council was being held. The tall Blackfoot and several warriors from each tribe were seated in a circle near where Wagner and the other two mountain men were tied.

"They'll go after the stock next," Allen said.

"We have a bigger problem," Nate informed him. "The Crow told me that more Blackfeet are on the way."

"How many? How soon will they get here?"

"I'd give my right arm to know," Nate said. Their small outfit might be able to hold out until Jenks and Thomas arrived, but not if the 200 warriors already there were reinforced by just as many, if not more. "Spread the word. Let everyone know that we'll be making a break for it before too long."

"Will do."

Nate scanned the compound and realized practically every last person was watching him, awaiting his command. In the crisis, they had turned to the one man they believed capable of saving them. It wasn't the greenhorn, who was nowhere to be seen. It wasn't the Sicilian, who although as powerful as a buffalo had only fought Indians once before. And it wasn't any of the other mountaineers, whose experience rivaled his but not their ability to make critical decisions on the spur of the moment. Nate had to accept that, live or die, the fate of dozens rested solely on his shoulders.

Gripping the rail, Nate issued directions. The woman and children were told to gather up whatever they wanted to take along, so long as it would fit into a parfleche. The men were divided up evenly between the four walls and instructed to help themselves to an additional rifle from the room Ashworth had dubbed the armory.

As everyone hustled to obey, Richard Ashworth came from his quarters. He walked a tad unsteadily thanks to the jug he had polished off a while ago, but he judged himself in full possession of his faculties. Adjusting his cape so that the frills on his white shirt caught the sunlight, he moved into the open. "Mr. King, a word with you, if you please!" he demanded in his most official tone.

Nate had more important matters to attend to, but he went down one more time. Prudently, he got in the first word to forestall useless questioning. "Booshway, you'd best grab your possibles and get set to head out. We leave in five minutes."

"We what?" Ashworth said, incredulous. Drawing himself up to his full height, he looked around at the people scurrying every which way, and went as white as a sheet of paper. "Are you demented?" he snapped. "Haven't I made it clear enough to you how much I have invested in this venture? We're not going anywhere!"

"Yes, we are," Nate said with finality. "More Blackfeet are coming, probably a lot more. By tonight there could be five hundred out there, even a thousand."

Ashworth gestured at the high walls. "We can hold off twice that number."

"Never in a million years." Nate minced no words. "Not with over half our brigade dead or missing. Unless we leave right away, the rest of us, including all the women and the children, will be butchered or taken prisoner and made to suffer in ways you can't even imagine. Do you want that?"

"No, of course not," Ashworth said, resentful of being manipulated. "But we still can't go. I absolutely forbid it!"

"Then you stay if you want," Nate said. He shifted to dash off and find his family when a hand the size of a grizzly's paw closed on his wrist.

"Hold it right there," Emilio said. He had listened to the two men, and he had no idea which one was right. But he did know which one the Brothers expected him to obey. "If Mr. Ashworth says no one is to go, then no one will."

Nate had to resist an impulse to smash the giant in the mouth. He met the Sicilian's troubled gaze. "I may not like you much, but I credited you with more sense than this. Do you want to be killed, mister? Because you will. If we don't skedaddle while we can, we'll be wiped out."

Emilio wavered. There was no denying the mountain man's sincerity. Nor could he deny that it would be pointless for him to die when there was nothing to be gained by his sacrifice. Easing his grip, he said, "Very well. We will be ready to leave when you are."

"What?" Ashworth screamed. "Has everyone here gone stark, raving mad? You're supposed to do as I want, imbecile! Not as this trapper dictates!"

Nate didn't stay to hear the Sicilian's reply. He reached his quarters as Winona, Zach, and Evelyn were emerging. His wife and son each had two bulging parfleches.

"It is the best we can do," Winona said. She regretted having to leave so many of their possessions behind. One of their heavy buffalo robes, in particular, she had spent days making. Yet she would gladly do without if it meant her loved ones would live.

Nate grasped her hand and headed for the north wall. Unknown to the Blackfeet and their allies, only the stock animals and spares were held in the corral attached to the outside of the fort. The personal mounts of every man, woman, and grown child were penned in a makeshift stable at the rear of the post.

Ashworth had raised a stink about it, but Nate had insisted. He'd learned his lesson well from his adopted people. Shoshone warriors routinely brought their most prized horses into their lodges to keep them from being stolen by marauding enemies.

Nate's foresight might just save dozens. He lowered a pair of rails and moved in among the milling animals. Locating the black stallion was simple since it was one of the biggest in the pen.

Winona's mare and his son's bay took a little longer. As he saddled all three, other mountaineers set to work imitating his example.

Nate was acutely conscious of the time factor. Everything had to be just right, or the war party would cut them off. Guiding his wife and children to a spot near the front gate, he paused to hug Winona and say, "No matter what happens, remember I've always loved you." Then he ran to where Henry Allen and a handful of men were loading rifles and flintlocks.

"Have all the women and kids in the middle," Nate said to the Southerner. "Watch for my signal."

"You can count on me."

Nate's next task brought him to the parapet on the north wall. The five mountaineers manning it acted relieved to see him, but they balked when he gave his order.

"You want us to do what?" one said.

"Abandon your post and get ready to ride out," Nate said again.

"But what about the stock?" the same man protested, indicating the huge herd that filled the outer corral. Beyond it, scores of warriors had gathered. "Those vermin will run the horses off any second now, and we're the only ones who can stop them."

"We want them to run the herd off," Nate said, much to their astonishment, and shooed the men down the ladder.

By Nate's reckoning, most of the war party would take part in stealing the horses since every warrior would want to get his hands on one or two. Relatively few of the Confederacy would stay on the south side of the fort, which would leave the lower portion of the valley wide open once he broke through them.

That was Nate's plan, anyway. He saw that more and more Indians were showing up every second in the trees nearest the corral, and he hurried to the southwest bastion to inform the pair of sentries that they were to get ready to ride out. Neither objected.

The compound was awhirl with activity. Mounts were being saddled, parfleches and saddlebags were being thrown on, items not needed were being discarded, women were collecting their offspring, men were lining up horses in an orderly file.

Henry Allen was largely responsible for achieving order out of the chaos. The Tennessean was everywhere, giving advice, lending help where it was needed.

Suddenly loud yipping broke out to the north. The war party was moving in on the stock sooner than Nate had anticipated! He was on the ground and speeding toward the armory before anyone else realized what was happening. "Mount up!" he hollered over and over.

There was one last thing Nate had to do. With his tomahawk, he busted the tops of three kegs of black power open and upended two of them on top of the stockpiled powder, balls, and guns. Grabbing the third keg, he upended it like the others, but this one he held on to as he backed from the armory and dashed to the spot where he had left his family.

Winona and Zach were on their horses. Nate took the reins to his stallion and moved next to the ribbon of black powder. Drawing one of his pistols, he cocked it, pointed it at the powder, then glanced up to insure all was in readiness. Most of the brigade had heeded him. Only a few had yet to climb on their animals. Allen and several others were standing by to open the gate.

Nate pulled trigger. At the blast, sparks and tiny flames shot up from the exposed powder. Crackling and hissing, the flames sputtered toward the armory at a brisk clip.

"Now!" Nate cried, and launched himself onto the black. The Tennessean and company tugged the gate wide open, and as was fitting, Nate became the first man out. He was smiling, confident that he had handily outwitted their enemies. He was wrong.

Over 70 warriors remained south of the fort. Some were to the east, some to the west, but the largest number were clustered around Little Soldier's body in the very middle of the cleared space, barring the most direct route out of the valley. The moment Nate appeared, they howled in fury and charged toward Fort Ashworth like a horde of crazed wolverines.

Chapter Twenty-three

It was too late to stop. There was no turning back. The brigade was committed to the course of action Nate had chosen. He angled to the east, where the smallest number of warriors were, and bore down on them at a gallop. A glance back revealed that all the mountaineers and their families were hard on his heels, staying in a compact group, the women and children in the center as he had directed.

Henry Allen, Wild Tom, and other reliable men were at the forefront, right behind Nate. They were the ones who would bear the brunt of the impending violence, and to a man they were as grim as the specter of death that hovered over all their heads.

Nate didn't see any sign of Richard Ashworth or Emilio Barzini. He hadn't thought to make sure they were with the group before riding out, and he couldn't afford to go look for them. The greenhorn and the Sicilian were on their own. Live or die, it was in their hands.

A piercing war whoop reminded Nate of the large body of warriors slanting to cut the brigade off. Even though the warriors were on foot, they stood a good chance of doing it; they were as fleet as antelope. Nate held his fire, saving his lead for when it would be most needed.

The warriors to the east had fanned out to prevent the brigade from getting past. Nate gauged how much ground the brigade had to cover before it reached them, then how much there was between the brigade and the 70 to 80 warriors rushing madly forward, and he concluded that the brigade would reach the east edge of the trees with perhaps a 30-yard lead.

The fly in the ointment were the 15 warriors who had fanned out in front of the woods. If they could slow the brigade down, delay it for just five to ten seconds, then the larger bunch would get there and it was doubtful any member of the brigade would ever get out of the valley alive.

As if reading Nate's thoughts, Henry Allen pulled alongside the stallion and hollered, "We have to break through that line or we're worm food!"

Nate nodded. Suddenly a horse whinnied stridently, and he looked around to behold one of the trappers catapulting to earth on a sorrel with an arrow jutting from its side. The man rolled clear and was picked up in seconds by a friend. But that arrow was only the first of many, as the charging warriors unleashed a hailstorm of shafts and lead balls.

Nate clamped a mental lid on the cauldron of anxiety roiling in the pit of his gut. He needed a clear head for what was to come. Any lapse, and the consequences would be too terrible to contemplate.

The 15 Blackfeet, Bloods, and Piegans ahead were elevating bows and lances and a few fusees. They, too, held their fire, and it wasn't hard for Nate to guess why. They planned to stop the brigade cold with a united volley. The ploy just might work.

Nate didn't care that he was one of their foremost targets. He bore straight down on them, the black stallion flowing like the wind. He had time for a hasty glance at Winona, and then he was close enough to open fire. He took aim as best he could.

At the very instant Nate's finger tightened, the brush behind the line of warriors parted, spilling out Clive Jenks and nine other brawny mountaineers who were on the Indians before the warriors had any idea the newcomers were there. Tomahawks, knives, and rifle butts flashed. Ten of the warriors were dead in a span of moments, their brains and blood splattered over the grass.

The five Indians who were left were brave men; they turned to do battle. Jenks and company hardly broke stride. And since there were two trappers for each warrior, the outcome was never in question. The red men went down without taking a single trapper with them.

Jenks knew what he was about. As soon as the last foe fell, he and his men darted to the south to get out of the way of the flying brigade.

By this time Nate was 20 yards away. He reined sharply to the right and halted. Allen and five others automatically did the same. When the main group started to slow, Nate motioned them on, bellowing, "Keep going! Keep going! Don't stop until you reach the Salmon! Ride! Ride!"

Nate glimpsed Zach as the brigade pounded on past. He smiled grimly, but had no idea whether his son saw. Then, wheeling the stallion, he pointed at the uneven phalanx of charging warriors, and leaped to the ground.

The other mountain men understood. Jenks and the trappers with him rushed forward to help, forming into a skirmish line. Allen and the five mounted men promptly dismounted, adding their rifles.

The 78 warriors belonging to the Blackfoot Confederacy never slowed. Why should they? They had the whites outnumbered. And they had just seen 15 of their fellows slain. Thirsting for vengeance, craving coup, screeching and whooping, they closed on the hated whites who dared defy them.

Nate dropped to one knee to take deliberate aim. "Don't shoot until I say so!" he shouted.

Thirty-five yards were all that separated the two forces. Then thirty. Then twenty-five. Nate would have waited even longer, but he had to give Jenks's men time to reach their horses, concealed in the trees. "Now!" he roared.

Seventeen Hawkens and Kentuckys cracked as one. Fifteen warriors in the leading line of warriors went down, clutching at shattered sternums or grasping at holes that blossomed in their foreheads. Those behind had to either leap over the bodies or slow down to avoid them. Most slowed. And it was then, as the momentum of the attackers was briefly broken, that a tremendous explosion rent the morning air, an explosion the likes of which none of the warriors had ever witnessed. To them, it was as if a hundred thunderclaps had sounded simultaneously. Sheets of flame and smoke spewed skyward above Fort Ashworth. To a man, the Confederacy froze to see the spectacle.

Not so Nate and the other trappers. They broke for cover, those mountain men who had mounts handy swinging up and covering the flight of those who had left theirs in the trees. In seconds the foliage closed around them.

Nate held back, watching the warriors. The Blackfeet, Bloods, and Piegans were still agape at the mammoth flames that engulfed the bowels of the post. Secondary explosions took place every few seconds, the scene reminiscent of a fireworks festival.

It wouldn't be long before the warriors realized their prey was eluding them. Nate slapped his legs against the stallion and entered the pines. Everyone else had gone. He brought the stallion to a trot and rode for over ten minutes without seeing a soul. A knoll hove into sight. Nate went to the top and placed a hand above his eyes to reduce the glare.

To the southeast a knot of trappers were crossing a meadow. To the northeast were a pair of riders who had strayed wide of the mark. One wore a flowing cape. The other was a human mountain. Nate galloped to the northeast.

Richard Ashworth was misery incarnate. He had never been so despondent in his life. Dazed by the disaster, he rode along not paying any attention to his surroundings, oblivious to where he was going.

"I'm ruined!" Ashworth breathed over and over and over. Tears dampened his cheeks.

It didn't seem real. Ashworth couldn't accept that his grand scheme had come undone, that he had lost everything. Everything! Every last piece of property he owned. Even the family estate. All of it was gone. Thanks to motley savages who slicked their hair with bear fat and traipsed around half naked! It was too ridiculous for words.

"What do I do now?" Ashworth wailed. "What do I do?" He was so lost in despair that it took a few moments for the statement he heard to register.

"We've gone far enough."

Wiping a cuff across his face, Ashworth glanced around. He had completely forgotten about his guardian. "Oh, Emilio!" he said sadly, reining up. They were in a small clearing in a stand of pines.

The Sicilian said nothing. He had a job to do.

Climbing down, he walked to Ashworth's horse and loosened the straps to the expensive carrying cases the dandy carried behind his saddle.

"See here?" Ashworth said, perplexed. "What the dickens do you think you're doing?"

"I don't think. I know," Emilio responded as he took the twin cases over to his own mount. He draped them over the back of the animal and tied them securely. Pivoting, he rubbed his hands together, savoring the moment. "I can't tell you how much I've looked forward to this."

"To what?" Ashworth said, his perplexity growing. He detected a cold gleam in the giant's beady eyes that was almost frightening.

Emilio moved slowly toward the expedition leader. "You have no idea how hard it has been for me to put up with you all these months."

"It hasn't been easy for me either," Ashworth said, indignant. "Having you hover over me every waking moment was enough to give a lesser man fits. Why your employers saw fit to send you along, I will never know."

"They had their investment to think of," Emilio said, "which is why they gave me certain orders."

"Orders?" Ashworth was growing more concerned by the second. The giant's countenance was twisted in raw hatred.

"The Brothers like to think ahead, to cover every contingency," Emilio said. "They were counting on you to come through for them, but in the event you failed, I was told to take certain steps."

Ashworth's whole body trembled as if from an

abrupt chill. At last he comprehended. "You can't be serious!"

"But I am. I'm to return what is left of the money. First, though, I get to show you how the Brothers feel about failure."

Too late, Ashworth attempted to flee. He raised the reins and flicked them once. Then hands three times the size of his own clamped onto his last decent shirt and heaved him from the saddle. The impact knocked the breath from his lungs. He struggled to sit up, but he was much too sluggish. From out of nowhere a ponderous foot slammed into his chest, pinning him in place.

"In the Old Country we have a name for men like you," Emilio said. He was in no rush. The Indians were far behind, and he wanted to indulge himself. "In English, it translates as foul-smelling weasel."

"Let me go!" Ashworth protested, trying to push the foot off him. It was like striving to lift a ten-ton block of marble.

Emilio leaned forward to apply more weight. He liked how Ashworth's face flushed red, and the feel of ribs sagging close to the breaking point under his sole. "It wasn't bad enough I had to let you lord it over me as if I were your servant," he said as if addressing a child who had misbehaved. "I also had to listen to all your whining whenever anything went wrong. I had to tolerate your moans and groans at every little inconvenience." He pressed hard. "It was disgusting. You are disgusting."

Ashworth barely heard. Acute pain racked his

whole body. Most excruciating of all was the agony in his chest. He was sure that it would stave in at any second. "Please!" he said.

Emilio frowned. "Groveling. How typical." He placed a hand on his knee and bent even lower. Ashworth gurgled and wriggled like a hooked fish. "I want you to know that I will enjoy this, that I have never looked forward to killing anyone as much as I have to killing you."

"No!" Ashworth wheezed, pounding at the foot that held him down. He screeched when something inside of him broke with a distinct crack. Moist drops burst from his nose.

"If I had all day," Emilio said, "I would do this right. Chop off your fingers one by one. Stick burning sticks into your eyes. Things like that. But since I don't have all day—" Sighing, Emilio wrapped his left hand around the other man's neck.

Ashworth felt his breath choked off, felt his body lifted effortlessly into the air. He kicked, but he might as well have kicked a brick wall. He struck feebly at the giant's chest, but it was like hitting solid stone.

"Good-bye," Emilio said, vibrant with the thrill of extinguishing another life. "Save a seat for me in the inferno." He squeezed, his fingers plying flesh as if it were so much clay, heedless of the warm blood that spurted onto his wrist. There were a few final convulsions, and the deed was done. Contemptuously, he cast the body down, wiped his hand on Ashworth's cape, and turned to depart.

"Not another step, you son of a bitch!"

Emilio knew enough to stand perfectly still. It surprised him that he had not heard anyone approach. He saw the other man he so wanted to kill gliding toward him and inwardly smiled. It was his lucky day.

Nate King had seen the two men enter the pines. Fifty yards out, he'd heard Ashworth cry out. Assuming that the pair had run into more hostiles, Nate had dismounted and sneaked closer. He'd reached the clearing just as the giant threw the lifeless husk that had once been the expedition's leader to the ground.

Now Nate circled around in front of the Sicilian, a cocked pistol in his right hand. He hadn't had time to reload the Hawken and left it with the stallion.

"I should have known it would be you," Emilio said good-naturedly.

"Shut up."

Nate looped around to where he could see Ashworth plainly. Any doubts he harbored that the greenhorn was dead evaporated when he saw Ashworth's ruptured throat. "Why?" he wanted to know.

"Does it really matter?" Emilio said, continuing to smile even as he slowly lowered his arms to his sides. A twist of both wrist, and a stiletto filled each hand, unseen by the mountaineer.

"No, I reckon it doesn't," Nate said. He thoughtfully regarded the Sicilian. "The question is, what do we do with you?"

There were no courts of law west of the Mississippi. The trappers lived by a very simple code: an eye for an eye, a tooth for a tooth. When a man committed rank murder, he usually answered to the friends of the victim.

Only in this case, Nate mused, the victim had no true friends. Few of the mountain men had grown close to Richard Ashworth. His standoffish ways had insured that he died unmourned, except for possibly Red Blanket.

"I'll take you along and let the others decide what should be done," Nate said. That was the fair thing to do. Were it up to him, he would shoot the giant and be done with it, but then he held a personal grudge. It was hardly right for him to set himself up as judge, jury, and executioner.

"Whatever you say," Emilio said with a shrug of his broad shoulders. As he shrugged, he flipped his left hand up and out, almost too fast for the human eye to follow.

Nate caught the movement barely in time. He pivoted, twisting as the slender blade sought his heart. In turning, he inadvertently held his right hand in front of his chest. The stiletto struck it a resounding blow and glanced off, catching him high on the forehead.

A burning sensation seared Nate's brow. He had been nicked, no more. Blood flowed. Not much, yet it got into his left eye and momentarily blinded him. Blinking to clear his vision, he extended the pistol at Barzini. Only the Sicilian was no longer there.

Nate swung to the left. As he did, a vise closed on his wrist. His arm was brutally wrenched so viciously it nearly broke. He had no choice but to drop the flintlock.

Emilio slid around in front of the mountain man and wagged his other stiletto in front of King's nose. "You are a disappointment, cur," he rasped while applying more pressure on the wrist. "Here I thought that you, at least, would be a challenge."

Forced to bend sideways or have his arm snapped, Nate gritted his teeth and glared at the complacent hulk. "I wouldn't want to let you down," he said, then kicked Barzini where it hurt every man the most.

Emilio had expected just such a move and was ready for it. All he had to do was shift his weight to deflect it with his thigh. He had done the same a hundred times in as many fights. But this time something went wrong. For as quick as he was, he wasn't quite quick enough. The kick landed solidly.

Pain lanced through him. Releasing King, he staggered.

Nate spun into a crouch, his Bowie clearing leather with the speed of thought. He sliced it across the back of Barzini's leg, then skipped out of reach of the stiletto.

Emilio, furious, took a step, intending to end their clash with a single stroke. But a strange thing happened. His left leg buckled, and he crumpled onto his left knee.

Like a tawny panther pouncing on prey, Nate swept toward the Sicilian's left side again. Barzini parried. As their blades rang together, Nate rotated to the right and slashed at his true target, the back of the giant's other leg.

Inexplicably, Emilio found himself on both knees. A hint of panic flared but he quelled it and tried to stand. To his utter consternation, he couldn't. His legs refused to respond. Glancing down, he discovered why. Both had been hamstrung.

Nate came to a stop a few feet in front of the crippled killer. He reversed his grip on the Bowie, holding it by the blade, close to his thigh. "I'll give you more of a chance than you gave that poor greenhorn," he declared. "Any time you're ready."

Emilio nodded. "A moment, please," he said, stunned by the suddenness of it all. He had always taken great pride in his skill, yet he had been beaten with the same ease he had so often beaten others.

Nate waited, watching the giant's right arm and nothing but the giant's right arm.

"I have but one regret," Emilio said wistfully. "Her name is Maria."

"Want me to get word to her?"

Emilio recoiled. "You would do that for me?"

"Why not? An enemy not worthy of respect isn't much of an enemy at all." Nate still didn't take his eyes off that arm. "Take the Blackfeet. They hate my guts, but I respect the hell out of them."

"I understand," Emilio said, his features relaxing, his mouth creasing in a smile. "I see the truth of it now. Of them all, you are the only one I judge worthy."

Nate was going to ask what the giant meant.

But in that instant the Sicilian's right hand shot up and out. Nate mimicked the movement, knowing that he had been a shade too slow, that both of them would go down. Yet only one blade flew true. His Bowie transfixed Barzini's ribs, thudding to the hilt, while the giant's stiletto streaked past his ear so close that it brushed the skin without breaking it.

Nate started to stoop, to grab his pistol, but it wasn't needed. The light had gone from the Sicilian's eyes. Wearing a quirky grin, Barzini keeled over. Nate touched his ear, saying aloud, "I wonder."

"That was a close shave there, hoss!"

From out of the trees ran Henry Allen and Clive Jenks. Neither wasted a glance on the bodies.

"We've got to light a shuck, pard," the Tennessean said. "Those Blackfeet and such are swarming out through the woods as thick as bees on a hive."

"We saw that you were missing and came back to find you," Jenks said.

Absently trailing them, Nate paused to grab hold of the reins to the giant's mount. "Glad you could join the festivities," he told Jenks.

"We would have joined sooner, but there were too many Injuns around the fort for us to get through to you," Jenks said.

"Any sign of Thomas and his party?"

Jenks raised a finger to his throat and cut from right to left. "We spotted a war party of more than two hundred Blackfeet northwest of the post. They were having their fun with Thomas's boys, or they'd of been at the post well before we got there."

So Nate had done the right thing, after all. As he swung onto the stallion, he gazed one last time at Richard Ashworth and the Sicilian. He should feel better now, he told himself, but he didn't. "Let's go," he said, and led his friends southward as if the hounds of hades nipped at the stallion's tail.

It was three weeks later that Scott Kendall stood in front of the King cabin and watched his wife and daughter wade in the shallow end of the lake. They were splashing and giggling and having a grand time. Vail Marie waved.

Kendall lifted the arm resting on his crutch and returned the favor. His daughter started pointing at something behind him, and at the same moment he heard the snap of a twig. Turning so fast that he nearly fell, he dropped his right hand to his pistol.

"Shoot me, and I'll never let you stay at my place again," Nate King said, riding into the open with Winona and Zach in his wake. Smiling, Nate unfastened the leather cases behind his saddle and tossed them to the speechless mountaineer.

Kendall found his voice. "Nate! Winona! You coons are a sight for sore eyes! But what in tarnation are you doing here so soon?"

Nate wearily climbed down. "I'll tell you all about it after I've slept for four days."

"Fair enough." Kendall hefted the wide strip

that linked the pair of carrying cases. "What's in here?"

"The money you need to take your family back to the States," Nate said, stepping to the doorway. He glanced around. "Call it a gift from the Ashworth Brigade."